UNAUTHORISED ACTION

Alan Hunt

Matador
9 Priory Business Park,
Wistow Road, Kibworth Beauchamp,
Leicestershire. LE8 0RX
Tel: 0116 279 2299
Email: books@troubador.co.uk
Web: www.troubador.co.uk/matador
Twitter: @matadorbooks

ISBN 978 1788032 650

British Library Cataloguing in Publication Data.
A catalogue record for this book is available from the British Library.

Printed and bound in the UK by TJ International, Padstow, Cornwall
Typeset in 12pt Garamond by Troubador Publishing Ltd, Leicester, UK

Matador is an imprint of Troubador Publishing Ltd

For Merrie, Charlie, Tori and Ronnie

AUTHOR'S NOTE
AND ACKNOWLEDGEMENTS

This story takes place in an imagined world in the Spring and Summer of 2005. It is set within a recognisable historical context, but any resemblance to real events or individuals is unintentional. The physical descriptions of the Foreign and Commonwealth Office and the Treasury, while broadly accurate, have been slightly modified for the purposes of the plot.

I am grateful, as always, to Meredith Hunt, Charlotte Hunt and Victoria Hunt Leyman for their support and critical input; and to Jorge Hay for vetting my rusty Spanish. Any inaccuracies or solecisms that survive are mine alone.

ACH April 2017

APRIL 2005:
UNFINISHED BUSINESS

CHAPTER 1

Showered and naked, Andrew Singleton surveyed his freshly shaved face in the bathroom mirror. As he braced himself against the slight movement of the ship, he had to admit that he was looking well. The exhaustion and pain of the last few weeks had finally receded, and he had regained some weight. He was lightly tanned from the voyage, his silver hair was neatly cut, somewhat shorter than had been his previous custom, and he was conscious of increasing physical strength. A stranger might have been forgiven for thinking that all was now well with him.

The stranger would have been wrong. During his waking hours he sought to keep the worst at bay by vigorous physical exercise: running, swimming, working out in the gym and endless walks around the deck. At breakfast and lunch he ate alone and frugally, but at dinner he allowed the head waiter to seat him with other passengers and accepted the invitations that came his way from the ship's officers. During the meal he drank a great deal of wine and spoke eloquently and expansively about world affairs. He was the very model of a *bon vivant*, a role that had once come naturally to him but now required conscious effort. All the while, he was staving off the inevitable moment when he would have to return to his cabin and risk sleep. For he knew that his dreams would be haunted by images of Elena and Marina – and, above all, of Birgit.

There were potential diversions. Unaccompanied women greatly outnumbered the single male passengers on the ship. In another life he could have been tempted to exploit this advantage. Now he had little appetite, either for the chase or the consummation. This was disconcerting for a man who, apart from the period of his disastrous marriage, had been an incorrigible womaniser. And he could see that it was puzzling to the well-groomed widows and divorcées he sat next to at dinner, whose mild flirtations he failed to reciprocate. He had accepted their invitations to play bridge after dinner – having half-heartedly protested that he had barely played since university – but had always retired before anyone began suggesting nightcaps in their cabin.

The other thing he had resolutely declined to do was participate in any of the shore excursions. The options had been many: Phuket, Yangon, Goa, Mumbai, Dubai, Muscat, Aqaba, Haifa and Limassol among others. He was averse under any circumstances to guided tours, but he had an additional motive for staying on board as the ship moved from South East Asia via the Indian subcontinent and the Middle East into the Mediterranean.

He found himself unconsciously fingering the scar on the left side of his upper chest. One inch lower and the bullet would have penetrated his heart. How much anguish might that have saved? It could not have brought back Elena or her delinquent daughter. Even his beloved Birgit would have been beyond saving – but at least he would have known nothing of her death. He would have died heroically, believing that he was an executed hostage, a victim of terrorists and of the Singapore Government's intransigence in the face of their demands. Instead he had lived, wracked with guilt, knowing that he had been nothing but a dupe.

That he might have wished to die then did not, however, mean that he wished to die now. Behind the never-ending shame and remorse lurked the shadow of fear; fear informed by memories of his incarceration and of the threat of personal extinction. Constrained though his professional and personal life had now become, his survival offered some hope of a road back, even if he could not at this moment imagine in any detail what that might be. Charitable work, perhaps, or... or what? No matter, he would not be taking any unnecessary chances on the way to the comparative safety of Europe.

The ship was bound for Civitavecchia. He could have remained on board until then, spent a couple of days with friends in Rome and then flown back to London to find out what, if anything, the Foreign Office had in mind for him. But his telephone conversation with the Permanent Under Secretary just before embarking in Singapore had made clear that, as far as the office was concerned, there was no rush.

"Really, Andrew," she had said, "the most important thing is for you to achieve a full recovery. Let's leave any discussion about the future until you feel ready."

"Whatever you say, Kirsty," he had responded.

He had decided therefore to disembark instead at Catania. One of his great regrets as a teenager was not to have climbed Mount Etna during his one and only previous visit to Sicily. The weather had been bad on the day, and the slopes had been closed. Given how relaxed the Foreign Office was about his return home, the fortuitous inclusion of Catania in the ship's itinerary seemed therefore too good a chance to miss. Not that he was in any shape to climb the whole mountain, but the cable car and a four-by-four bus would get him close enough for the final ascent. Once his Etna ambition had been achieved, he would base himself in Taormina for ten days or so, revisiting familiar places when he felt like doing so, eating pasta and drinking Sicilian wine. There were worse ways to convalesce.

He glanced at his watch. It was just before eight: time for breakfast. He dressed in a white linen shirt, chinos and loafers, slung a navy cashmere sweater around his shoulders, picked up his Panama hat and left the cabin to go up on deck. He very nearly collided with a woman walking past in the passageway and they went through the very British ritual of apologising extravagantly to each other before the woman recognised him.

"Andrew," she said, "is it true you're leaving us tomorrow?"

Her name was Rebecca Shearer, and she was by far the most sympathetic of his bridge partners – perhaps, he thought, because she had always behaved entirely correctly, with no hint of coquetry.

"Yes," he said. "Etna calls."

"We'll miss you," she said. "Take care." She said it seriously, with no hint of hidden meaning. He had learned earlier in the voyage that her husband had drowned when his dinghy capsized during a freak storm off the Isle of Wight three years previously. If Andrew had been minded to speak of his wife's death, he might have remarked on the fact that Elena had died in those same waters. As it was, he had consciously avoided saying anything that might have created some kind of bond.

"And I'll miss all of you," he said, equally gravely, choosing his words with care.

She nodded solemnly, and was gone. He might see her tonight at dinner, depending on the whim of the maître d', or at bridge afterwards. Would she then be gone from his life? He had told himself repeatedly in the last two months that, after the catastrophe he had perpetrated in Singapore, he was done with women. Certainly he felt no urgent need of a physical relationship. At the same time, he was saddened to be saying a definitive farewell to such a cultivated and intellectually gifted woman as Rebecca. She was a formidable bridge player, mainly because of her instinctive intelligence, but also because she appeared to have a near-photographic memory and was able to recall at will the order in which every card had been played in any hand. Her courteous, thoughtful and logical manner reminded him of someone. It had been niggling at him throughout the voyage who this person could be. It had to be someone he had known a long time ago, possibly someone with whom he had been in a relationship, but their identity had remained elusive, because it was not a physical resemblance he discerned, but one of general demeanour. It was only when he emerged on deck under a cloudless blue sky, as the ship approached Italian waters, that it suddenly came to him. Rebecca reminded him of Kirsty – or to be more accurate, of her current incarnation, Dame Gillian King, DCMG DCVO, Permanent Under Secretary at the Foreign and Commonwealth Office and Head of the Diplomatic Service. Not, then, the girl he had loved and lost at university but the accomplished, mature woman from whom on his return to London he would no doubt be receiving a formal admonishment for bringing the Service into disrepute.

***

Mohamed Hussein (although it was a name he now rarely used) sipped his morning coffee on the terrace of the Regency Tunis Hotel. The faint odour of camel urine, mingled with the scent of roses, bougainvillea, eucalyptus and mimosa, hung ambiguous and piquant in the still, warm air. Hussein had taken care to find a table in full shade and was nevertheless also wearing factor-fifty sunscreen. Aware still, but careless, of the residual pain at the bridge of his nose, he mentally rehearsed his timetable for the coming forty-eight hours. His formal business would take him to Madrid for several weeks and thence to Brussels, where he planned to stay for at least two months. But first he had unfinished personal business to complete, for which the time window was very narrow.

For Madrid and Brussels he had elected to be an Orthodox Jew, an identity that afforded him ironic amusement as well as relative security. For his immediate purposes he needed a different, temporary identity: he was a Tunisian merchant and would shortly be catching the overnight ferry to Palermo, where the following morning he would explain to the immigration official that he was in Sicily to meet an associate to discuss the terms of an olive oil contract.

It was true that he had a meeting the following day. It would take place in Cefalù, just down the coast from Palermo, but olive oil would not bulk large in the conversation. He was meeting a supplier to Cosa Nostra, and the subject under discussion was the purchase of arms.

***

The sun was well past its zenith now, as the ship continued on its increasingly calm way through the Mediterranean. Rebecca Shearer lay on a sun lounger, dressed in shorts and a long-sleeved shirt, her face protected by a broad-brimmed straw hat and sunglasses, an open book by her side. She was feigning sleep, because she did not want to engage in idle gossip with the woman lying on the neighbouring lounger. The latter was a perfectly nice person, whose travelling companion was confined to her cabin with a stomach upset. Rebecca felt slightly guilty about deceiving her, but could not face the triviality and lack of self-awareness that characterised the woman's conversation.

Am I a hopeless snob? she wondered. Would it not be an act of kindness to allow the woman to talk to her? At least she wouldn't ask any questions. Her profound lack of curiosity in anything or anybody other than herself had initially irritated Rebecca, who had, however, come to see that it was better than the intrusive questioning that was the alternative. Rebecca had less difficulty now in talking about her husband's death, but she preferred to give people the short version and move on to other things. Not everyone took the hint.

Andrew Singleton *had* taken the hint, limiting himself to polite condolences and then remaining silent, allowing Rebecca to determine which way the conversation would move. She had asked about his own situation, but he had said only that his wife had died some while back. There was obviously a good deal more to his story than that – her Singaporean friends had intimated that he had been involved in a kidnapping, although they were vague about the details – but she did not press him any more than he had pressed her.

Andrew intrigued Rebecca. He was an attractive man, but that in itself would not have been sufficient to account for her interest in him: she doubted that she could ever again feel the way she had about Robert, who had been a wonderful lover as well as the funniest person she had ever known. No, it was Andrew's enigmatic quality that had piqued her curiosity. Whenever she came across him during the daytime, he seemed withdrawn, almost antisocial; he was courteous enough, but was clearly not seeking company. Over dinner, by contrast, he seemed to come alive, speaking eloquently and knowledgeably on a wide range of subjects, although she noticed that he said nothing of his personal life. His bidding at post-dinner bridge was erratic and risky, but his intuitive card play frequently rescued an apparently doomed contract. She would have liked to know him better, to understand his apparent contradictions, but it seemed unlikely now that she would get the chance.

Why am I even thinking about Andrew Singleton? she asked herself. She had organised her life with great care since Robert's death. She taught mathematics at a comprehensive school in Peterchurch and socialised almost exclusively with a group of close friends in the Herefordshire village where she and her husband had lived for over twenty years. She volunteered each year at the Hay Festival, as she and Robert had always done, visited their married sons in London from time to time, and had taken to holidaying in remote parts of the British Isles with a fellow birdwatcher from the village.

The cruise had been a departure from that regular routine, an impulsive decision, taken after an old school friend, now living back in Singapore, had invited her to visit. "Why don't you take a boat home?" her friend had said. "Make a real break of it?" *Why not?* she had thought, perhaps, unconsciously, beginning to tire of the staid life she had constructed for herself. She had claimed a long overdue sabbatical to allow her to anticipate the Easter holidays by several weeks and had booked the cheapest cabin she could find on the alarmingly expensive cruise her friend had identified as ideal for her purposes. Had her friend had an ulterior motive? she wondered. Did she think Rebecca might meet someone to take her out of her self-imposed purdah?

This is nonsense, she thought, *get a grip.*

She opened her eyes and levered herself up on to her elbows. "Hello," she said to her neighbour. "I seem to have nodded off. What have you been up to today?"

CHAPTER 2

Andrew had checked into the hotel early, but his room was not ready, so he left his bags and went for a stroll in the late spring sunshine. The hotel was rather grand, but down at heel. It was located at the foot of steps leading up to the Via Crociferi, home to some of the finest examples of Sicilian baroque architecture: houses, palaces and churches, built from black lava and limestone after the great earthquake of 1693 and virtually unchanged since the eighteenth century. Andrew did not climb the steps. He chose instead to walk east and then, leaving Etna clearly visible against the cloudless sky behind him to the north, he turned south to make his way to the main square, the Piazza del Duomo.

Ignoring for a moment the cathedral, he crossed the square and descended steps beside a marble fountain into the archetypically Sicilian chaos that was the fish market. He pushed his way through the throng of vendors wielding knives and yelling across slabs of fresh fish, crabs and shellfish, until he found the restaurant he was looking for, amazingly still there and looking much the same as it had done over thirty years earlier. He booked a table for lunch, talking in halting Italian to the elderly owner, who politely pretended to remember him. Pausing briefly to enjoy the cool juice of a *spremuta d'arancia* bought from a swarthy street vendor, he then he made his way back to the main square and to the cathedral.

The cathedral was a massive building, with surviving elements of its Norman origins, plus granite columns salvaged from Catania's Roman amphitheatre, crafted into the post-earthquake baroque reconstruction. Once inside, Andrew was struck again, after all these years, by how light the interior of the cathedral was compared with its contemporaries in northern Europe. He stood for a while, absorbing the cool calm, momentarily at peace with the world. But his mood darkened when he moved on, past Bellini's tomb, and came to the Chapel of St Agatha, which housed the relics of Catania's patron saint. As a hedonistic teenager, in relentless pursuit of pleasure, he had barely registered Agatha's terrible story. Now, in middle age, he found himself unexpectedly affected by the thought of this innocent woman, subjected to horrific torture and executed for nothing more than saying no to the Roman ruler of the day.

By the time Andrew emerged from the cathedral it was nearly noon, and he determined to return to the hotel, unpack and shower before walking to the restaurant. To his surprise and amusement, however, he suddenly found himself among a familiar crowd of thirty or so people. The ship had organised a walking tour of Catania and the group had just this moment arrived in the cathedral square, where their guide was fighting with a defective amplification system to try to explain the story behind the fountain in the centre of the square, which was dominated by a black lava elephant bearing an Egyptian obelisk on its back. He spotted Rebecca Shearer lurking at the back of the group and made his way toward her.

"Well, well, well," he said. "Here we are again."

"Hello," she said, removing her earpiece. "Have you come to rescue me?"

"Is it that bad?"

"I'm sure it's all very interesting, if you're standing right next to the guide, but the sound system isn't working properly," she said. "I'm a bit adrift, to be honest."

"Come and have lunch with me instead." *Where did that come from?* he thought.

She hesitated. "Better not," she said. "The others wouldn't be happy if I just bailed out like that." She indicated two other women who had frequently made up their bridge four. They were both frowning with concentration and fiddling with the amplifiers strung around their necks. "Unless we ask them along as well, perhaps?"

Was she teasing him, ever so slightly? He felt his self-denying ordinance weakening.

"Maybe not," he said. "What time do you sail?"

"First thing tomorrow."

"How about dinner then?"

She hesitated again, then said simply: "That would be very nice."

Andrew gave her the map from the hotel he had been using to orientate himself.

"Here," he said. "My hotel is almost literally just around the corner. I'll see you there at seven. In the meantime, I'll spy out some suitable local hostelry."

***

Rebecca listened distractedly to the near-incomprehensible patter of the guide as it came through the distortion of her headphones. The guide, a jovial middle-aged woman, was fluent in English and evidently expert in her field, but her heavy accent alone would have been a barrier to communication. The complication of the defective sound system rendered understanding virtually impossible.

Rebecca caught something about the elephant in

13

the fountain having been, since the thirteenth century, a talismanic protection against the eruptions of Etna (not a very successful one, Rebecca reflected), then a reference to an inscription of some kind in honour of the martyred St Agatha. But she could not be confident that she had properly grasped what the guide was saying, and after a while she gave up and removed the headphones, resolving to absorb as much as she could visually and to look up the history in the guidebook later. Gazing now, absently, at the baroque façade of the cathedral, she found herself thinking about her chance encounter with Andrew Singleton, about his surprising invitation to dinner, and about her equally surprising acceptance.

Or had it been chance? Not that she believed that Andrew would have deliberately engineered the meeting. But what about her? Why had she taken the ship's tour? It wasn't the first of these tours in which she had participated. But Yangon, Goa and Mumbai were places she might never get back to; Sicily was practically a weekend break. What had decided her to sign up, and to persuade two of her shipboard friends to come too? (What was that about? Camouflage?) *Too late now,* she thought. *What will be will be.*

***

Andrew was in danger of being late for his appointment with Rebecca Shearer, something about which he felt unaccountably concerned. He had eaten a grilled, freshly caught swordfish for lunch in the restaurant at the periphery of the bedlam of the fish market. He had drunk no wine, resolving to leave that pleasure for his evening with Rebecca Shearer, and had opted instead for a cold Messina beer. Then, instead of immediately returning to his hotel, he had decided to combine walking off his lunch with looking for a suitable restaurant for dinner. He had unexpectedly come across a major landmark that had somehow escaped his memory altogether: the Castello Ursino, a thirteenth-century castle that had miraculously survived the great earthquake and now housed the city museum. There he had whiled away an hour or more before getting pleasantly lost in the maze of streets beyond the castle, the memories of his teenage visit deceiving him after so many years about the city's dimensions beyond the centre itself.

It was almost seven when he got to the hotel. A tour group had just arrived, and the lobby was thronged with people surrounded by luggage, all speaking German, while a young woman in a travel agent's uniform holding a pile of passports negotiated patiently with the reception desk. Andrew made his way politely through the crowd and headed towards the lifts. He had no doubt that the newly arrived tourists were engaged in perfectly normal conversation but they still all gave the impression of being involved in a monumental row. And then, hearing the spoken German, he experienced an unexpected wave of grief. *"Du bist der Boss,"* Birgit had used to say, with an inimitable combination of seductiveness and irony. Irony, because – certainly at the last – he was not the master of his own feelings. And now she was gone, dead because of him.

As Andrew walked, deep in thought, past the seating area in the lobby, a man stood up from one of the sofas and greeted him.

"Mr Singleton," he said. "Could you come with me, please?"

Andrew studied the man. He did not believe he knew the face, which was in any case partly obscured by tinted glasses, yet there was something oddly familiar about the stance, about the timbre of the voice. The man was dressed in an inexpensive, lightweight blue suit, with a white shirt and colourful patterned tie. He was carrying a raincoat over one arm.

"I'm sorry," said Andrew. "And you are?"

"Just come with me, please," said the man. The quiet authority in his voice belied his modest appearance. Where had Andrew heard that voice before?

"Where to?" Andrew said.

"Your room."

"What for?"

"You'll see."

Andrew was becoming irritated now. "I'll need a little more explanation than that," he said.

"Will this do?" said the man, stepping closer to Andrew and shifting the raincoat on his arm very slightly to reveal the barrel of a gun.

"Are you mad?" said Andrew, fear flooding through him.

"Your room," said the man.

Andrew made a bid to collect himself. "I don't know who you are," he said. "Why should I do any damned thing you say? Are you going to shoot me here in broad daylight?"

"This is a Beretta 93R machine pistol," said the other. "It's forty years old, but has been lovingly maintained by its former owner and thoroughly tested by me, so please do not be in any doubt that it will work. Unfortunately, as you may know, when repeatedly fired in burst mode it is *very* difficult to control. This means that one false move from you will almost certainly result in the death of everyone in the lobby of this hotel. Including you, of course. You decide."

Andrew looked around him at the crowded lobby. Was this man so insane that he would do what he threatened? It was surely a gigantic bluff. Or was it? Why had the man not simply followed Andrew into the lift and accosted him there, or outside his room? Was he playing a kind of lunatic game? And then Andrew saw Rebecca Shearer, some twenty yards

16

distant, emerge from the revolving doors at the entrance to the hotel. She smiled and raised a hand in greeting.

"Okay," said Andrew, avoiding eye contact with Rebecca. "Let's go now."

The man looked amused. "Good decision," he said. "You go first."

They were alone in the lift, but with the barrel of the gun now thrust into the small of his back there was no possibility of resistance. The corridor leading to Andrew's room was also deserted. Andrew held the key card against the pad and pushed open the door. The man shoved Andrew roughly in the back before he could try anything and he fell face forward on to his hands and knees.

"Get up and put the key card in the slot," said the man.

Andrew did as instructed. The other pressed the light switch: nothing happened. "Now put it in the right way up," he said, apparently unfazed by Andrew's amateurish attempt at deception. Andrew obeyed, and the light came on.

"Sit in the chair on the left," the man said.

Andrew sat in the chair indicated. The man sat across from him, the gun pointed at Andrew's heart. *Who are you?* thought Andrew. *Why do I think I know you?* There was something about the man, the way he moved, the rhythm of his speech. Andrew caught himself thinking that this was exactly the problem he had had in trying to decide who Rebecca Shearer reminded him of. There was no physical resemblance, but...

"We didn't really finish our discussion properly last time we met," said the other.

"You think we've met before?"

"Really," said the man. "I'd expected you to be a little quicker on the uptake."

"I think you're making a terrible mistake," said Andrew. "You must have me confused with someone else." But even as he spoke, he was desperately trying to decide what was so familiar about the man.

"Come now, High Commissioner," said the other. "You can do better than that."

"I'm sorry," said Andrew, startled to be addressed with the title he had so recently relinquished. "I really don't know who you are."

"It was such a shame about Birgit," said the other.

The room was not air conditioned and had absorbed considerable warmth from the sun throughout the day. But Andrew was suddenly cold.

It was the nose that had put him off. It was a generous, prominent nose suggesting a Middle Eastern provenance, Arab or Israeli perhaps, possibly Kurdish. Not the small, neat nose of the man he had known. Hussein, a man of mixed Malay and Indian parentage, the man who had held him hostage on a yacht in the South China Sea, the man responsible for the scar on his chest. A terrorist. And Birgit's former lover.

Once again, Andrew experienced fear, this time mingled with fury. "You," he said, still half-unbelieving.

"Very good," said Hussein. "You have to admit the plastic surgeon did an exceptional job. Sadly for him, it was his final commission – one can't be too careful about these things."

"How in hell's name did you know where to find me?"

"How did I find you last time?"

Andrew was silent. The location of his final, fated assignation with Birgit had been betrayed by a member of the High Commission staff whom Hussein had blackmailed. But Susan was now in London, facing disciplinary action; it could not have been her. That he was travelling by sea had been no secret: Michael Seng, the Permanent Secretary at the Singapore Foreign

Ministry, had bid him a formal farewell at the dockside, with the press in attendance. But he had thought that his decision to disembark at Catania had been known only to his Head of Chancery and to his Personal Assistant, who had informed the travel agent and made the hotel reservation. The travel agent, of course... But then he also recalled saying something about it to Michael Seng as they said goodbye, the devout Methodist doing his best to prevent his fundamental disapproval of Andrew's recent behaviour impair his professional courtesy. Had Michael, or the protocol officer who had accompanied him, spoken to someone else? And what about the ship's officers, with whom he had exchanged polite conversation throughout the voyage? Or his bridge partners? Andrew realised that the potential for leaks was considerable. But then again, he argued with himself, how had Hussein known his hotel?

"You'll need to be a bit more exact than that," he said finally.

"We'll see," said the other.

"What the hell do you want from me, anyway?" Andrew said. "What's your great game this time?"

"There is no game," said Hussein. "I'm going to kill you."

***

Rebecca Shearer stood for a moment, nonplussed, just inside the entrance to the hotel. Andrew Singleton had definitely seen her: he had been looking straight at her. Why then had he abruptly shifted his gaze and moved away? And who was the man he was with?

Her puzzlement rapidly gave way to irritation. What was she doing here anyway? What possible point had there been in having dinner with Andrew Singleton, a man she would never see again? Was it simple curiosity, an inability to resist the opportunity to delve behind the urbane mask to uncover the secrets that undoubtedly lurked there? Or was she unconsciously hoping for something else?

Well, he had certainly given the impression that he wasn't remotely interested in *her*. She checked her watch. The taxi had taken only twenty minutes from the port. She would give Andrew fifteen minutes. If he did not come by then, she could be back at the ship in time for a late table for dinner, maybe getting in a hand of bridge afterwards.

But even as she took a seat in the lobby, Rebecca began to feel uneasy. Why had Andrew blanked her? Why had he gone to the trouble of seeking her out in the crowd earlier and inviting her to dinner only to be so uncharacteristically rude? It had to have something to do with the man who was accompanying him. Had Andrew been under some form of duress?

The swarm of German tourists who had been in the lobby when she arrived were now making their way noisily to the lifts. Rebecca waited until they were all clear of the lobby, then stood up and went to the reception desk.

"Could I speak to Mr Singleton, please?" she asked.

"Of course, madam," said the receptionist, with elaborate courtesy. He was a young, rather pretty man, probably Eastern European from his accent. "Do you know his room number?"

"I'm afraid I don't," she said. "Is that a problem?"

"Not a problem," he replied. "One moment, please."

The receptionist tapped the keys of his computer and consulted the screen. "Room 402," he said. "I shall call him."

There was no reply from the room.

"Could you try again, please?" said Rebecca. "I'm pretty sure he's there."

The receptionist looked as though he was about to

demur, but he changed his mind. "Yes, of course," he said. "It is not a problem."

Once again, there was no reply. Maybe Andrew had gone to the other man's room, or to the restaurant.

"Could you try paging him in the restaurant?" she asked.

"Sorry?"

"Could you call the restaurant to see if he is there, please?"

"Of course. It is not a problem."

Andrew was not in the restaurant. *What now?* she thought. She didn't have his mobile number. Short of banging on the door of his room, she had no means of communicating with him. *Should I just go back to the ship?* But then she would never know what had caused Andrew Singleton to behave in such a peculiar way. *No,* she thought, as she walked towards the lift. *We'd agreed to meet. At the very least, I'm owed an explanation.*

***

"That's what you said last time," said Andrew, affecting a degree of bravado he did not feel. He had to keep the man talking, to exploit the other's vanity and love of his own voice. Six days of captivity alone with Hussein on a yacht in the South China Sea had given Andrew some insight into the other's character. The man was a natural conspirator, someone who enjoyed the conception, planning and execution of terror as much as its effect. He also had intellectual aspirations and had embraced with enthusiasm the warped notion of international relations theory Andrew's brother had taught him at Oxford. The prolonged debate about Islam and the West during Andrew's captivity had all been part of an elaborate act of misdirection designed to provoke the United States into war with Iran. But Andrew was in no doubt that Hussein had enjoyed the argument for itself – or rather had enjoyed his own part in it.

"You were part of the game last time," said Hussein. "Now you're just unfinished business."

"What took you so long?" said Andrew, essaying another tack. "Don't tell me you were afraid of the Singaporeans?"

"I'm not afraid of *anything*," said Hussein in a matter-of-fact tone. "But I'm not a fool. I knew your security would be relaxed once you left Singapore – and so it has proved."

"As far as you know," said Andrew, allowing the words to hang in the air.

"Well," said Hussein. "I'd say it was conspicuous by its absence – unless, of course, the rather nice-looking woman in the green shirt whose eye you were trying to avoid downstairs is in deep cover."

So Hussein had seen Rebecca. Was this good or bad? Had Rebecca seen *him*? Or did Hussein think she had? Was she now in danger too? *Christ, Andrew,* he thought. *You are a fatal man.*

"I was meeting her for dinner," said Andrew, striving to speak calmly. "She'll have given up on me by now – she's probably on her way back to the ship."

"Let's hope for her sake that's true," said Hussein.

"I still don't understand why you've waited until now," said Andrew, anxious to move the conversation away from Rebecca.

"Well, let's just say that the timing was fortuitous," said Hussein. "I have things to do in Europe, so I was coming this way anyway."

"What sort of things?"

The other laughed. "Oh, nothing as elaborate as last time, I can assure you. A straightforward assassination."

"Who?"

"I don't think I'm going to give you the satisfaction of

knowing that," said Hussein. "I want you to die in total ignorance, feeling stupid and frustrated."

"But why?" said Andrew. "I served your purpose before. It's not my fault the Americans didn't fall for it."

"Because you represent an atheistic, materialistic and corrupt society and deserve to burn in hell," said Hussein.

Despite himself, and the situation, Andrew guffawed. "Well, honestly, that is so much bullshit," he said.

"And I blame you for Birgit's death," said Hussein. "Her husband may have killed her, but it was because of you."

Andrew felt very cold again. "That is undeniable," he said. "And I live with the shame of that. But it's laughable that words of moral censure should issue from the mouth of someone like you – a terrorist guilty of murder and conspiring to cause the death of thousands of innocent people."

Now it was Hussein's turn to laugh. "Maybe it's just professional pride then. You're a loose end that needs tidying up."

"Here? In a hotel bedroom? With a machine pistol? I hope you have some kind of plan for your extraction."

"Oh, no," said Hussein. "The machine pistol is just for dramatic purposes – or if I really do find myself in a corner. I'm temporarily flying solo and one does need to have an ultimate fall-back position."

He reached with his free hand into his inside jacket pocket and pulled out another, much smaller gun.

"This is a somewhat more recent example of the genius of Beretta," he said. "It's a 21A Bobcat. As you will see, it is fitted with a silencer. These things are not brilliantly effective, but with the television on I doubt that anyone outside this room will hear anything untoward."

Hussein placed the machine pistol on the coffee table and took the television remote control from its holder on the bedside table. He switched the television on and scanned the programmes until he found BBC World. "Here we are," he said. "There's bound to be some noisy news before too long. Probably something from Gaza or the West Bank."

Andrew calculated his chances of reaching the machine pistol before Hussein shot him. They were close to zero – offering Andrew a hint of hope was no doubt all part of Hussein's cruel game. But what else was Andrew to do? Wait passively for death?

"Look," he said, gathering himself for one final effort to put the other off balance. "You and I both know that you're taking an enormous risk. If you get caught, that's not only the end of you but the end of your assassination plot, which I suspect is rather more carefully planned than this personal diversion. Is it really worth it? Walk away from here and I give you my word that I shall say nothing to the police, nothing to anyone, about this episode."

Hussein roared with laughter. "I'm pleased to see that duplicity remains part of the armoury of the British diplomat," he said. "I'm tempted to keep you alive a little longer just for amusement's sake. But no, it's time to get this over with."

The telephone rang, startling both men. "Well, well, well," said Hussein. "Maybe she hasn't gone back to the ship." They listened until the phone ceased ringing. Before either of them could speak, it rang again, then finally was silent once more.

"Well now," said Hussein. "What next, I wonder? Will she call the police? Probably not, I would say. What could she tell them that would convince them to take any action – that her date had stood her up? I'd say the odds are that she will now return to the ship, to complain to her friends about the unreliability of shipboard romances."

"You've got this all wrong – I hardly know her," said Andrew, as calmly as he could. "My guess is she wouldn't even bother to talk about it."

"You may be right," said Hussein. "On the other hand, maybe she'll come looking for you."

***

Rebecca stood before the door of Room 402 and hesitated. She thought at first that she could hear people speaking, but then realised, from the rhythm of the voices, that the sounds were coming from a television news programme.

What was she to make of this? That Andrew had failed to acknowledge their appointment in order to watch television? Or that he was not there and had left the television on? The latter was less likely if the hotel used electronic cards, as she now saw was the case. As an unaccompanied guest, Andrew would have only one card, which he would have taken with him, thereby switching off the power in his room. So, he was there. Unless, of course, she belatedly thought, he was *not* unaccompanied. Could there be a woman in his room? But what would that mean? What sense would there be in Andrew inviting Rebecca to dinner if he had never had any intention of honouring the invitation? Or, and another possibility occurred to her, had he had a better subsequent offer?

This is stupid, she thought. *It's not about you.* It had to have something to do with the man she had seen Andrew with. Maybe there was some television news bulletin he had wanted Andrew to see urgently. Yes, that was it. In five minutes' time, Andrew would be rushing down to the lobby, seeking her out to apologise for being so ungentlemanly and explaining that, not having her mobile number, he had been unable to ring her. Maybe she should just go down and order herself a drink at the bar and await developments.

But then, logic required her to ask, why had Andrew not answered his telephone? Was he so absorbed in what he was watching that he could not be interrupted? Had he fallen asleep? Or was he under some form of constraint?

Now you're being melodramatic, she thought. Well, there was only one way to find out. She knocked on the door.

AUGUST: ADAM

CHAPTER 3

The Foreign Office has its share of attractive women, but most people agreed that Kate Thomas was in a class of her own.

It was not just that she was beautiful, although she was certainly that. The delicate features, the silken, ash-blonde hair, the supple, athletic figure were in themselves enough to cause Adam White momentarily to hold his breath the first time they met. But Kate had more: an unconscious sensuality and a honeyed, musical voice which imbued the most everyday remark with the promise of something more. In keeping with her Welsh Nonconformist upbringing, she dressed, in the office, demurely, even chastely. Yet the effect of this modesty on those with whom she worked was perversely erotic.

The more imaginative of Kate's admirers claimed to detect a hint of something darker, some episode in her past which had left its subtle mark and made her even more alluring. Others purported to have observed an unexplained troubled air about her in recent months. But no one in the Foreign Office got close enough to Kate to unravel these mysteries.

Kate was also bright, and determined enough, when barely twenty-six, to have been given the number two slot in the Foreign Office Financial Control Unit. It had thus fallen to her to induct Adam into his new position as head of the unit. (She must, he realised, have thought him extraordinarily dim, because he could not afterwards recall a word of her introductory briefing.) Her intelligence and coolness of head had been further demonstrated by a limited secondment to the Foreign Office emergency unit following the July bombings in London.

There was much speculation in the office as to whether Kate had a permanent partner. She wore no rings on her fingers, was not heard to take private phone calls in the office, was never collected from work for the theatre or dinner. She lived alone in a small rented flat in Shepherd's Bush. Her personal file (to which Adam had had access in an earlier job in Security) revealed a brief relationship at Aberystwyth University with her married history tutor, membership of the Socialist Society, one conviction for possession of cannabis and a creditable upper second-class degree. Positive vetting had uncovered nothing further untoward since she had joined the Foreign Office at the age of twenty-two. She kept herself to herself, politely declining the invitations of her love-struck male colleagues. The latter did not give up easily. Indeed, they regarded Kate as a serious challenge: one of the boys in Middle East Registry had even opened a book on who would be the first to break down her resistance.

No one won the bet. Early one Tuesday in August, as storm clouds gathered over London and early risers bemoaned the probability of no play once more at Lord's, while the Foreign Office night duty staff prepared to hand over to their daytime colleagues and, in their flat off Archway, Alison Webster was shaking Adam White awake to tell him he was late for work, the body of Kate Thomas was found, fully clothed, floating in the dark brown waters of the lake in St James's Park.

CHAPTER 4

Alison Webster had asked Adam White to marry her as they lay side by side in bed on the night following her mother's funeral.

"If you're ready, Ali," he had said, in his soft Glaswegian burr. "But is this really the right moment to decide?"

Alison had to acknowledge that this was a fair question. She had used similar words to Adam less than eighteen months previously, when he himself had raised the possibility of marriage at a moment of great personal stress. "I just want what they had," she said.

Adam said nothing, but held her close to him and gently stroked her hair.

"I want unconditional commitment," she said. "Lifelong devotion."

Adam turned to look at her in the pallid light of the streetlamp shining through a gap in the curtains. "That's not exactly how I thought you saw your parents' relationship," he said.

Alison pulled him closer and kissed him lightly on the forehead. "I know," she said. "She was the mother from hell. But Daddy didn't see it like that. You saw how he nursed her in the final months."

"He's a fine man," said Adam.

"And so are you, Adam," she said.

He laughed self-deprecatingly, turning his head away. "I

don't quite think of myself in the same category as your father, Ali," he said. "I'm a lucky idiot, that's all."

She lifted her head to look at his dark profile in the gloom. "When we first met I thought it was all about sex and laughter," she said. "Now I know I need something else."

He turned his face back towards her, but it was in shadow and she could not see his expression. "I hope that doesn't mean no more sex and laughter," he said, and she knew now that he was smiling.

"Adam, I'm serious," she said. "I'm afraid."

"I don't understand," he said. "What are you afraid of?"

"Supposing we'd been caught in the bombings," she said. "Wouldn't that have been awful? To have died without having married?"

"Ali, the bombs weren't on our line," Adam reminded her. "We were never in any danger." His tone was gentle, but she sensed his mild impatience. For Adam, death would be final, leaving no room for regret.

"But one of us *might* have been," she insisted. "How would the one left behind have felt?"

Adam said nothing immediately. When he finally spoke, it was with quiet conviction. "Ali, legalising our relationship is surely not what's important," he said. "It's the relationship that counts."

"You don't get it, Adam," she said. "I know what a bitch I can be. I want to bind you to me, so you'll stay – even when I'm impossible. I want you to be like Daddy."

"I'm not your father, Ali," said Adam. "Don't think you'd be marrying your father."

"That's not what I mean," she said. "You know that's not what I mean." She seized his face in her hands and kissed him on the lips. "Make love to me," she said.

They had spoken no more of marriage in the two weeks since then. They had both been busy, but there was more to it than that. Adam had appeared excessively preoccupied with his new job, as though he regarded this as his last chance to salvage his career. She, too, had been under pressure, with a tricky negotiation on behalf of a major corporate client approaching the final stages, and a number of vital arguments concerning draft tax legislation in Iraq still to be fully researched. As a result, they had both been working long hours during the week and had barely exchanged more than a few words late at night or over breakfast. At the weekends, Alison had felt obliged to spend time in Pinner with her father, who had been physically drained by her mother's illness and in a state of near shock since her death. Adam had said he did not wish to intrude on their time together and brought home piles of paperwork to keep himself occupied in her absence.

Despite all this, it would not have been impossible for Alison to find a spare moment to say to Adam, in the full light of day, that she had been serious and would like to fix a date for their wedding. But she was waiting for Adam to raise the subject, and he did not.

Even now, today, as she kissed him goodbye before leaving the train at Tottenham Court Road, Alison was willing Adam to say something. But he merely squeezed her arm in a slightly distracted fashion and said: "See you later, Ali."

She stood on the platform, watching the train disappear into the tunnel, bearing Adam towards Embankment and the Foreign Office. Then she made her way to the eastbound Central Line platform. As she boarded the train to take her to Chancery Lane, she resolved to spend only one day with her father at the weekend. He was already much better, and would understand. Then she and Adam could have a proper talk.

***

Hoping to beat the rain, Dame Gillian King was striding to work along Victoria Street when she received a call on her mobile from her Private Secretary, Hilary Price. For a moment she stood still and could not speak. Then thirty years of professional experience kicked in and she began to walk again, even faster than before.

"Do we know what happened, Hilary?" she asked.

"She appears to have drowned, Permanent Under Secretary," he said. "She was in the lake in the park."

"Was it an accident?"

"The police are being non-committal pending a full post mortem," said Price. "But they're inclined to treat her death as suspicious."

"Oh God," said Gillian, as she turned into Dean Farrar Street, heading north. "Who identified her?"

"They found her handbag in the lake," said Price. "They've asked about next of kin for a formal identification. Personnel are on to that."

Gillian descended Cockpit Steps and came out into Birdcage Walk. Looking across to the park, she could see that the police had erected a tent at the edge of the lake and established an outer perimeter, with blue-and-white tape, stretching as far as the footbridge across the lake to the west and Horse Guards Parade to the east.

"They're also asking to speak to Kate's immediate colleagues," said Price. "They seem to think one of them may have been the last to see her alive. Security are making the necessary arrangements."

Gillian ran up Clive Steps and into King Charles Street. "I'm almost there," she said. "You'd better put the meeting back."

***

There was a police car parked in the Foreign Office quadrangle when Adam arrived. He gave it only a cursory glance, his mind on the business of the day, for which he was already late.

Adam was acutely aware that he could not afford to make a mess of his new responsibilities. He was lucky to have any job at all, and he knew it. His interview with the Head of Personnel on his return from Singapore had been as bad as he had feared.

"Adam, I'm afraid I'm going to have to admonish you formally," Julian de Crespigny had said, his rich baritone voice betraying a lifetime's consumption of vintage brandy and cigars. There was an unhappy expression on his toad-like face, as he adjusted the crisply ironed cuffs of his white Sea Island cotton shirt and shifted uncomfortably in his tailored navy mohair suit. "Are you sure you don't want a union representative present?"

"No need for that, Julian," said Adam. Even at such a moment he found himself calculating how much de Crespigny must have paid for the hand-stitched Italian silk tie he was wearing – probably as much as Adam had paid for his own entire outfit, he guessed. "I screwed up big time. I know that."

"To be precise," said de Crespigny, looking down at the single sheet of paper on his desk. "You suppressed evidence relating to the arrest of a British citizen, who might well as a result have been wrongly convicted and hanged for heroin smuggling. The Foreign Office is now facing a demand for compensation from Daniel Taylor's father, who is alleging – with some justification – that we failed to exercise our duty of care towards his son. You also risked prejudicing the close working relationship the High Commission enjoyed with the Singapore Narcotics Bureau. You are accordingly deemed to be guilty of unprofessional conduct and of bringing the Service into disrepute."

"I can't deny any of that," said Adam. "But Dan Taylor's

free. And, thanks to what I did, the SNB arrested the man behind one of the most extensive narcotics smuggling operations in South East Asia. So it's not all bad."

"Quite so," said de Crespigny, who seemed relieved that the formal part of the interview was out of the way. "I must say, Adam, you do seem to have a knack of getting into scrapes that somehow work out alright in the end. But there'll be no medals this time, I'm afraid. You broke the law and you're bloody lucky the Singaporeans aren't prosecuting."

"I know that," said Adam. "I'm ready to take my medicine."

In the event, he had got off lightly, with the loss of three salary increments and a time bar on promotion. Then he had been told to take indefinite leave until a suitable job could be found for him in London.

For several weeks Adam had laboured to keep Harry Webster's garden tidy, while Harry looked after Ruth. The stroke had left Ruth almost totally paralysed, and it was difficult for Adam to judge the level of her awareness, but Harry would not stray from her side for more than a few minutes at a time. Alison had had to begin work as soon as she and Adam got back from Singapore, because her firm had made her a take-it-or-leave-it offer. She went to her parents' house at the weekends, but even then her father had insisted on bearing the brunt of the caring.

The telephone call, when it came, was not quite what Adam had been expecting. He had more or less resigned himself to being relegated to a dusty corner of the office where the powers-that-be believed he could cause no damage. The Financial Control Unit was something else again. It was the nearest thing the Foreign Office had to an internal police force, dedicated to eradicating fraud committed by members of the Service. Its first head had rejoiced in the unlikely name of Roger Jolly. Some wag had pinned a picture of the skull and crossbones to his door and, from that moment on, the members of the unit had been known throughout the Service as 'the buccaneers'.

"You're lucky," had said the Deputy Head of Personnel, Jack Grey (whose surname fitted his personality like a glove). "Archie Drysdale's had a nervous breakdown. We need someone to run the unit urgently. You know about money laundering from your time in Security." He paused. "And you certainly know about drug money in South East Asia. So this is your chance to redeem yourself."

"Don't you have to run this past the appointments board?" Adam had asked.

"You're our only candidate," had been the terse reply. "You start this afternoon."

Lata Shankar rose from her desk as Adam entered her office. She looked tired and anxious – she was having more problems with her son, he supposed. She was not, as she normally did, wearing a sari, but a patterned cotton shirt and cream trousers. "Where have you been, Adam?" she said, worrying a strand of black hair with her fingers. "You've got visitors – Gerry Baxter from Security brought them along."

"Why didn't you call me?" he said.

"You're not answering your mobile."

Adam patted his pockets. "Damn," he said. "I was charging it overnight. I must have left it at home."

Adam walked through Lata's office and into his own. Two men were sitting in the chairs in front of his desk. They stood up as he entered and turned towards him.

"Good grief," said Adam, staring at the first man, who had a thatch of shaggy red hair and a face with ridiculously sharp features. "What's going on, Raymond?"

"Hello, Adam," said the red-haired man. "Long time no see."

It was, in truth, no more than eighteen months since Adam had last seen the Scotland Yard detective inspector whose name, Raymond Fox, so aptly suited his appearance. It had been at his last interview with Fox, when the latter was clearing up the final details of the murder case involving Adam's former boss, James Carter. But so much had happened since then – including the entire Singapore saga – that it seemed like a different world.

"Don't tell me you haven't heard," said the man's shaven-headed companion, whom Adam now recognised as a detective sergeant who had worked with Fox when he and Adam had first met. (What was his name? Roker? No, Coker. Phil Coker.)

"Heard?" said Adam. "Heard what?"

"Kate Thomas is dead, Adam," said Fox.

Adam felt a churning in his stomach and a strange thickness in his throat. "No," he said, sitting down heavily in the chair behind his desk. For a while he could say nothing else.

Then he said: "No, I hadn't heard."

"Was she a very close colleague?" said Coker.

Oh, Kate, Kate, Kate. Oh, sweet Jesus, Kate. "She was my deputy," said Adam.

"We know that," said Coker, glancing down at an organogram of the unit in his hand. Despite the humidity in the non-air-conditioned office, his face was dry and smooth. "But were you close?"

"I don't understand the question," said Adam, although in fact he understood it only too well. He was conscious that he was beginning to sweat.

"The thing is this, Adam," said Fox. He, too, was perspiring, and the tone of his voice was almost apologetic. "Miss Thomas's body was found in the park, only a matter of a few hundred yards from here. She was dressed for the office and we've just received confirmation that she didn't sleep in her bed last night. We don't have a final time of death yet. But it looks as though she may have been killed soon after leaving work."

"Killed?" Adam heard the question as though spoken by a stranger.

"We're assuming she was killed until we know otherwise," said Fox.

"So, you see," said Coker, "it would be very helpful to know when you last saw Miss Thomas."

"How did she die?" asked Adam. He was on automatic pilot, his spoken words unrelated to the racing of his mind.

"It looks as though she drowned," said Fox. "But we'll know for sure before the end of the day."

"When did you see her last?" said Coker, a hint of impatience in his voice.

"Last night," said Adam. "We were both working late."

"How late exactly?"

Too late, Adam thought. *Too bloody late for your good or mine, Kate. Oh, Jesus, Kate.* "She stayed until getting on for ten," he said.

"And you?"

"I left about half an hour later."

"Why were you in the office so late?" said Coker.

"I was working on a case which needed to be presented to the Legal Advisers first thing today," said Adam. "I wanted to make sure everything was ready and correct."

"And Miss Thomas?"

"She was working on something different," said Adam.

"Did she say she was planning to meet anyone last night?"

Adam closed his eyes and had a vision of Kate running for the door, calling over her shoulder as she tucked the tail of her shirt into the top of her jeans. "I have to go now, Adam," she had said. "I daren't be late."

"Yes," said Adam. "She didn't say who."

"At ten at night?"

"I think it was someone she knew pretty well," Adam said.

"Why do you think that?" asked Coker.

What had Kate said? "It's a very long story. I can't explain it. I don't understand it myself..."

"She said it was someone she'd known for some time," he said.

"But no name," said Coker.

"No," said Adam.

"Can you tell us something about the work Miss Thomas was doing, Adam?" asked Fox. "What does your unit actually do?"

"We're a kind of financial watchdog," said Adam, relieved to be moving on to safer ground. "We're trying to eliminate fraud."

"What was the particular case Miss Thomas was working on?" said Fox.

"It was a new development," said Adam. "We'd picked up some irregularities in the Madrid embassy account and she was looking into them."

"Irregularities?"

"Something to do with war pension payments," said Adam. "I'm not sure of the details."

"Do you know why she was working late on this particular case?"

Good question, thought Adam. *Why did you have to work so late, Kate? What was the pressing urgency?*

"She was very conscientious," he said. "She'd picked up something interesting and was keen to crack on with the investigation."

"I see," said Fox. "Well, perhaps we should know a bit more about this thing she was working on, just in case it has any relevance."

"I'll get someone to summarise what we have on the file," said Adam.

"Good," said Fox. "Now I think we need to talk to the rest of your colleagues, if that's alright with you. Maybe we—"

"Actually, I have one further question," said Coker, interrupting his detective inspector. "Did you see Miss Thomas again after you'd both left the office?"

"No," said Adam. He paused for a moment. "But I got a text message from her at around midnight asking if we could meet urgently."

"Oh, really?" said Coker, his expression a mixture of irritation and triumph. "Why didn't you tell us about this before?"

Why indeed, Adam? Why did you wait until they dragged it out of you? "I was coming to it," he said. It sounded hopelessly weak.

"From what you've already said, you obviously didn't meet her," said Fox.

"No," said Adam. "I tried to call her, but her home phone didn't answer and her mobile was switched off."

"You had her home number?" said Coker. "So you *were* close friends?"

"We all have each other's home numbers in case of emergency," Adam said.

"Weren't you worried when you couldn't make contact?" asked Fox.

"I left messages," said Adam. "I knew I'd be seeing Kate this morning. At least..."

"What do you think she wanted to see you about?" asked Fox.

"I assumed it was something personal," said Adam.

"Personal?"

"Yes."

"Do you want to be a little more precise, Adam?" said Fox.

Adam thought very carefully about his response. "She'd said something about wanting to escape from an unsatisfactory relationship," he said. "I thought it was about that."

"So you *were* close to her," said Coker, who seemed determined to prove a point.

"We were good friends," said Adam, wincing inwardly at the banality of his choice of words.

"And you've no idea who this other person was?" said Fox.

"No," said Adam. "Kate was a private sort of person."

"Show us the message she sent you," said Coker.

"It's on my mobile," said Adam. "I left it at home this morning. But it was a simple message, asking to see me as soon as possible."

"We'll need to see the mobile," said Coker. "One of our officers will go with you now to collect it."

"Actually, I've got something really urgent to do right now," said Adam. "Can I bring it to you later?"

· Coker began to say something, but Fox cut across him. "Later will be fine, Adam," he said. "Now, can we see the rest of your staff, please?"

"There are – were – only five of us," said Adam. "Ubaid Butt is just down the corridor. Steve Alford is on leave, and you've already met Lata Shankar, my Personal Assistant."

"Right," said Fox. "We'll talk to Ms Shankar first and think about whether we need to ask Mr Alford to break his holiday or not."

"He's in Italy," said Adam. "I hope you won't drag him back for no reason."

"We never do anything for no reason," said Coker, with a mirthless smile, which told Adam very clearly that his friendship with Raymond Fox would count for nothing if Coker had anything to do with it. "I expect we'll be back to see you again before too long."

***

"I've done a brief note, Permanent Under Secretary," said Hilary Price, placing a single sheet of A4 paper on Gillian's desk, as she walked into her office. "The meeting's postponed by fifteen minutes. I hope that's enough."

"Thanks, Hilary," said Gillian. "That's fine. You get on with things while I catch up."

One of the qualities that had helped Gillian King decide on her choice of Private Secretary had been Hilary Price's strangely old-fashioned habits of courtesy. While all and sundry in the office these days called her by her Christian name, Price always used Gillian's formal title, a custom which frequently drew secret smiles from others in meetings she was chairing. He sprang from his chair to escort visitors, however junior in rank, opening and closing doors for them and fussing over whether they were comfortable, or had enough milk in their tea. Any request he made for work to one of the Private Office team, or to a busy head of department, was always couched in the most apologetic terms, as though the person concerned were being asked to make a painful sacrifice rather than simply fulfilling their job description.

Hilary was also a sympathetic and thoughtful colleague and mentor. He had demonstrated this very effectively by his sensitive induction of Gillian's new Assistant Private Secretary, Sophie Smith, who had arrived in April, newly promoted and fresh from a posting in Singapore. Sophie was not entirely to Gillian's taste – she seemed brittle and had a mildly resentful air about her – but she was undoubtedly intelligent and had come highly recommended. Hilary had seen Sophie into the job very successfully and she was now involving herself diligently in all aspects of the work of Gillian's Private Office. Gillian was not sure whether there was more to the relationship than kindness on Hilary's part and gratitude on Sophie's, but at the least they appeared to have become friends.

Courtesy and empathy alone would not, however, have won Price the position. He had a good, analytical mind, honed at Eton and Cambridge, and the ability to condense the sometimes sprawling arguments of his Foreign Office colleagues into the kind of crystalline prose which pressurised ministers could absorb on the run without even breaking step. He also had the essential dispassion of a successful diplomat, his evident distaste for British involvement in the military intervention in Iraq, for example, never inhibiting him from faithful defence of British government policy.

An outside observer would probably have described Price as coming from the privileged, upper-class background typical of a British diplomat, when in fact such people in today's Foreign Office were very much the exception to the rule. To call Price's background 'privileged' would in any case have been an error. For Gillian had also been influenced (although she would not acknowledge this to anyone but herself) by the tragedy in Price's personal life. His father, a retired army officer, had been ruined in a stock market fraud and committed suicide, leaving Price's mother effectively destitute. Somehow she had got Hilary through Cambridge, making it possible for him to enter the Foreign Office. But such surplus as there was from his Foreign Office salary, which he maximised by leading an exemplary, frugal life, made little impact on his mother's accumulated debts. They lived together in a small flat just off Regent's Park, on the lease of which there were only eight years unexpired. Each day was a struggle to keep assorted creditors at bay. Security Department had expressed concern to Gillian that Hilary's financial difficulties made him a risky appointment. Gillian had weighed that risk against Hilary's many virtues and his prudent, sober lifestyle, and had given him the job. So far, he had rewarded her decision with unswerving loyalty and professionalism.

The first item on Gillian's agenda was an office meeting about the impending visit of the President of Iraq. She used five of the fifteen minutes delay arranged by her Private Secretary to brief herself on the details known so far of Kate Thomas's death. Then she spoke to the Head of Personnel by telephone.

"Julian, we're going to have to put some kind of circular round the office," she said. "And we'll need a press line."

"I've spoken by telephone to all the private offices," said de Crespigny. "We've had no press contact yet, but the standard line is to refer all enquiries to the police. I rather thought we should wait for formal identification before putting out anything in writing. Her mother's on her way from Cardiff."

"You're right, of course," said Gillian. "Is someone going to be with her?"

"Welfare have a volunteer meeting her off the train and looking after her while she's in London."

"I should see her after she's identified the body."

"We'll arrange a time with Hilary," said de Crespigny.

"Thanks. How are Kate's colleagues taking it?"

"They're pretty shaken, not surprisingly. We suggested they take the day off, but they seem to prefer to keep working."

"That's probably for the best," said Gillian. She paused. "Congratulations on Madrid, by the way."

"I'd have waited for Paris, you know," said de Crespigny.

"I think the bird in the hand was the right decision," said Gillian. *Why do we have to play these games?* she thought. Both she and de Crespigny knew that she would have resigned rather than see him as Ambassador in Paris.

"No doubt you're right," said de Crespigny, possibly a little too smoothly. "And I know how much I owe you in that regard, Gillian."

***

For several minutes after Fox and Coker had left, Adam sat staring into the distance, trying not to think of Kate Thomas's drowned body being fished from the muddy waters of the lake in St James's Park. But he could not rid his mind of the image, or of the inter-cutting flashes of a different Kate, alive and fragrant, far too close, the pressure of her breast against his chest, her radiance threatening to dissolve his self-control, her hands slipping up and around his neck, seizing the back of his head, pulling him to her. And then, once more, a glimpse of her farewell, over her shoulder, as she tucked her shirt into her jeans. "I have to go now, Adam. I daren't be late."

There was something wrong with these fragmented images, a nagging, indefinable anomaly which troubled him, even through the overwhelming sense of loss – and, yes, guilt – but he could not give it conscious articulation.

He shook himself out of his reverie. He was due with the Legal Advisers in twenty minutes. He must focus on Tashkent for the next hour. Then he would study the Madrid file.

***

Ginny Ballesteros sat on a plastic chair in the corridor outside the entrance to the morgue, waiting for Gwyneth

Thomas to emerge following the identification of her daughter's body. Ginny had opted to stay outside, because she knew that the horror of the moment was not one to be shared with strangers. She had identified the badly burned remains of her first husband, James, in the company of the excitable wife of the Deputy Head of Mission in the Embassy in Santiago: it had been the worst experience of her life. Her second husband, her beloved Diego, had died in her arms in the same hospital barely a year later, but that had been a peaceful, almost joyous release.

Ginny knew she was not being entirely rational. Gwyneth Thomas would be surrounded by police and morgue staff, so there was no way that the moment would be private. Nevertheless, Ginny was convinced it would be wrong to expose the body of Gwyneth's dead child to the eyes of yet another stranger.

The doors opened and Gwyneth came out, leaning heavily on the arm of the shaven-headed detective sergeant. Ginny went and put her arms around her, saying nothing.

"I still thought it might have been a mistake," said Gwyneth, her small, quiet voice betraying the faintest of Welsh accents. "Well, there we are. It wasn't."

She seemed calm, almost resigned. But her fine-boned face was as grey as her hair, and she looked older than her fifty-odd years.

"Let's get a nice cup of tea, shall we, Mrs Thomas," said the detective sergeant, whose name was Coker. "Then I must ask you a few questions, if you don't mind."

"I think Mrs Thomas should have some time to herself first," said Ginny.

"No, really, dear," said Gwyneth. "I'll be fine. Let's get it over with."

They went to a nearby Starbucks and sat nursing

coffees. The detective sergeant made no attempt at finesse. "We need to know if your daughter had any men friends," he said. "Or if you know of anyone at all who might have had a grudge against her."

"I didn't see much of Kate once she came to London," said Gwyneth. "She was very much her own person, you know."

"Did she mention anything, on the telephone, or in letters?"

"She didn't write much," said Gwyneth. "Only the odd e-mail."

"On the phone then? Or when she visited?"

Gwyneth thought for a while. "She never said anything specific," she said. "But there was something a bit different about her these last few months. She called less often, for one thing."

"Less often?"

"Yes. I'd normally get a call from her on a Sunday evening, just to pass the time of day, you know? But lately I was lucky to get a call once or twice a month."

"And how else was she different?"

"She seemed a bit distracted. She used to tell me where she'd been, what she'd done, that sort of thing. But she started being very vague, almost as though she didn't want me to know too much."

"So she gave you no names?"

"She used to mention the names of girlfriends, sometimes a boy she'd been out with."

"Could you give me the names, please?" said Coker, pulling out a notebook.

"Oh, they were just first names," said Gwyneth. "I can't remember them all. Sarah, I remember. And Lucy. And Rachel. And there was a boy called Michael."

"But nothing lately?"

"No, like I say, she seemed to go all vague in the last few months."

"Did she talk about her colleagues at work?"

"She used to talk about her boss. Archie, I think his name was. She said he was a bit odd. The work was getting him down. I think in the end he suffered some kind of breakdown."

"Did she say anything about her new boss?"

Gwyneth thought for a moment. "Nothing much," she said. "Just that he was completely different from Archie."

Ginny studied Gwyneth's face as she spoke. Was it her imagination or was Gwyneth's expression marginally more strained than before? Could she be concealing something? But why should she? Ginny put the thought from her mind.

Coker suddenly changed course. "Did Kate have any other close family?" he asked.

"No," said Gwyneth. "My husband was killed five years ago and I've no other children."

"Your husband was killed?" said Coker.

"Yes," said Gwyneth. "He was knocked down by a hit-and-run driver."

As though she had until that point been anaesthetised by shock, the enormity of the situation suddenly seemed to dawn on her. "It was just her and me," she said, her voice tailing off.

"What about friends in Cardiff," said Coker, clearly oblivious to the shift in mood.

"I'd like to go now," said Gwyneth.

"I just need to know—" said Coker, but Ginny interrupted him.

"Mrs Thomas needs to rest," she said. "Surely this can wait until tomorrow."

Coker looked irritated, but did not insist. "We'll take a taxi," said Ginny. "So as not to take you out of your way, Detective Sergeant."

Ginny gave the taxi driver the address of her flat in Pimlico. The Foreign Office had booked Gwyneth into a small hotel at the back of Paddington Station, but Ginny knew she should not leave her alone in the anonymity of a London hotel.

"She used to win all the races at school, you know," said Gwyneth suddenly. "She ran so fast, it broke my heart."

Ginny said nothing, but placed her hand gently over Gwyneth's where it lay slackly by her side.

The taxi turned off Victoria Street and into Vauxhall Bridge Road. The rain that had been threatening all morning finally began to fall, slowly at first, then more insistently. There was a distant peal of thunder, somewhere to the north. Almost as though she had been waiting for the rain, Gwyneth began to cry. Ginny put her arms around her and held her close, still saying nothing, for there was nothing she could say which would make any difference.

***

Alison was home late, but still arrived before Adam. She had been engaged in meetings all day. The negotiations were at a delicate stage and the managing partner, Richard Sheinwald, had asked her to ensure that she did not allow the other team out of her sight. They had all eaten a sandwich lunch in the boardroom and not even left the room for tea or coffee. On a short visit to the bathroom, she had switched on her mobile and picked up a message from Adam asking her to call him, but there had been no time to do so.

Alison dumped her briefcase in the narrow hallway, hung up her dripping raincoat and scarf and went through to the kitchen. She set the kettle to boil and then suddenly remembered Adam's message. She telephoned his office and got an answer phone message. When she dialled his mobile number, she was surprised to hear it ringing in the bedroom.

"One day it'll be your head," she smiled to herself and went to unplug the phone.

Alison trusted Adam absolutely. Only once, at the very beginning of their relationship, had he kept something from her, and then it had been for the best of motives. So she could not account for the impulse which impelled her to listen to his mobile messages. They were, in any case, a mundane collection of routine communications, including a number from herself about various household issues. Nor could she explain why she then turned to his text messages and found herself scrolling through them. But within seconds she was sitting, frozen, on the bedroom floor, staring in disbelief at the handset. She did not hear the front door of the flat opening a few minutes later.

"What are you doing on the floor, Ali?" said Adam, as he came into the bedroom.

"Who's K?" said Alison, without turning round.

"Kate," said Adam. Something in his voice made her turn to look at him. His hair was wet from the rain, his pale, boyish face troubled. "Kate Thomas at the office," he said. "She's dead, Ali. I tried to call you to tell you."

Alison had a brief vision of a disconcertingly beautiful girl she had seen when collecting Adam from the office one night several weeks back. Her momentary twinge of jealousy was immediately eclipsed by guilty shock. "Oh, my God," she said. "What happened?"

"She drowned in the lake in St James's Park," said Adam. "The police think it might have been murder."

"Murder?"

Adam said nothing. He sat on the bed, rubbing his eyes.

"She wanted to see you last night," said Alison, standing up and handing him the mobile.

"Yes, but I couldn't reach her," said Adam.

Alison recalled that Adam had hung behind in the kitchen after she had come to bed the night before. Exhausted from the office, she had been asleep before he joined her.

"Do you know what she wanted?"

"No."

Alison debated with herself and decided to keep her counsel. She had intended to confront Adam. She could not believe that he was capable of deceiving her. And yet, he had seemed distracted in recent weeks – and the girl had been beautiful. But now she was dead, which changed everything. Adam would not know that Alison had seen all the messages in his inbox. He would not know that she had seen the message he had received an hour and a half before the request from Kate for an urgent meeting. He would not know that she had read the words which had brought her close to being physically sick: *We'll find a way. There has to be a way. K.*

"I'll get supper," she said. "You look all in."

CHAPTER 5

"Thanks for coming by, Adam. Do you have time for a coffee? We can probably let you have your phone back in half an hour."

Adam glanced at his watch, then grunted his assent and sat in the chair by Raymond Fox's desk. Fox brought two coffees back from the machine in the corridor and handed one to Adam.

"Thanks for this, by the way," said Fox, indicating the folder of papers on his desk. "Did anything strike you as possibly relevant when you put it together?"

"We seemed to have nothing hard to go on," said Adam. "But Kate had picked up something interesting in the pattern of payments being made to people drawing military pensions."

"Interesting?"

"Yes," said Adam. "We regularly run random checks on different Embassy accounts over a selected period of years to see if there are any unexplained variations in the figures. If the computer picks up a noticeable increase in expenditure on stationery, say, or on building maintenance materials, there may be some kind of fiddle going on."

"And this had happened in Madrid?"

"No," said Adam. "Quite the contrary. The amount disbursed in pensions over the last five years or so has been remarkably constant."

Fox's freckled forehead creased in puzzlement. "I don't get it," he said.

"Most of these pensions date from the Second World War," said Adam. "It would be a miracle if at least some of the pensioners haven't died in the last five years. So the payments should be declining."

"You mean someone's drawing pensions for people who are dead?"

"It looks like it," said Adam.

"Any clue as to who it might be?"

"Well, immediate suspicion must fall on someone in the locally engaged staff in Madrid," said Adam. "If it's been going on for five years or more, that pretty well rules out any current UK-based member of staff."

"Do you have any names?"

"They're listed on the file," said Adam. "One person who works in the Defence Attaché's office and two in the Embassy accounts section."

"Do they have any idea you're on to them?"

"I don't know," said Adam. "Kate sent a personal message to the Chargé d'Affaires on Monday evening alerting him to her suspicions and proposing that she visit to investigate."

"Has he replied?"

"No," said Adam. "I was planning to call him this morning after seeing you."

Fox appeared to think for a moment. "It may be irrelevant," he said. "The best thing would be for you to continue as you would have done anyway."

"There is one other slightly strange thing," said Adam. "This wasn't such a new discovery. There's a note on the file from my predecessor dated October of last year ordering the discontinuation of the investigation because of the absence of *prima facie* evidence of wrongdoing."

54

Fox looked more interested. "So why do you think Miss Thomas opened the case up again?" he asked.

Adam smiled bleakly. *Kate, Kate, stubborn, lovely Kate.* "Because she was her own woman," he said. "If she thought she was right, she wouldn't let it go. Once Archie left, there was no one to stop her."

"Archie?"

"Archie Drysdale, my predecessor."

"And where can we reach him?" asked Fox.

"He's in Whittington Hospital," said Adam. "He's undergoing treatment for a depressive illness."

Fox's telephone rang. He listened without speaking, then muttered a quick word of thanks. He looked up at Adam, his expression subtly changed.

"Adam, did you delete any messages from your mobile before bringing it here today?" he asked.

Adam was aware suddenly that his hands were damp. The rain of the previous day had done little to take the humidity out of the atmosphere, although today Fox appeared untroubled by it. Adam looked steadily back at Fox. Raymond knew him well enough to recognise the truth when he spoke it.

"Yes," he said. "I deleted a personal message from Kate."

"Why, Adam?" said Fox, an expression of mild exasperation on his sharp features. "You must know we have ways of recovering these things."

"I didn't think you'd be looking," said Adam.

"We didn't need to look," said Fox. "It was still in her own mobile. Why did you do it, Adam?"

"Because it wasn't relevant to the investigation into her murder," said Adam. "And I don't want to hurt anyone."

Fox was silent for a while. He looked unhappy. Finally he spoke.

"Adam, are you still telling me there was nothing between you and Kate Thomas?" Fox said.

Nothing? No, Raymond, I can't say nothing. Because for a terrible moment...

"Not in the way you think," Adam said. "The message was an aberration. A momentary fit of madness."

Fox sighed. "I'm prepared to believe you, Adam," he said. "But I'm not alone in this investigation and for the average observer that message is highly material."

"I'm telling you it's not," said Adam.

Fox thought for a few seconds before speaking again. "I probably shouldn't be telling you this," he said. "But you'll find out soon enough. We've had the interim post mortem report. First, Kate Thomas didn't drown. There was no water in her lungs. From the bruising on her face, and traces of silk fibre in her mouth and nostrils, our working hypothesis is that she was suffocated. Second, she had very recently had sexual intercourse. There were no injuries which would confirm rape, but there was a very small puncture of the skin just below the jawline, which suggests use of a knife, perhaps to intimidate. And there were fragments of hair and skin beneath her fingernails, which are now being subjected to further analysis."

Adam tried to suppress an imagined image of Kate struggling for breath, a cushion over her face, those elegant fingers scrabbling for purchase on the killer's face to force him away. But he could not block out the actual memory of the kiss, the hungry, unplanned, all-consuming kiss, or of Kate's hands kneading the back of his head and clutching his hair as she pressed against him.

"Do you want a DNA sample from me?" he said.

"I don't think we have any choice, Adam," Fox said. "And we're going to have to hang on to your phone for the time being."

Gillian King had rescheduled her Wednesday morning appointments to allow Gwyneth Thomas to catch the train of her choice back to Cardiff. It was a small enough gesture; there was no real urgency about the courtesy call by the new Portuguese Ambassador or the briefing from the Finance Director on the expected shape of the next budgetary negotiating round.

Hilary Price ushered two women into Gillian's office. At first glance they might have been sisters. They were both slim, with neat features and grey hair cut in a short, no-nonsense style. But, with a shock of recognition, Gillian saw that the younger woman was Virginia Ballesteros.

"Come and sit down, Mrs Thomas," said Gillian, gesturing to the sofa in front of her desk. "Virginia, how are you?"

"I'm well, Gillian, thank you," said Virginia, settling herself unobtrusively into a chair off to one side.

Gillian had not expected to see Virginia, although she realised on reflection that it had always been possible. She knew that Virginia was a Welfare Section volunteer, because Julian de Crespigny had very sensibly cleared the appointment with her. It was not unusual for widows of members of the Service to volunteer for such work. It was unprecedented for the dead husband to have been a murderer.

"What a lovely office," said Gwyneth, looking around at the stately room, which was furnished in late Victorian style, its walls splendid with portraits of long-dead viceroys and princes.

"Thank you," said Gillian, as coffee was served and Hilary Price withdrew. "I had a bit of a fight to restore it to its former glory, but I think it was worth it. At least these high ceilings help to keep the place cool in this sticky weather."

Gillian waited until she judged that Gwyneth Thomas was well settled before speaking again. "Can I say once more how sorry we all were to learn of your daughter's death, Mrs Thomas?" she said. "I've written to you, but I wanted to speak to you directly as well. Kate was an outstanding officer and a much valued colleague."

"That is a comfort," said Gwyneth. Her face was calm but drawn, terribly drawn, as though she had not slept the night before. There was no trace of irony in her voice.

"Is there anything we can do for you, Mrs Thomas?" asked Gillian. "Please do ask and we'll help if we can."

"What I want most of all is to take Kate home," said Gwyneth. "But I can't, apparently."

"The police are insisting on further tests," said Virginia. "They can't say exactly when Kate's body will be released."

"I'll get someone to ask them not to delay unreasonably," said Gillian.

"And I want the police to stop asking me questions about Kate's private life," said Gwyneth. "I spent an hour with them this morning and they kept going round and round the same track. They seem to think she had enemies, or a jealous lover or something. But Kate wasn't like that. She just wasn't."

"I know she wasn't," said Gillian, although she had in truth met Kate only once, briefly, on the latter's induction course. "But they just want to get to the bottom of this terrible business and find the person responsible."

"But she was attacked in the park," said Gwyneth. "It must just have been some madman."

"I'm sure that's true," said Gillian, knowing that this was what Gwyneth needed to believe. "But they have to explore all the avenues. It's their routine. They mean no harm."

Gillian saw Virginia consulting her watch. "How are you for time?" she asked.

"We should be going quite soon," said Virginia.

Gillian reached for Gwyneth's hands and took them in both of hers. "Please ask us for anything you need," she said. "Anything at all."

As the two women left, Gillian said to Virginia: "How's the research going?"

"Not bad," said Virginia. "I'm about to begin the book now, although I'll have to go back to Chile one more time to verify some of the detail."

"Will that be okay?" asked Gillian.

"It will be difficult," said Virginia. "But I have to do it."

***

It was mid-afternoon and the negotiations had reached their final stage. Richard Sheinwald had been speaking for five minutes without pause. His sentences were formulated with characteristic precision and his arguments flowed logically and inevitably towards a conclusion which would produce the optimal result for his client while leaving the people on the other side of the table with the impression that they had themselves achieved all that was legally feasible. No one seemed to discern any contradiction between Richard's self-deprecatory manner and his exotic, central European charm.

Alison had been responsible for researching the material she now heard Sheinwald deploying. She had in fact constructed a detailed, verbatim brief for him to use, but Richard had transmuted her correct, pedestrian prose into controlled oratory. Sitting beside him, Alison could not see the movements of Richard's fine, dark features. But she could see the effect they were having on the woman who led the opposing legal team. The other side had made a mistake, Alison thought, in sending a woman to negotiate with Richard, even someone as tough and glamorous as Veronica

Buckingham. Or had they? If Richard had a weakness, it was to regard any attractive woman as a prospect for conquest. Maybe the opposition knew exactly what they were doing.

Now that Richard had taken charge, and despite her best intentions, Alison found her concentration wandering. She had promised herself she would put Kate Thomas's text message out of her mind. There had to be an innocent explanation. And yet…

Alison tried to remember what Adam had ever said about Kate. Nothing she could recall that might have aroused her suspicions. In fact, almost nothing at all, now she came to think of it. And wasn't that strange in itself? When Adam had come home three months ago, after his first day in the new job, what had he and Alison talked about? Adam had described his discussion with the Finance Director, Simon Shakespeare, to whom he would be reporting: "a very cold fish", according to Adam. He had spoken of his Personal Assistant, Lata, an Indian woman whose son had a drug problem. He had observed how remarkably well Lata seemed to get on with another of his colleagues, Ubaid, whose family were from Pakistan. He had given a long, convoluted account of the history of someone called Steve, who seemed to be plagued with a disastrously complicated love life. But what had he said about Kate? "And then there's my deputy. A girl called Kate Thomas. Seems nice enough. Welsh – and pretty bright." *Seems nice enough, Adam? Seems bright? Was that the best you could think of?*

Stop it, Alison told herself. But she could not. What else had Adam said about Kate over the following few weeks? Always very routine stuff, and never more about her than about the others. In fact, decidedly less. He'd talk of Lata's latest clash with the probation people, or of Steve's impossible girlfriends, or of Ubaid's difficult interview with

Security about certain of his friends at the local mosque. But whenever he mentioned Kate it was work-related. "Kate's uncovered something a bit suspicious in the Caracas account." Or, "Kate told me something interesting about Archie Drysdale the other day." Never anything personal. Never, "Kate's mother's not well," or, "Kate's got a new man," or even, "Kate's a mysterious one – none of us knows what she gets up to in her spare time."

In the absence of further information, Alison had initially formed a mental picture of a quiet, conscientious, possibly dowdy girl. Unaccountably – or rather logically, given Kate's Welsh parentage – Alison had thought she would be pale and dark-haired. And then one night she had collected Adam from the office in the Mini to meet friends for supper in Clapham. She had been totally unprepared for the breathtaking woman who had waved at Adam as she ran for a bus in Whitehall.

"Who's *that?*" Alison had said.

"That's Kate," Adam had replied. "Haven't you seen her before?"

"You bloody well know I haven't," she had said. "Bloody hell, Adam, she's a knockout."

He had laughed and kissed her on the neck. "I prefer crooked noses and lopsided grins," he had said. Typical Adam. And she'd believed him. She *still* believed him. But what did the text message mean? And why in heaven's name hadn't she simply asked him? Was she still so insecure in their relationship, after all they'd been through together, that she preferred not to know the truth?

"Would you be able to do that, Alison?" Richard was saying.

"Of course," said Alison, suddenly aware that she had not been listening. She thought fast. "But can I just make a detailed note of the requirement?"

She saw some amusement on the faces of the other legal team.

"I agree," said Sheinwald, who appeared, with his customary sensitivity, to have divined Alison's predicament. "It's as well to be absolutely sure what we're talking about. Now, Veronica, you asked for the final revised draft agreement by close of play today. Did you mean by six? Or would seven be early enough?"

"Seven will be fine, Richard," said the leader of the other team, her voice betraying the slightest hint of huskiness. It had been a long negotiation, thought Alison.

"Good," said Sheinwald. "I'll bring it along myself. Maybe we can have a small celebratory drink in anticipation of your client's signature."

When the others had left, Richard took Alison to one side. "Are you okay?" he said.

"It was a momentary lapse, Richard. I'm sorry. Thank you for not making a big deal out of it."

"Is everything alright at home?" It was a sincere enquiry, she thought. Since she had rebuffed Richard's one and only proposition, just before rejoining the firm, his dealings with her had been impeccably correct.

"The Foreign Office girl who was killed worked for Adam," she said. "It's been a bit of shock."

"I'm so sorry," said Richard. "Are you sure you're alright to get this done this afternoon?"

"Don't be silly, Richard," she said. "I'll be fine."

***

Adam realised he had been staring at his computer screen for ten minutes or more without actually reading the document he was supposed to be checking. The Legal Advisers had agreed to the proposed action on the Tashkent case. The officer concerned was on leave in the UK, so it was simply a matter of inviting him to come for a chat with the Head of Personnel so that he might be confronted with the evidence of his wrongdoing and formally suspended from duty pending a full disciplinary panel. It was the detailed brief for Julian de Crespigny that Adam was in the process of polishing. Or at least he was supposed to be.

Had Ali seen Kate's first text message? She had gone to bed early the previous evening, saying she was tired. She had been up again early that morning and out of the flat before he had properly woken up. He was an idiot not to have told her. He should have realised the police would find out somehow, which meant that Ali would know as well before long. And what had he and Ali said so recently about always being open with one another? Tonight. He would tell her tonight, before things got out of hand.

The telephone rang. It was his direct number, so Lata had not intercepted the call.

"Adam? It's Archie Drysdale."

"Archie. How are you?" said Adam. Archie sounded terrible and probably knew it.

"I heard about Kate," said Archie. "The police came to see me. It was bloody awful."

An interesting sequence of statements, thought Adam. Not bloody awful that Kate was dead, but bloody awful that the police had been to see him.

"What did they ask you about?" said Adam.

"Not on the phone, Adam," said Archie. "I need to see you."

"Of course," said Adam. "I'll look in on you tonight on my way home."

"Can't you come sooner?"

"You know how things are here, Archie. I can't just drop everything."

"Okay," said Drysdale, although he sounded far from happy. "Come around eight."

***

Ginny Ballesteros was also finding it difficult to concentrate. After months of painstaking work she had assembled a mass of detailed material on the role of the British in the early development of Chile. The origins of the project, many years earlier, had been different. She had intended a comparative study of the history of the British in Venezuela and Spain. But with Diego's encouragement she had included Chile in her researches and had been so fascinated by what she had learned that she had in the end decided to focus exclusively on that country.

Now it was simply a matter of writing the book. She had been looking forward to this moment, when she would actually begin to create something, something she could dedicate to the memory of Diego and the happy but bitterly brief time they had spent together.

Instead she found herself thinking about what Gwyneth Thomas had said to her as they sat drinking tea waiting for the platform announcement at Paddington.

"Virginia, you've been so kind," said Gwyneth. "I'd have been lost on my own, you know."

"Call me at any time if you need to, Gwyneth," said Ginny. "Any time, I mean that."

Gwyneth appeared to think for a moment. Then she said: "I don't know why I'm telling you this, but I wasn't entirely honest with the police."

So there had been something, thought Ginny. She set her cup down carefully in its saucer. "Not honest, Gwyneth?" she said.

"They had no business digging around for scandal in

Kate's life," said Gwyneth. "It was a terrible accident what happened to her. Her private life has nothing to do with it."

Ginny said nothing, waiting for Gwyneth to continue.

"This new boss of hers, Adam," said Gwyneth. "She was in love with him."

Oh, sweet Lord, thought Ginny. "Kate told you that?" she said.

"Yes. I'd not heard from her for weeks. Then about two weeks ago she called me. She apologised for being strange in recent months. And she said this Adam person was such a wonderful man she was sure things would work out well for her."

"Wait a minute," said Ginny, momentarily confused. "Is this Adam White we're talking about?"

"Yes," said Gwyneth. "Do you know him?"

"Yes, I do," said Ginny. "Or I did. I haven't seen him for some time. He was…" Ginny paused. Gwyneth really did not need to know that Adam had been the person who had unmasked James. "He was someone my late husband used to work with."

"Is he a good man?"

"He's a lovely man," said Ginny. "But I thought he was as good as married to someone else."

"I know," said Gwyneth. "Kate told me. But she didn't see that as a barrier. She was convinced she could win him over."

"Gwyneth, I really think you should have said something about this to the police," said Ginny, though her heart was heavy as she said it.

"But it wouldn't have been fair," said Gwyneth. "If this Adam really was committed to another girl, then nothing would have come of it anyway."

Ginny was silent for a moment, puzzling over Gwyneth's words. "Are you saying Kate's feelings weren't reciprocated?" she said finally.

"I can't be absolutely sure," said Gwyneth. "But Kate's dead now, so it's over, whatever it was. There's no point in ruining someone else's life – or Kate's reputation."

"Gwyneth, I know Adam White reasonably well," Ginny said. "I don't think he'd want you to keep this information from the police. Not if…" She paused. "Not if it might be relevant to their enquiries."

"But it isn't, is it?" said Gwyneth, almost defiantly.

Ginny hesitated. She could think of any number of reasons why Kate's attraction to Adam might be significant, but it would be pointless, and hurtful, to try to persuade Gwyneth of this.

"You won't say anything to the police, will you?" said Gwyneth.

"But, Gwyneth, why have you told *me*?"

"I don't know," said Gwyneth. "Maybe I thought you'd guessed already."

Ginny hesitated again. "Let me at least talk to Adam White about it," she said.

"If you feel you must, dear," Gwyneth had said.

Ginny stared at the words on her computer screen:

"The history of the British contribution to what is now modern Chile is not unique. It shares many features with other British adventures in Latin America – and, indeed in other parts of the world. But it does have unique features, and it is on these which this book will focus…"

How terribly original, she thought. She deleted all the text and decided to leave the introduction to the book until she was done with the main body of the work.

But still she could not bring herself to concentrate. She

sighed. It had to be done. She picked up the telephone and called the Foreign Office.

***

It had been a difficult day, and Gillian King was looking forward to a rare free evening. She smiled to herself. 'Free' was a relative term, meaning only that she had no official engagement (and then only because the Korean Ambassador had gone down with flu and cancelled his dinner). She had a bulging case of papers to catch up with after the supper she would be hastily improvising in the kitchen of her tiny flat just off Victoria Street.

Gillian had barely put down her briefcase and set a pan of soup to heat on the hob when the telephone rang.

"Gillian, I'm sorry to bother you. It's Bill Cambridge."

Gillian turned off the hot plate and sat down at the kitchen table. A call, at home, from the Assistant Commissioner responsible for homicide investigation at Scotland Yard did not bode well.

"Bill," she said. "It's been a while. What can I do for you?"

"It's rather bad news, Gillian, I'm afraid," said Cambridge.

***

Adam had intended to pass by the flat before going to the Whittington. Alison had been tied up at work all day on an important negotiation, but had left a message with Lata that she would be home around seven thirty. He wanted to clear up any misunderstanding between them before doing anything else.

But Ginny Ballesteros had given the impression that she needed to speak to him urgently and it made more sense to call at her Pimlico flat before heading for north London.

"Come in, Adam," said Ginny. "Thank you for getting here so soon." She looked much older than the last time he had seen her, even though it had been not much more than eighteen months previously. Dressed in a t-shirt and old blue jeans, she still had the slim figure of a young girl. But her fair hair, which she had cut severely short, had turned almost completely grey, and her neat features had become painfully gaunt.

"Hello, Ginny," he said. "How are you?"

"Oh, you know," she said, with a slight shrug. "I'm keeping myself busy with the book." She gestured to the corner of the small flat, where a computer sat on a desk surrounded by sheaves of papers. There were more piles of papers on the floor by the desk and boxes of what looked like black-and-white photographs. Apart from this hint of mild untidiness, the rest of the flat was scrupulously neat and clean, its furnishing minimalist but not unwelcoming. The paintings hanging on the walls were identifiably Latin American. Over the fireplace hung a large photograph of a handsome, grey-haired man on a horse, with snow-capped mountains in the background.

"You drink beer, don't you?" said Ginny, disappearing into the kitchen.

"Thanks," said Adam. He was touched that she remembered. The last time she had seen him drinking beer had been in the moonlight on the terrace of the Ambassador's residence in Santiago. That seemed a very long time ago. Before this current nightmare, before Singapore, at a time when he had known Ali only a few months, when life had seemed so uncomplicated. Ginny, her husband James and Adam had been discussing, over dinner, the mysterious deaths of two colleagues, men for whose murder it ultimately transpired James himself had been responsible. Ginny had never subsequently spoken to Adam about his role in James's exposure and violent death. Had this been deliberate avoidance on her part? Probably not. By all accounts, she had not loved James for a long time before the end. And she had been fully occupied, once the police business was over, with building a life with Diego in Chile. Such a short life, in the event. Adam reflected on his own relative good fortune. Ginny, by comparison, had endured so much tragedy: first the death of a child, then widowhood, not once but twice.

"I was very sorry to hear about Diego," Adam said, when Ginny had returned and they had both sat down.

"We had a wonderful year together," Ginny said. She looked at Adam unflinchingly, her grey eyes shining, almost luminescent, and he was reminded of the Ginny of before.

She took a sip from her mineral water before speaking again. "Adam, I've been looking after Kate Thomas's mother," she said.

"I had no idea," said Adam, initially startled. But then he remembered seeing something in a Personnel circular, when he and Ali were in Singapore, something about a new cohort of Welfare volunteers. Ginny's name had been on the list and he had remarked on this to Ali, saying that it must have taken courage for Ginny to offer her services. "How is she?"

"Not good, as you can imagine," said Ginny. "But, Adam, she told me something I must share with you." She hesitated, as though looking for the right way to say something difficult and delicate.

Adam put down his beer. "Share with *me*?" he said.

"Yes," said Ginny. "She told me... she said she thought Kate was in love with you."

Adam had not been remotely expecting this. "Her mother knew?" he said. "I had no idea myself, until..." He stopped, not sure how to finish the sentence.

Ginny spoke again, swiftly. "She didn't tell the police, because she didn't think it was relevant."

"It's not," said Adam.

"Adam, how can you know that?" said Ginny.

"Because no one else knew," said Adam. "Even I didn't until..." He stopped again. What right had Ginny Ballesteros to know what had happened on Monday night? "... until she said something to me the night she was killed."

"Her mother knew," said Ginny. "Why should she be the only one?"

Adam said nothing. Was he defending the indefensible?

"Even so," he said at last. "It's not relevant." But as he spoke he realised how empty that claim was now beginning to sound. If Kate already had a lover, and she had confessed to him the way she felt about Adam, then there was no denying the relevance of this fact.

Ginny looked at him with slightly raised eyebrows. Once more he got the full benefit of those steady grey eyes.

"Okay, Ginny," he said. "You win. I'll talk to the police about it."

***

It was nearly eight when Adam changed from the Victoria Line to the Northern Line at Euston. He had promised Archie Drysdale he would see him at eight, so there was no time to stop off at the flat. Adam cursed the absence of his mobile. He should have rung Ali from Ginny's flat to explain. He would have to try to call from the hospital.

The Whittington Hospital stood on the lower slopes of Highgate Hill. In the fifteenth century there was a leper hospital on the site, but the current building, constructed to handle a smallpox epidemic, dated from the mid-nineteenth century. The building sat side on to the main road, its imposing Victorian neo-classical façade apparent only after entering the main car park.

To Adam's surprise, Archie was waiting for him by the main entrance. He was wearing a raincoat buttoned to the neck over jeans and sneakers. His face, which Adam had remembered as being plump and florid, was haggard and yellowish, and beaded with sweat.

"Come on," said Drysdale. "Let's get out of here. I'm dying for a drink."

"Is that allowed?" asked Adam.

"Fuck what's allowed," said Drysdale. "Let's go."

They walked the few hundred yards to the St John's Tavern and sat down at a corner table. "I'll get them in," said Drysdale. "A pint?"

Adam nodded. Drysdale returned with two mugs of bitter and what looked like double whisky chasers. "Not for me, thanks," said Adam. "I'll stick to beer."

"Suit yourself," said Drysdale, taking a generous pull at one of the whiskies.

"Aren't you on medication, Archie?"

"Just giving it a helping hand."

"What's up, Archie?" said Adam.

Drysdale looked at him appraisingly, barely suppressing a belch. Except when they had occasionally met in the corridors of the Foreign Office, the two had seen little of each other since their initial arrival in the Foreign Office. They had shared no overseas postings and their interests were too dissimilar to bring them together when in London. Drysdale had evidently lost weight recently, especially around the neck, but he remained formidably bulky.

"Aren't you supposed to do that the other way round?" asked Adam.

"Can't fucking wait," said Drysdale.

71

Adam was conscious of the time ticking on. "What did you want to see me about, Archie?" he said.

"You look fucking fit," Archie said. "No wonder…" His voice trailed off. "I'm a fucking mess," he said, his voice registering self-disgust. He knocked back the rest of the first whisky and took a long draught from his beer.

"Did you have her?" said Drysdale. "The police said you had."

"Well, they're wrong," said Adam, suddenly cold with despair. "Archie, what is it? What was so urgent you had to see me today at all costs?"

Drysdale drank again from his beer. "She opened up the Madrid file again, didn't she?" he said.

"Yes," said Adam. "Is that connected to her death?"

"I warned her," said Drysdale. "I shut down the investigation. You shouldn't have let her open it up again."

"Why, Archie? Why did you shut it down?"

"Because Shakespeare told me to, that's why."

"For what reason?"

Drysdale belched into the back of his hand. "No reason. He just told me to lay off and give him the file."

"But there's hardly anything on the file," said Adam.

"Not now there isn't," said Drysdale. "Shakespeare shredded all the good stuff."

"But that's outrageous, Archie," said Adam. "People go to jail for that sort of thing."

Drysdale shrugged. "It would have been my word against his," he said. "The individual documents meant nothing on their own. It was only when I brought them all together it began to make sense. Shakespeare would have destroyed the whole file if he could, but too many people knew it existed, even though they knew none of the details. So he just told me to put a note on the file to say the evidence was inconclusive."

"And all this without giving you any reason?"

"He just said if I knew what was good for me I'd forget all about it. So I did. Or at least I tried."

"But, Archie," said Adam. "If you thought there was a genuine case of fraud, why didn't you go over Shakespeare's head? You could have gone straight to the Permanent Under Secretary with something like this."

Drysdale avoided Adam's eyes. "I didn't dare," he muttered. "I was frightened. I began to think people were following me, bugging my phone, that sort of thing. I was scared shitless and it all seemed like too much trouble. Then they sent me to the loony bin. Christ, it's hot in here."

Adam watched as Drysdale, the sweat pouring down his face, tugged open his raincoat collar to reveal the top of his pyjamas. "Do you really think Kate's death was connected to the pensions fraud in some way?" Adam asked.

Drysdale belched again, this time openly, before taking another slug of whisky. "Christ only knows," he said. "But it seems like too much of a coincidence. There's something really fucking funny going on, that's all I know."

"Did you say anything to the police about any of this?"

"No fucking fear," said Drysdale. "I just gave them a lot of flannel about lack of real evidence of wrongdoing in the pensions payments. I think they're more likely to be pursuing the jealous lover theory myself."

"Then why are you telling me?"

"Christ knows," said Drysdale. "Guilty conscience, maybe. And I thought I'd better warn you the police have got you nailed as – what do they call it? – a material witness."

"Archie, you must tell the police about this," said Adam.

Drysdale had started on the second whisky. "No way," he said. "I've retreated into mental illness and alcoholism. That way they know I'm no threat – whoever they are."

"Supposing I tell the police I know you know something," said Adam.

"I wouldn't do that, pal," said Drysdale. "I'll tell them you're lying. They'll think you're trying to divert attention from the fact you were her lover."

"But I wasn't her lover, Archie," said Adam, patiently.

"Yeah, right," said Drysdale. He finished his beer and tossed back the rest of the whisky. "Your round, I think."

Adam checked the time. "Archie, I'm sorry," he said. "I should already be at home. Besides, don't you think...?"

"One more drink," said Drysdale, slurring his words. "For old times' sake."

Adam hesitated. Maybe if he stayed a little longer he would learn something more from Drysdale, something which might provide a clue as to why Kate was killed.

"One drink," said Adam. "Just let me make a quick call first."

***

Ali was running late. She had accompanied Richard to the meeting with Veronica Buckingham at the latter's office in the City in case there were any last-minute questions about the final version of the agreement. There had, inevitably, been a need to clarify one or two minor points, but Richard had been able to deal with these to Veronica's satisfaction.

"God, I need that drink now," Veronica had said, her voice even huskier than earlier. "I think I'm coming down with something. A touch of champagne should help, I fancy. You'll join us, won't you, Alison?"

Richard had smiled warmly at Alison, as though to make clear how welcome she would be. Her first instinct had been to say no. She needed to get home to speak to Adam. And it did not take a genius to deduce that at some stage of the evening Richard and Veronica would have plans that did not include her. But then she realised that they needed her with them so that they could make an unsuspicious exit from the building, so she relented to the extent of one drink. After what seemed an eternal taxi ride, they crammed into the Lounge Lover in Whitby Street. Richard ordered champagne cocktails. Whether or not the other two were playing some kind of game involving postponement of gratification Alison could not be sure, but they kept pressing her to stay for another drink, and then another. Finally, she escaped, but it was well after eight when she arrived home in Archway and she was ready with her apologies before she realised the flat was empty.

Muttering crossly to herself, and realising that she was a little drunk, she began rooting around in the refrigerator looking for something to eat. Her search was interrupted by the doorbell.

Alison had a curious sense of déjà vu when she opened the door and saw the red-haired man in the crumpled, lightweight grey suit.

"Detective Inspector Fox," she said, extravagantly. "This is just like old times."

"Is Adam home, Alison?" said Fox.

"No, he bloody well isn't," said Alison. "And I don't know where the hell he is, either."

Fox looked at a loss. "He's not at the Foreign Office," he said. "He left some time ago, as far as we can establish."

"Come in," said Alison, opening the door wider. "You might as well wait for him."

As she spoke, the telephone began to ring. "That may be Adam," said Alison. "Do you want to talk to him, if it is?"

Fox hesitated. "No, I'd better not," he said. "I'm late home myself." He paused again. "I just wanted to warn him that we're going to have to ask him to come in for questioning first thing in the morning."

Nicole looked tired, but she always did these days. Raymond kissed his wife on the cheek and said apologetically: "I know, I've missed the kids again. I'm sorry."

"It's in the oven," she said, looking up briefly from the television. "I didn't wait. I didn't know how long you'd be."

"I should have called," he said. "I'm really sorry."

She said nothing. She was watching *Wife Swap*, a programme she knew he hated.

"I'll just nip upstairs and see them first," he said.

"Don't wake them up," she said. "And don't let your supper burn."

Tracey and Samantha were in the same room, a source of some indignation to Tracey, who thought that eight was more than old enough to be spared the hassle of sharing with her five-year-old sister. Raymond knew it was time they moved, but there was nothing bigger they could afford in Lewisham and it wasn't feasible to move further out – unless Raymond transferred to another force, which he was reluctant to do.

Raymond looked at his daughters in wonder as they slept. Could they really be his, with their straight brown hair and olive complexion? They looked for all the world like miniature versions of their mother.

Max, however, had red hair, although still only the faintest of wisps. He lay on his back in the cot in the spare room, eyes closed, oblivious to the final, decelerating notes still emerging from the musical mobile above his head. A kind of peace settled over Raymond's shoulders as he watched his son sleeping.

When he went downstairs, Nicole had switched off the television and had laid his supper out on the kitchen table. She had poured him a beer and was sitting sipping a cup of coffee. She was no longer angry with him. She rarely was for more than an hour at a time.

"What was it today?" she said.

He drank from his beer glass and forked some lasagne into his mouth. "Do you remember Adam White?" he said.

She frowned. "Yes," she said. "He was the Foreign Office man you thought had murdered the Argentinian Ambassador."

"The British Ambassador in Argentina," said Raymond. "All the evidence pointed towards him and he had a strong motive – the man had ruined the life of someone he regarded as practically his sister. But it turned out he was completely innocent."

"And?"

"It's happened again. This girl, Kate Thomas, who was found in St James's Park – all the evidence links him to the crime. But I can't believe he did it."

"What does Phil think?"

"Phil would lock him up tomorrow," laughed Raymond.

"Well," said Nicole. "Phil's been right before, hasn't he? Just because this man was innocent then doesn't mean he's innocent now."

"I know," said Raymond. *God, she looks tired*, he thought. "But it just doesn't feel right."

CHAPTER 6

The atmosphere in the interview room was markedly different from that when Adam had seen Raymond Fox the previous day. Fox had been concerned but sympathetic when they had parted company. Today his manner was formal, even distant. He sat on the other side of the interview table, his notebook and two freshly sharpened pencils lying in front of him. Alongside him lounged Coker, smooth-headed, cool and undisguisedly hostile. A faint smile played round his lips as he gazed at Adam, repeatedly clicking a ballpoint pen open and closed as though limbering up for a game of hand wrestling. A uniformed policeman stood unobtrusively by the door.

"Are you sure you don't want your lawyer present, Adam?" asked Fox.

Coker's smile broadened into a sardonic grin. *Yes*, thought Adam. *You would find that funny.*

"I'm quite sure, thanks, Raymond," he said. "And I'm here voluntarily, as you know," he added, looking at Coker. *Shades of my interview with Julian*, he thought. Except that Julian had already known the truth about everything there was to know about Adam's behaviour in Singapore. Fox and Coker only *thought* they knew the truth about his relationship with Kate.

Adam had not played much chess in recent years, but he found himself remembering that, as a boy, he had always suffered his worst defeats when he moved first. In his daily life and work, the chess analogy scarcely applied. He had always had a tendency, for better or worse, to charge into situations head-first. He had begun to temper this impetuosity of late, although he was not entirely convinced that thinking about things always produced a better result.

But this was not a chess game either. It was poker, because neither side knew, although they strongly suspected, what cards the other held. Mindful of his undertaking to Ginny Ballesteros, Adam was tempted to make a statement and get it over with, but something persuaded him to wait for the questions.

Finally Fox spoke. "Adam, I'd like you to reflect again on your answers to our questions about your relationship with Kate Thomas."

"We didn't have a relationship," said Adam. "Not in the sense you mean."

"Adam, we have a DNA match with the skin and hair fragments found under her fingernails," said Fox.

"I thought as much," said Adam. "Kate kissed me goodnight when she left the office. She must have put her hand on my neck."

"'Must have'?" said Coker, his face twisted in disbelief. "You don't remember?"

Oh yes, thought Adam. *I remember.* Kate had been wearing a pale pink cotton dress all day, but had disappeared into her office to change before leaving. She had emerged in jeans, her shirt half tucked in, fiddling with one of the buttons and frowning. "Can you help me with this, Adam?" she had said. "It seems to be stuck."

"Yes, she put her hand on my neck," said Adam.

"Why did you say nothing about this before, Adam?" said Fox.

"Because it wasn't relevant," said Adam.

"Not relevant?" said Coker. "Do me a favour. She tells you she's seeing another man and you're sticking it to her late at night in the office and you say that's not relevant?"

Adam suppressed an urge to hit Coker in the face. "She kissed me," he said. "That's all."

"You had sex," said Coker.

Adam turned to Fox. "This is bollocks, Raymond," he said. "You know it's bollocks."

"You used a condom, of course," said Coker. "It's always wise to take precautions, isn't it?"

"You know bloody well you have no evidence to prove that," said Adam.

"She had sex with somebody, Adam," said Fox.

Is that possible? thought Adam. Was it conceivable that within a matter of hours Kate was making love to someone else? Raymond had said there had been no evidence of rape, so she must have done so willingly. But then what did her text messages mean?

"What happened after you 'kissed her'," said Coker, his tone laden with sarcasm.

"Kate went home," said Adam.

"Just like that?" said Coker. "No plans to do it again? No arrangements for another meeting?"

"How many times do I have to tell you? We didn't do anything," said Adam.

"Adam, you've got to explain the situation," said Fox. "You said it was Miss Thomas who kissed you."

"That's right."

"What did she say?"

"How do you mean?"

"Come on, Adam," said Fox. "Don't play games. This is serious. She kissed you. You say nothing else happened. What was that all about?"

Adam was silent for a while. *I'm so sorry, Kate*, he thought, before he spoke.

"She said she loved me," said Adam. "I said it was impossible – that I was going to marry Alison."

"This would be Miss Alison Webster?" said Coker, consulting his notes.

"Yes."

"How did she react?" asked Fox.

"I don't think she believed me. She said she was going to break off her existing relationship. I said she mustn't do anything on my account."

"What did she say to that?"

"Nothing, really. She suddenly realised how late it was and said she had to go."

Adam saw her again, that backward glance, the slim hand tucking the shirt into her jeans. "I have to go now, Adam. I daren't be late."

And suddenly Adam knew what had been worrying him.

"What time did Kate die, Raymond?"

"We ask the questions here," said Coker, irritably.

Fox ignored Coker. "As best we can tell, sometime between midnight and three in the morning."

"You said she was dressed for work?"

"That's right."

"And so you thought she hadn't been home that night."

"Yes."

"What exactly was she wearing?"

Fox consulted his notes. "A white shirt, a navy skirt, black woollen tights, black court shoes, white cotton underwear, a gold chain necklace, no rings."

Adam thought hard. "Apart from the gold chain, she wasn't wearing any of that when she left the office."

"What are you getting at, Adam?" said Fox.

"Kate had been wearing a dress," said Adam. "A pink

81

cotton dress. She changed into a shirt and jeans before she left."

"Colour?"

"Blue denim jeans and a blue check shirt, long sleeves."

Fox made a note. "That does seem strange," he said.

Adam had another thought. "Did she have a bag?" he said. "A sports bag of some kind?"

"She did have a bag," said Fox. "Not a sports bag. A handbag."

"What was in it?"

Fox consulted his notes again and read out a list of items.

"No Foreign Office pass?" said Adam.

Fox read through the list again. "No," he said.

"I saw her leave the office dressed in a shirt and jeans, carrying a grip," said Adam. "And she couldn't have left the building without using her pass."

"She went and changed," said Coker. "What's the big mystery?"

"Into office clothes?" said Adam.

"Maybe she was going to stay with someone and then go straight to the office in the morning," said Fox.

"Without her pass?"

"She could have mislaid it," said Fox. "We'll check her flat."

"What about the woollen tights?" said Adam. "In this weather?"

"This is bullshit," said Coker. "We only have your word for it she wasn't wearing these clothes when she left the office."

"You can check with the security guard on duty when she left," said Adam, although he was far from confident that the guard in question would in fact remember. Kate's pass opened an electronic gate, requiring no intervention from the security staff.

"What about CCTV?" said Fox, who seemed to think that Adam's point had some relevance.

"Only at the main entrance," said Adam, remembering now a battle he had lost with Finance when he had been working in Security Department. "If she left by the park entrance, there are no cameras there. It's for staff only, so we've never bothered."

"What exactly are you driving at anyway, Adam?" said Fox.

"I'm saying that Kate went home – or somewhere – and that someone killed her, God knows why. Then they dressed her in her office clothes and dumped her in the lake to give the impression she'd been on her way home from the office."

"And who exactly do you think would do a thing like that?" said Coker.

"I don't know," said Adam. "Maybe it had something to do with the case she was investigating. Or it could be the person she was in a relationship with."

"This is crap," said Coker. "Because you're the only one we know for sure was with her on Monday night."

***

With the deal now lacking only the signatures of the two principals, Alison had the opportunity to catch up on a pile of routine paperwork that had accumulated over the previous week. She asked her legal assistant to intercept all her calls, closed the door of her office and sat behind her desk. But instead of reaching for the paper at the top of her in tray she buried her head in her hands and began to weep silently.

She was not entirely sure why she was crying, although a monumental hangover was not helping. Recollection of her conversation late the previous night with Adam was undoubtedly the proximate cause, but other pressures had been building up over recent weeks which were suddenly released. Being back at work full time had been exhausting and nerve-wracking. In particular, the tensions surrounding the intricacies of the just concluded negotiations had been greater than she had expected. But, above all else, her mother's sudden illness and death had come so fast that Alison had had no time to make her peace with her. They had been so different and yet so similar: the vain, shallow, beautiful mother and the plain, clever, resentful daughter, both of them capable of terrifying bouts of bad temper. Alison's father had assured her that her mother loved her and just had difficulty expressing it. But Alison could only remember the fights, the snobbery, the curled lip when she had committed herself to Adam. "He has no money," Ruth Webster had said. "His family were nothing. And on top of it all, he's a Roman Catholic – or was. Surely you can do better than that." Why had she not understood what was happening when her mother began to attend the synagogue regularly? Why had she assumed that the medication she had stumbled on was for her father?

Alison had not wept at the funeral, not even at the moment of the solemn rending of garments. She had stood, pale and dry-eyed, her father on one side and Adam on the other, listening to the chanting of psalms and staring, still unbelieving, at the simple wooden coffin in which her mother's body lay, wrapped in a plain white shroud. Ruth's face, according to Jewish custom, was unadorned by any trace of the cosmetics which, in life, had been so central to her social survival. Alison knew she should be feeling more than this strange, flat emptiness. Her mind told her there had been a tragic, ongoing miscommunication between her and Ruth, but the wellspring of her emotions remained dry.

Everything in the end had happened so rapidly, the imperative for burial within twenty-four hours of death precluding any possibility of adjustment. So perhaps, finally, she was crying for her mother, and grieving for so many lost opportunities. How often had Alison met fire with fire when a laugh and an affectionate embrace might have disarmed her mother? How many times had Alison's father slipped unobtrusively away to tend his garden rather than watch the two people he loved most in the world locked in bitter combat? He had loved her mother, despite all Ruth's pettiness and irritability. And suddenly he was alone, when he had always imagined that he would go first. So, she was weeping for her father as well.

Alison wiped her face with a tissue and composed herself. There was nothing to be done now about her mother and there was no point in wallowing in remorse. She would do her best to remember the better times and would devote herself as far as possible to her father's happiness. It was her relationship with Adam which needed to be resolved.

Did she believe him? Had there been nothing between him and Kate Thomas? "It was an aberration," he had said. "I don't know what got into her."

"Did you try to stop her?" Alison asked, hating herself for the question.

"It happened so fast," he said.

"Did you enjoy it?" she said, hating herself even more.

He did not answer immediately. His expression was agonised. He seemed to be choosing his words with extraordinary care. "Ali, I'm a man," he said finally. "You saw her."

"You bastard!" she shouted. "You bloody bastard! You bloody, bloody bastard!"

They were sitting facing each other across the kitchen table. He looked at her sadly. "Ali, I'm trying to be honest," he said. "I've tried not talking about it at all, which was stupid. Now I'm trying to be as truthful as possible."

Well, I asked for that, thought Alison. *But, just this once, couldn't you have lied, Adam? One little white lie in which no one could possibly have found you out?*

"She told you she loved you," she said.

"And I told her I was marrying you."

"But she wasn't going to give up, was she? What did she say? 'There has to be a way.'"

"I don't know what she meant by that," said Adam.

"You said she was going to break up with this other person," said Alison. "Presumably she was planning to try to break us up as well."

"It wouldn't have happened, Ali," said Adam. "Bloody hell, you know me better than that."

"The trouble is, we'll never know now, will we?" she had said, regretting the words the moment they were out.

Alison took the first letter from the pile. It contained a routine request from a long-standing client for advice on the technicalities of shifting an offshore account out of Jersey and into the Caymans. Alison logged into her computer and began to compose a reply. She had hurt Adam by doubting him. But she sensed that he was too ashamed to dispute what she had said, because it was no more than the truth. The seed of uncertainty had been sown in both their minds. He had not demurred when she had said she would go to stay with her father for a while. And she had not argued when he suggested he sleep on the sofa that night, even though what she really longed to do was hold him in her arms and weep into his chest. *How easily an apparently perfect relationship is soured*, she thought, and pressed the printer button.

***

Gillian King would not normally have agreed to see the Head of the Financial Control Unit at such short notice. For better or worse, much of her day was pre-programmed by her Private Office, and any gaps in her schedule were gratefully seized as an opportunity to grapple with the relentless stream of paperwork which poured across her desk. She had, in any case, set aside the period between eleven and eleven thirty to read through the security plan for the Iraqi President's visit.

For Adam White, however, she made an exception. She did so because he had twice in the last two years demonstrated courage and determination in the face of great personal danger, even though in the most recent case the rules had obliged her to agree that he be formally disciplined. Prudence would nevertheless have dictated that she refuse his request for a meeting: he might not yet be the prime suspect for the murder of Kate Thomas, but Bill Cambridge had made clear that the police had no one else in the frame for the time being. So it was only her instinctive faith in Adam's integrity which made her override Hilary Price's cautionary advice.

"What can I do for you, Adam?" Gillian asked, after she had waved an uncharacteristically tight-lipped Price out of the room and Adam had sat down by the coffee table. He looked tired, she thought, harassed rather. And no wonder.

"Thank you for seeing me," he said. "I realise this is irregular, but I couldn't think of what else to do."

"We have ten minutes," said Gillian. "Oh, by the way, I should say that you and Andrew were right about Sophie. I wasn't sure at first, but she's doing very well indeed now."

"That's good to know," said Adam. "She's not an easy girl, but she's very capable." He paused. "It was very sad about Andrew, though. Even now, I still find it difficult to believe."

Gillian was initially startled by this belated expression of sadness, which threatened to open up a wound that had barely begun to heal. Then she realised that, although she had signed Adam's formal letter of admonishment, she had not seen him face-to-face alone since his return from Singapore. *I wonder if he knows about Andrew and me,* she thought. It was unlikely: no member of the Service under forty seemed able to conceive of her having any life at all before her current position. Aloud, she said: "So do I. The whole experience must have taken a greater toll than we realised."

They were both silent for several seconds. Then Gillian said: "Spit it out then. What's the problem?"

"I've just spent two hours with the police," said Adam. "They're convinced there was something going on between Kate Thomas and me. And they think that has something to do with her death."

Adam paused, as though hoping for a word of encouragement. Gillian remained silent, not wishing to suggest she had a view one way or the other on what the police believed.

"They're wrong," said Adam. "It's connected to a financial scam in the Embassy in Madrid."

Ah, thought Gillian. *So that's it.* "Go on," she said.

"Kate had reopened an investigation Archie Drysdale had closed," said Adam. "I talked to Archie about it."

"You went to see Archie Drysdale?"

"Yes," said Adam. "He said he'd stopped investigating on Simon Shakespeare's instructions. But he also said he didn't go any further because he was afraid."

"Afraid? Afraid of what?" asked Gillian.

"He didn't say exactly," said Adam. "But he did seem genuinely scared."

Gillian thought for a few seconds. Then she spoke with some care. "Adam, you know that Archie is very ill, don't you?"

"I know he's depressed," said Adam. "And I suspect he's an alcoholic."

"It's worse than that," said Gillian. She hesitated. "I can't break medical confidentiality," she said. "But let's just say he sees threats where none objectively exist."

"You mean he's paranoid?"

"I mean exactly what I said," said Gillian.

Adam looked uncertain. "Then why is Kate Thomas dead?" he said finally.

"Adam, I don't know," said Gillian. "Let's leave that to the police, shall we?"

"What about the Madrid investigation?" said Adam. "Why couldn't Archie pursue it?"

"Have you spoken to Simon about this?" said Gillian.

"No," said Adam. "I thought that he might possibly… oh, I don't know what I thought."

"I think you should speak to him before you do anything else," said Gillian.

"I was planning to go out to Madrid myself," said Adam. "I spoke to the Chargé d'Affaires yesterday and he's happy for me to visit."

"Speak to Simon first," said Gillian. "Just to be on the safe side." She paused. "I'm sorry the police are giving you a hard time, Adam," she said. "Have you spoken to the union yet?"

Adam looked suddenly angry. "I don't need to speak to the union," he said. "Everyone keeps suggesting I need the union, or a lawyer. I haven't done anything."

"All the more reason to have their support," said Gillian.

Adam shook his head. "No," he said. "Thanks, but no."

When Adam had left, Gillian called in Hilary Price. He looked distracted.

"Are you alright, Hilary?" Gillian asked. "You're not still cross with me for seeing Adam White, are you?"

Price appeared to recover his composure. "That was, of course, absolutely your decision to make, Permanent Under Secretary," he said.

"Is there something else, then?"

For a moment, Price's delicate features were expressionless, as though he were making some rapid mental calculation. Then he smiled and shook his head. "No, no," he said. "I'm fine, really."

At another time, Gillian might have probed further, because she was not convinced that Price was fine at all. But she had urgent business to execute which would not wait.

"That's good to know," she said. "Now, get me Simon Shakespeare on the telephone as fast as you can. Then I'd better speak to Bill Cambridge and the Head of MI6 – in that order."

Gillian picked up the Iraqi visit security plan and rapidly scanned the executive summary while she waited for the call to Simon Shakespeare. *Chinese walls*, she thought. *So much of my life these days consists of Chinese walls.*

. "Simon," she said, when Shakespeare came on the line. "We've got the same problem again… Yes, I know. We'll need the same recipe, please."

***

When she was a child, Ginny Ballesteros had played a game whenever the telephone rang in her parents' house. One ring was good news, two rings were bad, three rings were good again, four were bad, and so on. She would try to stop her mother from answering the phone if it was on an even-numbered ring, but she was not always successful. Was it a trick of the memory or was it always on those occasions that her father had been calling to say his ship had been delayed, or that there was a tricky disciplinary issue to be resolved with one of the ratings, or simply that he had to stay in Portsmouth overnight for some otherwise unexplained meeting with his commanding admiral? Ginny's mother had never questioned these casual excuses, although Ginny fancied she could now recall a permanent, distant sadness in her demeanour in that relatively innocent time. That was before the women began calling the house to ask to speak to him, women who had also been cheated, women who did not know of each other's existence, let alone of Ginny or her mother.

Even in adulthood, Ginny often found herself counting the rings before she picked up the telephone: odd, even, odd, even, odd, even... But she had at least sufficient self-discipline not to try to time the lifting of the receiver to coincide with a supposedly lucky odd-numbered ring. Her fate was what it was and would be. There was no way of manipulating it by playing childish games.

She picked up the telephone on the sixth ring, telling herself that it was nonsensical to think that this would be unlucky. After the terrible mixture of tragedy and euphoria she had experienced in the last two years, what more could await her?

"May I speak to Virginia Ballesteros, please?"

The woman's English was correct, but her voice was heavily accented, the 'g' in 'Virginia' pronounced as a strongly aspirated 'h'.

"Speaking," said Ginny. She could feel an unaccountable surge of adrenaline. She knew, God knew how, what the woman was going to say.

"My name is María Carmen Dominguez," said the other. "I think we need to meet."

***

Adam left the office early, still troubled but marginally less frustrated. His meeting with Simon Shakespeare had got him no further with his concerns, but at least he now knew where he stood.

Shakespeare was not a man who gave the impression

of enjoying his job at the best of times. Having narrowly missed a much coveted ambassadorship in Latin America, he found himself now situated between a gung-ho axe-wielding Treasury on the one hand and endlessly profligate Foreign Office directors on the other. To the former he was an apologist for waste and inefficiency; to the latter a ruthless, unimaginative bean counter.

Today, however, Shakespeare seemed to be finding life especially painful. Adam surveyed his bony, bird-like face, the grey hair swept austerely back, the equally grey eyes peering at him with undisguised distaste through rimless glasses. At their first meeting, Adam had found himself speculating what someone like Shakespeare did for recreation. Would it involve whips and uniforms? He had been suitably ashamed to discover subsequently that Shakespeare, a former county tennis champion, was happily married with three teenage children.

"You went to see the Permanent Under Secretary," said Shakespeare. His tone was neutral, but the statement sounded like an accusation.

"I thought it was urgent, Simon," said Adam. "You were over at the Treasury."

"Only for a one-hour meeting," said Shakespeare. "It wouldn't have killed you to wait until I got back."

Adam said nothing.

"You talked about the Madrid pensions," said Shakespeare.

"Yes," said Adam.

"I thought Archie Drysdale had closed the file," said Shakespeare.

"He did," said Adam. "Kate Thomas opened it again."

"I gave Archie explicit instructions to close it," said Shakespeare. "It should have stayed closed."

"Do you want me to close it now?" asked Adam.

"Yes," said Shakespeare. "You should be concentrating on Tashkent. That's the real can of worms."

"I just wanted to be sure," said Adam. "Archie seemed pretty worked up about it. And Kate—"

Shakespeare interrupted him. "Close the file, Adam," he said. "Take my word for it. There are no grounds for investigation."

"Whatever you say, Simon," said Adam. Five years ago, he would have argued the point, lost his temper even, in the face of such crass pulling of rank. Today he was that little bit more circumspect, that little bit more capable of suppressing his emotions.

Was it his imagination, or had Shakespeare's face betrayed a flicker of relief at his acquiescence? It was immaterial. He had no intention of closing the file. On returning to his office he telephoned the Chargé d'Affaires in Madrid to secure his agreement to a visit the following day. "Can we keep this between you and me, for the moment?" said Adam. "There may be ramifications at this end, so we've got to keep it pretty tight."

Time was also tight, but manageable. The Tashkent case would come to a head on Monday. The rest of Adam's in tray consisted of routine accounts irregularities which could be dealt with by correspondence in the coming week. He would take the last flight to Madrid that evening and have the whole of Friday, plus the weekend, for his investigation.

Lata had left a message to say that she had been summoned to her son's school at short notice. Adam put his head round the door of Ubaid's office.

"I'm out all day tomorrow," said Adam. "I'll be on the duty officer mobile if anyone needs me."

Ubaid smiled and lifted his hand without looking away from his computer screen.

"Gotcha, Adam," he said, in an accent leaving no doubt about his Hackney origins.

Adam made his way out into King Charles Street and down Clive Steps into St James's Park. His mind was on his mission in Madrid, but he was also recalling the brief flash of misery he had seen on Gillian King's face at the mention of Andrew Singleton's name. *How little we all really know about each other,* he thought. He had believed he knew Andrew Singleton well. As High Commissioner in Singapore, Andrew had shown himself to be intelligent, urbane, glamorous – and a shameless philanderer. He had admittedly been much diminished by his kidnapping and by the deaths of his daughter and his mistress. Nevertheless, he had seemed relatively serene when he bade farewell to Adam at the docks in Singapore. Adam could not have believed Andrew capable of what he had later done in the unpredictable obscurity of a hotel room in Sicily.

***

Gillian King had ten minutes free before leaving the office for her evening engagement, a symposium at Chatham House on the West and Islam. She was determined to read through the Iraq visit security plan before she left, but her best intentions were again thwarted.

"Hello, Bill," she said, after Hilary Price had put the caller through. "What marvellous revelation have you got for me now?"

"It's worse than we thought," said Cambridge. "We've completed forensic tests in Kate Thomas's flat. There are DNA matches for Adam White in several places."

"You mean—?"

"Yes, including in the bedroom."

"But I thought the bed hadn't been slept in?"

"It was carefully made up," said Cambridge. "We assumed it hadn't been used. Now we think the killer may have made it up again afterwards."

"I find this so difficult to believe," said Gillian. *When will I stop saying that?* she thought.

"I'm afraid there's more," said Cambridge.

"More? What more could there be?"

"We've identified a body which was found lying on the road in Archway in the small hours of this morning. It took us a while because it was dressed only in pyjamas, jeans and a raincoat."

A vague misgiving stirred within Gillian. "Did you say Archway?" she said.

"Yes," said Cambridge. "We thought it was suicide at first. The bridge is a favourite spot."

"It was Archie Drysdale, wasn't it?" Gillian said.

"Yes," said Cambridge, sounding surprised. "Another one of yours, I gather."

"How do you know it wasn't suicide, Bill?"

"Well, we can't be absolutely sure," said Cambridge. "But we've got witnesses who saw him in a pub that night not a hundred yards away. He was having a violent argument with someone, someone answering exactly to the description of your man, Adam White."

CHAPTER 7

The British Embassy in Madrid had been located on the same site in Calle Fernando el Santo, a generous stone's throw from the fountains of Plaza de Colón, since the early part of the twentieth century. The Embassy's original building was an elegant palace, once owned by the Marquis of Alava. With the expansion of the Embassy's responsibilities after the Second World War, the palace became increasingly impractical. In the 1960s it was demolished to make way for a brand new building, circular in shape in homage to that undying symbol of traditional Spain, the bullring. Forty years on, like so many of its contemporaries from that aggressively modernist architectural era, the building was badly showing its age (and, indeed, was shortly to be abandoned).

The building's circular design was also not without practical problems. The curvature of the walls was a feature to celebrate in the Ambassador's large and imposing office. In the modest quarters of the Embassy's underlings the mild distortion was barely noticeable. But, in the medium-sized offices, the irregular shape meant that no arrangement of the furniture ever looked right, and visitors had a persistent sense of being slightly drunk.

Adam sat in one such office, that of the Chargé d'Affaires, Christopher Robin, a name which, coupled with its owner's babyish face and (now fading) golden curls, had no doubt invited much childhood teasing. Adam guessed that even now Robin had to put up with the occasional ill-suppressed smirk when introducing himself to colleagues for the first time.

"This is a bit of a business, isn't it?" Robin said.

"Well, it certainly looks suspicious," said Adam. "But we don't know for sure, of course. I really need to look at the detailed files of all the war pensioners to see whether we can identify any cases that warrant further examination. Can I do that without alerting anyone we may be on to them?"

"I think so," said Robin. "But only if we bring the Defence Attaché into it."

"I'd rather not do that just for the moment," said Adam. "Ideally, I'd like to have at least a preliminary look through the files without anyone knowing but you."

Robin hesitated, a decent man wrestling with his natural loyalty to his colleagues and a desire to do the right thing.

"They're not classified files," he said finally. "They'll be in a locked cupboard in Luis Moreno's room. His key will be in the Defence Section key box. I can get it for you when he goes to lunch."

"Thanks," said Adam. "In the meantime, I can speak to Alicia Espinosa and Guillermo Vasquez in Accounts."

"I hope you're up to speed on the new accounts software," said Robin. "Because that's what they think you're here to talk about."

"I know enough to bamboozle anyone who hasn't seen it before," said Adam.

"Good," said Robin. "I'll get the Management Officer to take you down."

***

Bill Cambridge rang Gillian King soon after she entered her office on Friday morning.

"It looks as if White's done a runner," said Cambridge.

"What?"

"We sent people round to his flat first thing this morning," said Cambridge. "There was no sign of him – or his girlfriend. We're trying to get hold of her now."

"Has anyone checked in the office here?"

"Yes," said Cambridge. "We spoke to his Personal Assistant. She simply had a message to say he'd be away for the day. His mobile seems to be switched off."

"I'll see what we can find out and get back to you."

Gillian rang Simon Shakespeare. "Do you have any idea what Adam White's up to?" she said.

"I told him to concentrate on Tashkent," said Shakespeare. He swore quietly. "You don't think—?"

"It's possible."

"Do you want me to check with Christopher Robin?"

"No," said Gillian. "The less anyone else knows the better. You'll have to leave this to me."

***

The last time someone from Scotland Yard had visited Alison in her office – some eighteen months previously – it had been Raymond Fox. This time it was a rather unprepossessing man called Coker, but their missions on each occasion were similar.

"I don't know where Adam is," she said. "He didn't tell me where he was going."

"He didn't say anything this morning?" said Coker, lounging discourteously in a chair in front of Alison's desk. "He told his Personal Assistant he was going to be out all day."

"No," said Alison. "He didn't say anything." It was none of Coker's business that she had not been at the flat since the previous day.

"We're going to arrest him, you know," said Coker. There

was an irritating note of satisfaction in his voice.

Alison kept her voice steady. "Don't be ridiculous," she said. "Because she kissed him? Because she told him she loved him?"

Coker laughed, an ugly barking sound. "Is that what he told you?" he said. "He was screwing her, and you know it. When she got too serious, he had to shut her up."

"You have no evidence to support such foul allegations," said Alison, as coolly as she could.

Coker smirked. "Did he tell you about going to her flat?" he said.

Alison felt cold. "What exactly do you mean?" she said.

"He didn't, did he?" said Coker. "Do you know where he was between midnight and three in the morning on Monday night?"

"He was with me at the flat."

"Sure about that, are we?"

No, damn you, thought Alison. *No, I'm not sure.* She had been asleep before Adam came to bed, so she had no idea what time it had been. What she did know was that Adam had overslept the following morning.

"Look, Detective Sergeant Coker," she said. "I don't care what you think you know about Adam. You're wrong."

"We've got DNA traces of him all over her flat," said Coker. He paused for effect. "Including, of course, in the bedroom. She had his skin and hair under her fingernails. He's the last person we know for sure saw her that night. I'd say it's open and shut, myself."

Alison felt sick. But then she remembered how this had all happened before, when things looked equally bad, when Raymond Fox, intending no harm and knowing no better, had sown the seeds of doubt in her mind about another murder. Adam had been innocent then. He was innocent now.

"There'll be an explanation for that," Alison said.

"Then why has he run away?" said Coker.

"He hasn't run away," said Alison.

Coker stood up. "If you hear from him, let me know at once."

"I'll tell him you were asking after him," said Alison.

Coker gave her a sour look. "Don't be clever with me. Your boyfriend's in deep trouble. And if you don't co-operate, we'll have you for being an accessory after the fact."

The flash of anger Alison experienced was a welcome sensation. But still she kept her voice calm. "You can't bully me, Detective Sergeant Coker," she said. "I can think of at least three formal complaints I could make about your behaviour in the last ten minutes."

"Lawyers don't impress me," said Coker. "And you don't impress me either. No wonder he went looking for it elsewhere."

Alison smiled. "Well, Sergeant Coker, I'm really rather relieved to hear I don't impress you. But, just so we understand each other: if you repeat any of the things you've just said to me in front of a third party you'll find yourself facing allegations of slander, defamation of character and harassment."

Coker looked as though he were going to spit at her. "You've got to be joking," he said.

"Let's see if the Independent Police Complaints Commission agree with you, shall we?" said Alison.

Coker laughed, again that ugly, barking laugh. "I think you'll find the IPCC have got a bit more to worry about these days than your poor little hurt feelings," he said.

He was right, of course. Unlawful killings, excessive force used when detaining terrorist suspects, allegations of high-level corruption – these were the daily fare of the IPCC. By comparison, a complaint, without witnesses, about

Coker's lewd and bullying behaviour would be very unlikely to prosper.

"We'll see about that then, shall we," said Alison, reaching for her telephone.

Coker rose from his chair. "Go ahead," he said, but there was the faintest note of uncertainty in his voice. Alison punched the first number that came into her head into the phone and watched while Coker backed away, his hands held up in a gesture of half-surrender.

As Coker left her office, Alison heard her father's puzzled voice at the other end of the line. "Hello, Daddy," she said. "Sorry, I called you by mistake. I'll see you tonight."

When her father had hung up, Alison sat thinking back over her exchange with Coker. She felt her aggressive anger fade away, to be replaced by fear and uncertainty. Where was Adam? And had he really been in Kate Thomas's flat the night she was killed?

***

Even in middle age, María Carmen was everything Ginny had feared and expected. Diego had described her as having been beautiful, and she still was. The eyes flashed, dark and angry, much as Ginny had imagined them. The skin was smooth, a striking olive colour, the hair jet-black and lustrous. She was simply dressed, in jeans and a t-shirt bearing the slogan UK OUT OF IRAQ!, but still managed to look vital and elegant. Ginny felt pale and dull by comparison.

They sat, sizing each other up, in a restaurant on the corner of Sloane Square, surrounded by late morning shoppers from Peter Jones. Both women had preferred a neutral venue. Ginny had no desire to let Diego's former lover into her own life, and yet she had not been able to resist the temptation to meet her. María Carmen herself, although she had taken the initiative in making contact, did not seem ready to take Ginny to her own home.

"I'm puzzled," Ginny said, after they had been served, both opting for a niçoise salad. "Why now? And what for?"

María Carmen poked at her salad with a fork. "There was no point while you were with Diego," she said. "Now, I'm curious."

"About me?"

"Yes, I guess. But also about Diego."

Ginny felt suddenly angry, as though a precious, private memory was in danger of being sullied. "He was the most wonderful man I'll ever know," she said.

María Carmen lit a cigarette, even though she had not yet finished her meal, at which she continued to pick. She must have detected a hint of a wince on Ginny's part. "You don't mind?" she said, waving her hand so as to distribute the smoke from the cigarette all around them. She clearly had no intention of extinguishing it, whatever Ginny might say.

"How did you find me?" asked Ginny.

"I guessed you'd come back when Diego died," said María Carmen. "And there aren't that many people in London called 'Ballesteros'."

"What do you want?"

The other woman smoked in silence for several seconds. Then she said: "I was an idiot."

Ginny said nothing. Her food was untouched. She was not hungry. She wanted to go, but something held her back. She needed to know what this woman had to say.

"Did Diego tell you why we split up?" asked María Carmen.

"Yes," said Ginny. It was a day she would never forget, the day Diego had confessed to her his most shameful act, the day – perversely – she had finally understood that she loved him.

"What did he tell you?"

"He said he hit you."

"Did he tell you why?"

Ginny hesitated. Did she really want to rake over these cold ashes? "He said you'd both had a lot to drink," she said. "You swore at him and he lashed out without thinking."

Unpredictably, María Carmen laughed, but only for a moment. "I couldn't believe it," she said. "He was always such a goddamned saint. God knows why he tolerated me for so long."

"Did you love him?" asked Ginny. Why was she asking this question of this virtual stranger?

"I've always loved him," said the other woman. Suddenly, Ginny's anger was dissipated and she felt a wave of sympathy, even gratitude, for the woman sitting before her. The legendary María Carmen, whom she had always pictured in fiery, beautiful youth, was now a sad, disappointed woman, someone whose inability to forgive had condemned her to a lifetime of regret. Someone who had made it possible, so many years later, for Ginny to find love with Diego, however briefly.

"Why did you never make contact with him?"

María Carmen stubbed out her cigarette in the remains of her meal. "Don't you think I've been asking myself that question for the last twenty years?" she said. "I suppose at first I wanted him to come begging. Then, after a while, I just dreamed of a chance meeting. And then he went back to Chile and I realised it would never happen."

"That was lucky for me," said Ginny.

"Yes," said María Carmen. "I hadn't expected anything like that to happen. Not after so many years had passed."

"Nor had Diego," said Ginny. "Nor had I, if it comes to that."

María Carmen looked at her appraisingly. "You're not what I expected," she said.

"Oh, really?"

"Yes," said María Carmen. "I must say I thought Diego would have chosen someone a bit more – how does one say? – a bit more colourful."

Ginny felt her sympathy rapidly evaporating. Diego had said that María Carmen always spoke her thoughts, without a hint of self-censorship, but it was still hard to take such rudeness. "Diego didn't choose me," she said evenly. "It just happened. We didn't mean it to happen."

"Well, I guess you made him happy," said María Carmen, in a sudden change of mood. "That's what counts."

The fact was, thought Ginny, that she and María Carmen had loved two different men. María Carmen's Diego, young, radical and passionate, was far removed from the courteous, gentle Diego of middle age with whom Ginny had fallen in love.

"Have you never…?" began Ginny.

"Oh, I've had plenty of men," said María Carmen. She paused while she lit another cigarette. "But no," she said, exhaling smoke. "No one like Diego."

"Diego said you were very active politically," said Ginny. *What am I doing?* she thought. *I'm engaging this woman in polite conversation.*

"That was part of the problem," said María Carmen. "Diego could only think about his beloved Chile. I wanted to fight every fight there was to fight here."

"Why didn't you go back to Nicaragua when the Sandinistas came to power?"

"That would have been too easy," said María Carmen.

"I see you're still active," said Ginny, nodding at the other woman's t-shirt.

María Carmen's face darkened. "All that time campaigning to kick the goddamned Tories out and now the other lot are just as bad."

Ginny was about to respond when María Carmen's mobile rang.

"Yes?" said María Carmen. "Is it urgent?" She made a face. "Well, if it's that urgent, you can pick me up. I'm in Sloane Square – it's on the way... Yes, I'll see you outside the Tube station."

María Carmen stubbed out her second cigarette. "I have to go," she said. "You want to meet again?"

"Is there any point?"

For a moment María Carmen's face softened. "I don't know," she said. "Take my card anyway."

Ginny studied the card, which described María Carmen as a freelance journalist and contained a mobile telephone number but no address.

"I'll pay the bill," said Ginny. "If you're in a hurry."

"Then we'll have to meet again, won't we?" said María Carmen.

As Ginny emerged from the restaurant, she was in time to see an open-top BMW pull up outside the Underground station. The driver leaned across to open the passenger door to allow María Carmen to get in. Ginny caught a glimpse of a well-chiselled, suntanned face, a thatch of straw-blond hair and the most incredibly bright blue eyes, before the car sped away in the direction of the King's Road.

***

Luis Moreno was a small, dark-haired man in his early forties. He was dressed neatly in a short-sleeved white shirt, grey trousers and black loafers. He wore a plain blue polyester and silk tie bearing the discreet gold insignia of a British defence equipment manufacturer. He sat behind a tidy desk, looking relaxed, pleasant and as unlike a criminal as

Adam could imagine. And yet Adam knew, from his rapid scrutiny of the Defence Section files, that at least a dozen of the pensions Moreno was currently paying related to people who were almost certainly dead. Having sat for most of the morning with the two members of the local staff who managed the day-to-day running of the main Embassy account, Adam was reasonably confident that they were innocent of any wrongdoing. Picking schedules apparently at random to demonstrate elements of the new accounts software, he had several times returned to the pensions payments schedule without this having any noticeable effect on their composure. In any case, their involvement appeared to be limited to recording the pension transactions and he could not see how they could have actually got their hands on any money.

"I'm sorry this is such short notice," said Adam to Moreno. "We had a last-minute cancellation and we brought forward the Madrid programme to fill the gap."

"There's no problem," smiled Moreno. "In what can I help you?"

Either this man was a *very* smooth operator, thought Adam, or he was completely innocent. "Well, I'm really here to explain the new software to the people in Accounts downstairs," he said. "But Alicia suggested I have a word with you as well while I'm here."

Actually Alicia had done no more than shrug her shoulders when Adam asked if he should speak to Moreno, but Adam did not want to give the impression that the idea had been his.

"Well, I really don't involve myself too much in what they do," said Moreno. "I have a cash imprest which Alicia replenishes once a month."

"But not all your payments are by cash, presumably," said Adam.

"No, of course not," said Moreno, smiling. "They're mostly by cheque."

"And you hold an Embassy cheque book?"

"Yes," said Moreno. "But, as I am sure you will know, I'm not an authorised signatory. Only UK-based staff can sign cheques."

"So, remind me how it works," said Adam. "Because this could be relevant when the new software comes in."

"I prepare the cheques with payment vouchers," said Moreno. "The Defence Attaché authorises them and puts the first signature on the cheques. Then they go on to the Management Officer or another UK-based member of staff for the second signature."

"And then they come back to you?"

Moreno made a slight grimace. "I know what you're going to say," he said. "They should be recorded in the account first. But it's not always practical if there's someone waiting to be paid."

"What sort of payments are we talking about?" asked Adam.

"By far the biggest category is war pensioners who've settled in Spain," said Moreno, without missing a beat.

"I see," said Adam. "Well you may have a bit of a problem shortly, because the new software will generate a cheque only when an entry is made in the account." *Unless, of course, you override it manually*, thought Adam. *But try sweating on that for a moment.*

"Oh well," said Moreno, who did not appear remotely troubled by the news. "We'll just have to do it a bit differently in future. I'll work something out with Alicia."

Adam could still not decide whether Moreno was a cool customer or genuinely innocent. But before he could try another tack, Moreno's telephone rang.

"It's for you," said Moreno, handing the phone to Adam.

"Sorry to interrupt, Adam," said Christopher Robin. "I need to see you upstairs urgently."

***

Gillian took a call from an irate Julian de Crespigny.

"You've got to intervene, Gillian," said Julian, his normal rich baritone betraying the faintest trace of a squeak. "Vauxhall Cross are giving me the bum's rush."

"I'm sorry to hear that, Julian," said Gillian, her heart sinking. "What exactly is the problem?"

"I can't get to see Jonathan Blood," said Julian. "How am I supposed to brief myself adequately on that side of things if the head of the outfit doesn't make himself available?"

"Haven't they offered you any briefing at all?"

"Yes, of course," said Julian irritably. "With some young sprog who thinks the Cold War's ancient history. It's not good enough."

"I can imagine Jonathan's very tied up right now," said Gillian. "They're going through a pretty comprehensive overhaul."

"If you'll forgive me for saying so, Gillian, that's absolute bollocks," said Julian. "Blood's got a legion of management consultants working on all that. He can spare me an hour to tell me what his people are up to in Spain."

Gillian sighed, she hoped inaudibly. "I'll see what I can do, Julian," she said. "But in the meantime, to be on the safe side, I think you should take the briefing they're offering. At the very least it will give you a heads-up on any issues Jonathan may raise with you." Just in time she stopped herself from referring, as she had in her previous conversation with Julian, to the bird in the hand. There was no point in gratuitously provoking Julian. But there were very good reasons why, at

108

least for the immediate future, the Head of MI6 would wish to avoid a meeting with him.

***

Christopher Robin had absented himself from his office with a muttered excuse, leaving Adam sitting alone at the coffee table with a large, balding, extremely ugly man in shirtsleeves and red braces, whom Robin had introduced as Freddie Gardiner.

"I imagine you know who I am," said Gardiner, tugging his tie loose at the collar. The voice was surprising: deep, cultivated, gravelly. If Adam had closed his eyes, he might even have imagined he was listening to Julian de Crespigny. But Gardiner's hulking, dishevelled figure was as different as imaginable from the Head of Personnel's squat, toad-like elegance. As he spoke, Gardiner was lighting a cigarette and looking around vainly for an ashtray in which to deposit the match end. The Embassy in Madrid evidently operated a no-smoking policy, to which Gardiner did not personally subscribe. He fetched a plant pot from the windowsill and set it down on the table in front of him.

"I can guess," said Adam.

"I've got two messages for you," said Gardiner. "Don't talk to Moreno again. And go home at once."

"I don't think I can do that," said Adam.

Gardiner glared at him. "You'll do what you're bloody well told," he said.

"You have no authority to tell me to do anything," said Adam.

Gardiner thought for a moment, taking a series of puffs at his cigarette. "Alright," he said. "I'll ask you nicely. Please do what I ask."

"Tell me why I should."

"I can't do that, old boy," said Gardiner. "You'll have to trust me."

"Look," said Adam. "I'm investigating a potentially serious fraud. One of my colleagues has just been murdered, possibly because of this investigation. My predecessor was warned off—"

"*You* were warned off," interrupted Gardiner.

"Yes, I was," said Adam. "But I'm an awkward bastard."

There was silence for a while. Finally, Gardiner stubbed his cigarette out in the plant pot and sat back with his arms tightly folded. "If I tell you what this is about, will you promise to get on the next flight back to London?"

"It's a deal," said Adam.

"Moreno's been on the fiddle for almost as long as he's been working in the Embassy," said Gardiner. "Seven, maybe eight years, by my reckoning."

"Then why doesn't somebody do something about it?"

"Because nobody knows," said Gardiner. "Well, none of your lot, anyway. I only discovered what was going on about six months ago."

"I don't get it," said Adam.

"One of my people met someone who knew someone whose girlfriend worked in the bank where Luis was parking all his money. You know how these things can just drop into your lap sometimes."

"I still don't get it."

Gardiner lit another cigarette. "He's mine now," he said. "That's all there is to it."

"Are you telling me you're letting him get away with theft of public funds just so you can run him?" said Adam indignantly.

"We've told him to cool it," said Gardiner. "He won't be doing it any more. He doesn't need to now."

"But that's outrageous," said Adam.

"Not if it's in the interests of national security," said Gardiner.

"What does that mean, exactly?"

"It means that my big boss and your big boss have agreed that Luis shouldn't be touched because he's too valuable to us."

"You've got to tell me more than that."

Gardiner shook his head, exhaling as he did so and creating random smoke patterns around his head. "No more, old boy. That's it."

Adam started to say something, but decided against it. He'd hit a blind alley and had better acknowledge defeat. But what of Kate? Did this mean her murder had nothing to do with the fraud investigation? Was Ginny Ballesteros right? Had Kate's lover killed her out of jealousy? In which case, wittingly or not, Adam bore the responsibility.

"Okay," Adam said. "You win. I'll go home tonight."

"Good," said Gardiner. "Oh, by the way. Don't tell anyone what I told you, understood? Not anyone. Not even – actually, especially not – Winnie the Pooh."

***

Gillian rang Bill Cambridge late in the afternoon.

"He's on his way back," she said. "The British Airways flight from Madrid tonight."

"Thanks, Gillian," said Cambridge. "I won't ask how you managed it, but thanks."

"Bill, I hope you know what you're doing," said Gillian. "I know this young man. None of it rings true to me."

"All the more reason for us to have a good talk to him," said Cambridge. "We won't take any formal action unless we're good and sure."

***

Raymond Fox always felt mildly intimidated in the presence of his Assistant Commissioner. Bill Cambridge had the build of a heavyweight boxer and the square chin and resolute eyes of a comic-book hero. He wore his iron-grey hair in a crew cut, he dressed smartly but without fussiness, and exuded a kind of relaxed, controlled strength, rather like a lion at rest. His voice, soft and with the faintest of Lancashire accents, did not quite fit his heroic appearance. But what he had to say was always crisp, to the point and imbued with solid logic. To be in the same room as Cambridge made Fox feel slight, untidy and fallible.

Cambridge had his back to Fox when Raymond entered the room. He had his hands thrust into his trouser pockets, looking through the window down to the throngs of office workers buying sandwiches on the corner of Broadway. He turned and smiled, a generous smile designed to put Fox at his ease. In this, it was only partially successful.

"Sit down, Raymond," he said. "Tell me about Kate Thomas."

Raymond was puzzled, as he had been when first summoned to Cambridge's office. He had already filed his reports, which his DCI had copied as a matter of routine, to the Head of Homicide Investigation. It was unusual for the Assistant Commissioner to involve himself in the details of such a case.

Cambridge evidently sensed Fox's bewilderment. "The Foreign Office find it difficult to believe," he said. "I know what the physical evidence is. I want your gut feeling."

Fox hesitated. "I don't think he committed either of them," he said, finally.

Cambridge sat down behind his desk. "That's not exactly what your reports say," he said.

"That's because all the evidence we have points in his direction," said Fox. "He's the last person we know saw Kate Thomas the night she died. He admits they kissed each other, although he initially tried to conceal the fact. She had sexual intercourse with someone that night. We can't be sure who it was, but she had fragments of Adam White's hair and skin under her fingernails. His prints and DNA traces are all over her flat."

"And in the case of Drysdale, you have witnesses who saw them arguing in the St John's Tavern, and White's DNA on the lapels of Drysdale's raincoat."

"That's right."

Cambridge drummed gently on the desk with his fingers. "When you interviewed him, White made a big thing out of the clothing Kate Thomas was wearing when she was found. As far as I can see from the report, you haven't traced the bag with the other clothing yet."

Fox shook his head. "No," he said. "Her other colleagues have confirmed what she was wearing during the day – the dress pretty much as Adam White described it. But no one can tell us what she wore when she left the office. I think the security guards were watching television. There's no sign of the bag White said she had, or of her office pass."

"And no witnesses who saw her after she left the Foreign Office?"

"No," said Fox. "We've looked at every CCTV camera on her normal route home, we've put out a public call, we've talked to her neighbours. Nothing. She appears to have vanished from sight."

"Did White not know we'd find his prints and DNA at her flat?"

"Obviously not," said Raymond.

"And there's no sign of this other man White says she was involved with?"

"None. We only have what White told us Kate Thomas said to him."

"And yet, despite all this, you personally think he's innocent. Why?"

"I know him," said Fox. "I just don't think he's capable of it."

Cambridge sighed. "You're the second person to tell me that this afternoon," he said. "Why not?"

Fox shrugged. "How do you know these things?" he said. "He's just not."

"That's not very scientific, Detective Inspector."

"You asked me for my gut instinct, sir."

"Fair enough," said Cambridge. "But with Kate Thomas it might have been something done on an impulse – it could even have been an accident."

Fox shook his head. "I don't believe it," he said. "And what possible motive could he have for killing Archie Drysdale?"

"You don't think Drysdale could have been Kate Thomas's other lover? That both murders could have been acts of jealousy?"

"We did consider that, briefly," said Raymond. In fact it had been Coker who had suggested the idea, his face flushed with triumph at the prospect of nailing Adam White as a double murderer with the perfect combination of motive, opportunity and forensic evidence. "But it made no sense. Drysdale had been hospitalised for several weeks. And, in any case, she was planning to leave the other man, whoever he was."

"So White says," Cambridge reminded him.

"What about the text messages?"

"Could they conceivably have been forged?"

Raymond did not speak immediately. It was possible. The situation could have been the opposite of that described by Adam. He could have been rebuffed by Kate Thomas, have

114

killed her in a jealous rage and then sent forged text messages to himself from her mobile.

"I hadn't thought of that," he conceded, finally. "We'd better see if we can get a fix on where the two phones were at the time of transmission."

The expression on Cambridge's face was neutral, but Raymond felt bound to apologise. "I'm sorry, sir," he said. "We should have done that already." And then because he felt he had to, he added: "But my stomach still tells me he's innocent."

***

Adam was in the taxi, which was struggling through the Friday afternoon Madrid traffic on the way to Barajas, when he finally switched on the duty officer mobile phone. There were several anxious voice messages from Lata, telling him that any number of people were trying to locate him. There was one from Raymond Fox – Lata had obviously given him the number – saying that he needed to see Adam urgently. And there was a text message from Ali, who must also have spoken to Lata. The message read:

Adam. Where r u? Police going 2 arrest u. Love u. Trust u. Call me. Ali

Adam sat back in the taxi and considered his next move. Gardiner must have known what the police planned to do. He had simply fed Adam a line designed to get him out of the Embassy and on a plane back to London. How much, if any, of what Gardiner had said was true?

Well, if people wanted to play dirty, they could not expect him to honour promises extracted under false pretences. "Change of plan," he said to the taxi driver. "Find me a nice cheap hotel near the centre somewhere. I think I'll stick around in Madrid a little longer."

LUKE

CHAPTER 8

In his small rented flat in Hounslow, immediately beneath the flight path to runway number one at Heathrow Airport, Luke lay in bed and calculated the pros and cons of the previous week. As he did so, he gently massaged the golden fuzz covering his chest and hummed tunelessly to himself. Every minute or so, a heavy jet aircraft lumbered overhead, bearing human cargo from Australia or India or elsewhere in Asia, soon to be disgorged into the corridors of Terminal Three and, ultimately, out into the Saturday morning traffic on the motorway. There had been a time when Luke had fantasised about getting hold of a shoulder-borne rocket launcher and shooting down one of these aircraft while leaning out of his bedroom window. But it had only been a passing phase.

It was going to be another fine day. He was looking forward to the trip. He liked flying. He particularly enjoyed flirting with the air hostesses, and who knew whether he might get lucky again? But on this trip, he reminded himself, he had to concentrate on the essentials. All the other arrangements were set up: María Carmen's friends had come through even better than expected. He just needed the final piece of information and the money.

Suddenly, Luke thought of Kate. He saw her, naked, kneeling in the corner in his other place, her body dimly lit by the laptop screen. He saw her head turn as he approached, the puzzled expression on her face, the unspoken question on her lips.

He swung his legs out of bed with a grunt and made for the shower. It had had to be done. Just as it had with Major Whitlock. He had thought that Kate might be different, but in the end all women were the same. This way, at least, there had been no argument, no remonstration. He ran the shower as hot as he could bear and worked up a lather of shampoo in his blond hair. Five days now, and not a whisper from the police. Yes, on balance, it had been a good week.

***

Gillian had risen early, as she invariably did, even at weekends, even after a short night like the one she had just had. She had the slightest of headaches, for which she held herself entirely responsible. The previous evening she had been at the Indonesian National Day before dining with some old LSE friends. The opportunity to relax for a few hours, away from the incessant pressures of the office, had proved too tempting to resist. She had probably had one whisky too many after dinner, and fancied she could imagine her father frowning down at her from his Presbyterian heaven. *Kirsty*, he would be saying. *You can take the odd dram now and then, but you're old enough to know when to stop, lassie.* She had always been Kirsty at home, had been even when she first came to London. Switching to her first name on joining the Foreign Office had been a conscious attempt to mark the final transition to adulthood. How often, these days, she longed to be Kirsty again.

She decided to walk quickly in the park to clear her head before eating breakfast and tackling the pile of paperwork

Hilary Price had apologetically placed in her weekend box the previous evening. It was warm and sunny, no longer so humid, and there were already small bunches of tourists about, consulting maps and looking happily lost. A tiny Japanese girl asked Gillian the way to Buckingham Palace as she made to cross Birdcage Walk.

The park was a mass of flowers and blossom, the grass lush and green, the foliage of the trees luxuriant. And yet, Gillian had a sense that the transition to autumn could not be far off. *June is a better month*, she thought. *Everything is beginning, blooming, on the verge of fruition. Everything still remains possible.*

As she paused on the bridge over the lake to look east towards where glimpses of the Foreign Office and the Ministry of Defence were just visible through the trees, she thought of Kate Thomas. That poor, unlucky girl. A destroyed life, a wasted talent. *How do you explain that, father? What does your God say about that?*

She had expected to hear further from Bill Cambridge the previous night, but in the relaxed company of her friends she had temporarily forgotten about Adam White. Now it was her Private Secretary who called her on her mobile as she turned to walk home.

"Adam White wasn't on the plane," said Price. "Or on any of the flights from Madrid last night, as far as the police can tell."

"Oh, dear God," said Gillian. "Could he have flown to another airport?"

"They're checking. He certainly won't get in any other way now. There's a general warning out at all ports and airports."

This news alarmed Gillian. "This mustn't get out of hand, Hilary," she said. "I hope they're not putting a call out to the Spaniards or anything."

"They're meeting in half an hour to decide what to do next."

"I'd better have a word with Bill Cambridge," said Gillian. "Have you spoken to Vauxhall Cross?"

"Yes. They're as worried as the police, as you can imagine."

"They were supposed to sort this out," said Gillian. "I'd better talk to them."

"It might help if we brought Christopher Robin into the link," said Price.

"No. The whole thing's risky enough as it is," said Gillian. "I'll see you in the office in fifteen minutes."

***

Alison and her father had been working non-stop in the August sunshine for over two hours. The garden had always been Harry Webster's passion. Since his retirement it had provided almost his only occupation. It was a place of order and beauty he had created for himself, a place above all where he could retreat from his wife's appalling temper. But, since the onset of Ruth's sudden, final illness, Harry had spent no time in the garden. The grass had grown wild, the weeds had multiplied, the pests had flourished unchecked. Adam had come from time to time to cut the grass and tidy as best he could, but he had barely managed to keep chaos at bay.

Now, finally, Harry had felt the desire to tackle the garden once more. Alison had happily worked alongside him. She remembered how, when not much more than a toddler, wearing shorts and a pair of rubber boots far too big for her, she had tottered around the lawn, picking daisies while her father planted and pruned and weeded in the nearby flowerbeds. Later, he had given Alison her own patch of earth, where she had sown seeds of mixed annuals, solemnly purchased with a whole week's pocket money from the garden centre halfway between their house and Pinner Underground station. Her mother had scoffed at her ambition and said her plants would never grow. But she had watered them, and talked to them, and squealed with delight when, by some miracle, most of them had in due course sprouted and flowered. Much later she worked out that her father must have been secretly weeding the bed and watering and fertilising her seeds to ensure that she would not be disappointed. Which of her parents, she wondered, had contributed most to her academic achievements and her success as a lawyer? Had she wanted to please her father or to defy her mother? She had not consciously set out to do either, but looking back she had to accept that something other than personal ambition had been driving her.

As a teenager she had discovered other pastimes, and her father had planted her patch with flowering bushes. She realised, as she weeded now around the base of a hydrangea in full bloom, that this was the very patch she had herself cultivated nearly twenty years previously.

"Coffee time," said her father. Alison made instant coffee in Ruth's still spotless kitchen and they sat in the sunshine at the patio table.

"Let's have it, Ali," said Harry.

"What do you mean?"

"Come on, sweetheart. You've been here for two days now. You haven't mentioned Adam once in that time. What's wrong?"

Alison felt curiously composed. When things had gone wrong between her and Adam in the past, she had experienced desperation and tearfulness. Now, her trust in him was absolute, however bad things looked.

"The police suspect Adam of being involved in the murder of the Foreign Office girl they found in St James's Park," she said.

"Oh, my God," said Harry, setting down his mug of coffee abruptly. His rugged, irregular features were filled with alarm. "Why on earth would they think that?"

Alison hesitated. Her father need not know everything. "They think something was going on between them," she said. "And Adam was the last person they know saw her alive."

"What does Adam say?"

"He says it's nonsense, of course," she said. And then, perhaps a little too quickly: "And I believe him."

"Then why are you here with me?" said Harry. "Why aren't you with Adam?"

"I came to be with you, Daddy, to help you."

"Ali…"

"Oh, alright," she said. "I doubted Adam momentarily, but I was wrong. And now, in any case, he's away on a job."

"Away?"

"Yes," said Alison. "I don't know exactly where." This much was true. Adam's brief, reassuring reply to her text message had not revealed his whereabouts – no doubt deliberately, so that she could legitimately claim not to know where he was if the police questioned her.

"Why didn't you say anything about this before, Ali?"

"It's taken me a while to understand how things are," she said.

"So, I take it you don't need any advice from me."

"Just tell me I'm right to trust him, that's all."

Harry smiled and took her hands in his. "Of course you are, sweetheart. You know that."

***

Gillian had spoken to the Head of MI6 and agreed on a modified plan of action. As ever, she felt mildly guilty about bypassing her own Security Department and the regular intelligence liaison staff, but that had been the agreement. Bringing in Simon Shakespeare had been inevitable when Archie Drysdale started making a nuisance of himself, although MI6 had not liked it.

Now she had to speak to Cambridge.

"I'm sorry, Bill," she said. "We thought he'd be on the plane. We're trying something else now."

"In other circumstances, we'd be speaking to the Spaniards by now," said Cambridge. His mild Lancastrian accent betrayed no impatience, but Gillian, who had once spent three weeks with Cambridge on a senior management course at Henley Staff College, knew him well enough to sense his puzzlement.

"I'd ask you not to do that, Bill," said Gillian. "Give us another chance to get him back."

"I get the feeling this is not just about avoiding scandal," said Cambridge.

"Bill, once he's on British soil you can arrest him with all the fanfare you want. I can't really say any more."

There was a short pause. Then Cambridge said: "Gillian, is there someone in my building who knows more about all this than I do?"

Gillian mouthed to herself a word for which her father would not have forgiven her.

"As I said, Bill, I really can't say any more," she said, her tone as neutral as she could manage.

"Thanks, Gillian," said Cambridge. "I get the message. I'll wait twenty-four hours. After that I won't be able to restrain my people. This is, after all, a murder investigation."

"Thanks, Bill," said Gillian. "I'm very grateful."

"This is a personal favour to you, Gillian," said Cambridge. "Twenty-four hours, no more. After that, I'll need a direct instruction from the Commissioner himself if I'm not to proceed."

***

By three in the afternoon it had become intolerably hot in the Plaza Mayor in Madrid. It was not the humid warmth which had characterised recent days in London, but a searing dry heat straight from the Sahara. The shutters of the balconied houses surrounding the square were all tightly closed, their privileged occupants no doubt enjoying a Saturday afternoon siesta in the cool dark within. In the centre of the square, the equestrian statue of Philip III looked down to where his subjects had once gathered to witness the autos-da-fé, public executions, bullfights and sundry festivals designed to brighten up the otherwise brutish lives of the underclass of seventeenth-century Madrid. Today, all the long-dead king would see was swarms of tourists seeking refuge from the baking heat of the centre of the square by retreating to the many restaurants and cafés which surrounded its fringe.

Adam had been forced to move from his original position to a table in the shade, where he sat now, sipping his second cup of post-lunch coffee. Not for the first time in Adam's life, having embarked impetuously on a course of action, he had initially been at a loss about how next to proceed. He had only one thing to go on. When interviewing the accounts staff the day before, he had managed to get hold of an internal staff list which included home addresses and telephone numbers. He was reasonably confident Gardiner did not know he had this. For want of a better plan, he had made his way early in the morning to Luis Moreno's apartment block and waited for something to happen. Almost immediately, Moreno had emerged from the building and strolled down the street, smoking a cigarette. Adam had followed him discreetly to a kiosk on the corner of the Paseo de la Castellana, where Moreno had bought newspapers and a copy of *TIME* magazine before returning straight home. Nothing had happened then for two hours. Adam had been on the verge of giving up when Moreno appeared again, this time accompanied by an elegant young woman and three small children. They had walked to the Castellana and taken a bus, which Adam had also just managed to catch. They had alighted at the Puerta del Sol and walked through the Calle Mayor to the edge of the Plaza Mayor, where they had spent an hour or so browsing in shops selling stamps, antique books and relics of Hemingway's Spain. Finally, they had gone into one of the restaurants facing on to the square for lunch. To Adam's surprise, they had chosen to eat inside. He had not dared to follow too closely, so had settled himself instead at one of the outside tables where he could just keep the family inside in sight. Moreno and the woman and children had eaten their way through an astonishingly large meal of roast lamb and were now tucking into a variety of puddings. Throughout the meal, various people in the restaurant had come to greet them at their table, giving the impression that they were regular customers.

Not wishing to be caught by a surprise move, Adam had restricted himself to a salad and mineral water, a decision he was now beginning to regret. But at least his hunger kept him alert. Suddenly, he saw Moreno glance casually at his watch, then pat his shirt pocket, shake his head and say something to the woman Adam assumed to be his wife. She looked in her bag and shook her head in return. Moreno shrugged and said something again and then stood up from the table. Adam ducked behind his newspaper and watched as Moreno came out of the restaurant and turned to go down one of the many narrow, crooked side streets leading off the square. Adam threw down a handful of notes and followed him as closely as he dared.

Moreno went into a tobacconist shop and Adam watched from outside as he bought cigarettes. But, when Moreno came back out, he did not return to the square but hurried further down the street and around a corner. Adam broke into a run to avoid losing Moreno and was just in time to see him pushing aside the dangling beads in the doorway to a dusty bar. *What the hell*, thought Adam, and followed him in.

Moreno had gone straight to a table and sat down. Adam lingered by the bar and watched. Moreno looked at his watch impatiently and then all around him, as though he had been expecting someone to be there before he arrived. This was not the impassive, relaxed Moreno Adam had interviewed the previous day. He looked jumpy and fretful, as though under enormous time pressure. Then the beads rustled behind Adam and he saw Moreno relax. Adam turned to see a blond-haired man in sunglasses enter and go straight to Moreno's table. Moreno said something angrily as the man sat down, at which the other appeared to laugh. The man flicked his fingers at a waiter and ordered drinks, while Moreno continued to grumble. Finally, Moreno pulled a fat envelope from inside his shirt and pushed it across the table towards the man, who took it without looking. Moreno was talking again, and the man shrugged as he lit a small cigar. Moreno stood up to go. The other waved his cigar at him absently and took a swig from his glass of anís. Adam turned away as Moreno swept through the bead curtain.

Now Adam had to decide: to follow Moreno back to his family or to stay with the stranger. After a few seconds of uncertainty, he decided to do the latter. If need be, he knew where he could find Moreno later.

***

"Twenty-four hours?" Coker's expression was a mixture of dismay and contempt. "The old sod's gone soft in the head."

Raymond was himself surprised, and in truth mildly relieved, that the Assistant Commissioner had put an approach to the Spanish police authorities on hold, a decision conveyed to him by his mystified DCI. But he was in no mood for a lengthy discussion with Coker about Cambridge's motivation. "He must know something we don't know," he said. "At least it gives us a bit of time to tidy up a few things. Are we sure we've now interviewed all of Kate Thomas's friends?"

"We've spoken to everyone we found in her address book and on her e-mail list," said Coker.

"What about her work computer?"

"Nothing," said Coker. "Nothing but official e-mails."

"What about the names we got from her mother?"

"She only had Christian names, but they all seemed to fit the people we interviewed."

"And they all said the same thing?" said Fox. "That they hadn't seen that much of her recently?"

"Pretty much, yes."

"Any more neighbours still to be traced?"

"No. We've talked to them all. No one saw anything."

"And you're sure there was nothing interesting in the recent phone calls she'd made?"

Coker gave Fox a sceptical look. "Are you still trying to find some mystery lover boy?" he said.

Fox shrugged. "I just want to eliminate all other options," he said.

"That's crap," said Coker. "And you know it."

"The phone calls, Phil?"

"I told you before, Raymond," said Coker. "No strange men. Just her friends, the office, the occasional telephone purchase, that sort of thing." He sniggered. "And, of course, deeply incriminating text messages to your friend on her mobile."

"Point taken, Phil," said Fox, making a mental note nevertheless to take a further look through the telephone company call records. "So, there are no more loose ends for the moment?"

"Well, we're still showing photographs to people who travelled on buses and the Underground between Whitehall and Shepherd's Bush on Monday night," said Coker. "And we're still asking anyone to come forward who might have been in the vicinity of St James's Park from midnight onwards. No takers so far – surprise, surprise. And, as you know, not a trace of her on any of the CCTV cameras."

"We may get another lead once we find out exactly where she was when she texted Adam White on Monday night," said Raymond.

"If it was her who sent the text in the first place," said Coker, who had seized with alacrity on the thought planted in Raymond's mind by the Assistant Commissioner that Adam might have forged the message.

Raymond ignored what Coker had said. "If there's nothing else doing, maybe you should take the rest of the day off then, Phil," said Raymond. "Get a spot of rest before Sunday, if that's the earliest we're likely to be able to talk to Adam White."

Coker smirked. "Trying to get rid of me, Raymond?" he said. "Got some new line of enquiry you don't want me to argue you out of?"

Fox laughed. "You know me too well, Phil," he said.

Then, unbidden, he had a sudden vision of himself sitting with Nicole and the children in the afternoon sunshine in Greenwich Park. Nicole was wearing the primrose yellow dress he'd bought for her birthday. In his mind, the tiredness had gone from her face and she looked the way she had when they first met: relaxed, smiling, inviting. *The hell with it*, he thought. *Sunday's almost certainly gone out of the window.* "No," he said decisively. "I'm going home too."

"Good for you," said Coker, who clearly did not believe him. "Me, I think I'll have another little chat with Miss Webster, just to pass the time."

Warning bells rang in Raymond's head. "I don't think that's such a good idea, Phil," he said. "You said yourself it didn't go so well yesterday."

"She's an uppity little cow," said Coker. "And she knows more than she's saying."

Raymond knew he should forbid Coker from going to see Alison. But Coker, being Coker, would go anyway. Raymond felt suddenly tired. Once again, he saw the yellow dress and the sunshine. "Okay," he said. "But for crying out loud, don't be too aggressive."

***

Alison was preparing tea for her father when her mobile rang. She did not immediately recognise the number, then realised it was Adam's office mobile. She almost wept with relief when she heard Adam's voice.

"What's happening, Adam?" she said.

"Listen, Ali, I need you to do me a favour. There's a man arriving at Heathrow on the British Airways flight from Madrid tonight. He's blond, in his late twenties, with very blue eyes – although actually he may be wearing sunglasses. He's wearing blue jeans, a black shirt and a black linen jacket.

He has no luggage. Follow him and find out where he lives."

"That's it?"

"That's it. Don't talk to him. Don't let him see you. Just get his address."

"Bloody hell, Adam. What's this all about?"

"I don't know, Ali. But this guy's up to something and it may be connected in some way with Kate's death."

"Adam," she said despairingly. "What are you doing? I thought you'd put all this sort of thing behind you."

"I know, I know," he said. "But what do you want me to do? The police think I did it. I've got to prove it's not true."

"When are you coming back? Where are you anyway?"

"I'll be back as soon as I can figure out a way of avoiding the police. Better you don't know any more than that. I'll be in touch."

***

If Adam had been trained in intelligence fieldwork, a number of things might have alerted him to the fact that all was not as it should be when he returned to his hotel on Saturday night. The first, of which he subsequently had only the faintest recollection, was the mud-spattered white Mercedes with CD plates parked in a nearby side road and partially obscured by the abundant foliage of one of the stately sycamore trees which lined the streets. The second was the momentary widening of the porter's eyes when Adam asked for his key. This he saw clearly – unlike the car – but could not interpret. The third was the slightest of noises at the base of the stairs as he turned, after stepping into the lift, to pull closed the rickety brass concertina door.

Adam was, in any case, totally lost in thought. He had followed the blond stranger on foot around Madrid for nearly two hours that afternoon. The man had strolled through the cool, green oasis of the Retiro, briefly visited the Prado and then sat in an outdoor café for twenty minutes, close by Plaza de Colón, drinking a coffee and smoking a cheroot. Then, without warning, he had hailed a passing taxi and was gone. Cursing, Adam had wasted several minutes finding a taxi for himself and took a calculated risk in telling the driver to head for Barajas as fast as he could. His guess proved to be correct: the stranger was just alighting from his taxi at the airport as Adam's taxi drew up. Adam had stayed close enough to him to learn the flight for which he checked in, but not close enough to discover his name. As a result, he knew he was asking a lot of Ali, but he felt he had no choice.

What had Moreno given the man? It could have been money – it had looked like money – although Adam's guess was that it was something more. But what? Nothing to do with pension fraud, that was for sure.

Adam slid the key into the room door. The fourth thing he should have noticed, as he did so, was the light just visible under the crack in the door. But by the time this had registered the door was open, and Adam was startled to see a familiar, bulky figure lying on his bed, smoking a cigarette and balancing an ashtray on his considerable paunch. Adam moved to back away, but he felt his arms pinioned from behind by someone who clearly did that kind of thing for a living.

"At bloody last," said Freddie Gardiner, stubbing out his cigarette and swinging his legs off the bed. "What the blue blazes do you think you're up to?"

***

Alison was convinced the task Adam had set her was impossible. Arriving passengers at Terminal One emerged from the customs hall in a continuous stream and there was no way of knowing on which of the many flights being processed they had been travelling. Adam had said her quarry had no checked luggage, which narrowed the possibilities considerably. But without checked baggage there would be no tell-tale labels to assist her. The man Adam had described would certainly be striking. But suppose he had changed clothes on the aircraft or disguised himself in some way? And even if, by some miracle, Alison were to identify the right man, how could she be sure of keeping track of him once he cleared customs? He might have a car parked in the long-term car park. Or be met by a friend. What should she do then?

In the event, everything was a lot easier than she could have hoped. There was the slightest of pauses in the flow of travellers coming out of the customs hall. And then, in the vanguard of the next group of arrivals, she saw him. He was wearing a black baseball hat, and his jacket was wrapped carelessly around his waist. But the blue jeans and the black shirt matched, as did the strands of blond hair sticking out from underneath the cap. So, too, did the absence of luggage. But the clincher was the piercing blue eyes, which momentarily appeared to lock on to Alison's own before she hastily raised her copy of *The Independent* to hide her face.

The man was making for the Underground, which gave Alison further basis for hope. Maybe this would not be so difficult after all. She already had a travel card, so she held back while the man bought a ticket and then followed him at a discreet distance.

He got out at Hounslow East. Alison was the only other person to leave the train, but luckily there were several people boarding and she managed to keep them between her and the man until he was clear of the platform. At the top of the stairs down to the street she waited to see which way he would go before descending two steps at a time to make sure he did not get too great a start on her. The man walked towards the High Street, where he crossed over and took an alleyway running down the side of a block of shops. The alleyway continued past a school and then opened out into a short stretch of road before becoming once more an alley, which ran down the side of a park and led to a stone bridge over a railway. Finally, the alley opened once more into a road, which the man followed until he came to a T-junction. He crossed the road and almost immediately turned into a gateless path leading up to the front of a dilapidated semi-detached house with greyish-brown pebble-dash walls. Alison watched from behind a tree as the man let himself into one of two doors at the front of the house, which had evidently been converted into two flats.

Alison walked as casually as she could across the road and past the front of the house, making a note of the number. She did not dare go closer to the house to see whether there were any name cards next to the doorbell. So she walked to the end of the road and checked its name. *Mission accomplished, up to a point,* she thought. Now she should go home and wait for Adam to make contact.

There was a pub on the corner with tables and benches outside. Alison looked at her watch. It was still only just after ten. She had a clear hour or more before she had to start worrying about the last Tube. It was a balmy night. If she sat and had a drink outside the pub she would be able to keep an eye on the front door of the man's house. Maybe he would have a visitor, or go out again. At all events, it was worth hanging on that little bit longer if she could find out something which would help Adam. She bought a white wine spritzer and, avoiding a table dominated by semi-drunken teenagers, settled herself down at the corner of a table occupied by what appeared to be an extended Indian family celebrating someone's birthday. The light was now fading fast, but she made a show of reading her newspaper to ward off any danger of being invited to participate in the revelries. *I'll compromise*, she thought. *I'll wait for half an hour. Then I'll go home.*

***

"You've really caused no end of trouble," said Freddie Gardiner, brushing the loose ash from his shirt front on to the faded carpet of the hotel room. He had exchanged his rumpled shirt and red braces for a pale pink Ralph Lauren polo shirt and white chinos, expensive extravagances that were wasted on his ungainly figure. "Alright, Tim, I don't think he's going to attack me. Why don't you wait outside?"

Adam felt his arms released and turned in time to see the flash of disappointment on the face of the man behind him. Tim had the build of someone who had played a lot of rugby. Adam calculated that they were about the same weight and height. In a fair fight, Adam would probably have held his own. But nothing about the other's demeanour gave the impression he had any concept of what a fair fight might be.

"How the hell did you know where I was staying?" said Adam as the door closed behind him.

Gardiner laughed sardonically. "Christ, you're so thick, aren't you?" he said. "As soon as Luis told us he'd seen you watching him, all we had to do was get hold of the taxi driver who took you to the airport."

"Moreno saw me?"

"Of course he saw you. You're a bloody amateur."

"I might have switched taxis at the airport," said Adam.

"Yes, but you didn't, did you?" said Gardiner. "So I rest my case." He sighed theatrically and helped himself to a miniature bottle of whisky from the mini-bar. He poured the whisky into a glass and took a generous swig, before sitting back down on the bed. "Why in God's name didn't you just go home? That was the understanding."

"Why didn't you tell me the police were planning to arrest me?" said Adam.

Gardiner raised his eyebrows. "How do you know that?"

"Never mind how I know," said Adam. "The point is *you* obviously knew and didn't tell me."

"Yes, well," said Gardiner, momentarily on the back foot. "It wouldn't exactly have encouraged you to get on the plane, would it?"

"Look," said Adam. "I'm innocent of Kate Thomas's murder. Her death is in some way linked to the pensions fraud – or something else Luis Moreno is mixed up in she may have stumbled on."

Gardiner gave an exasperated snort. "I told you yesterday, Luis is one of mine."

"That doesn't mean he may not be involved in something else as well," said Adam.

Gardiner regarded Adam with undisguised anger. "Will you please do me a favour and leave this to the professionals?" he said.

"Alright," said Adam. "How about this? Moreno met someone today and handed over a package. It looked as though it contained money."

"So?"

"Well, who was this person he met? What was the money for?"

Gardiner gave him a look of unremitting hostility. "You know, if things were different, you'd be sitting in a Spanish jail now, awaiting collection by Scotland Yard. You'd be going home in handcuffs, not standing here arguing the toss with me."

"Well, why aren't I?"

Gardiner was silent for a while, as though composing his thoughts. When he spoke, his tone was marginally more emollient. "Look," he said. "I don't give a monkey's about what the police want you for. And if it's any consolation I don't think they *are* planning to arrest you – not yet anyway. They just want to talk to you. All I'm concerned about is that you're trampling all over my patch and making a bloody nuisance of yourself."

Adam shook his head. "But you're missing the point. Kate Thomas's death is connected with Moreno in some way."

"You're wrong," said Gardiner. "It's got nothing to do with Luis."

Adam had remained standing during this exchange. Now he pulled the chair away from a small desk in the corner of the room, turned it towards Gardiner and sat down. "You want me to go home and surrender to the police?" he said. "You've got to do better than that."

Gardiner tossed the rest of the whisky down his throat. "They told me you were a stubborn bastard," he said. "I think I'll just leave you to Tim."

Now it was Adam's turn to laugh. "I may be thick," he said. "But now you're being absurd."

Gardiner gave him a puzzled look. Then he looked affronted. "I'm talking about an escort to the airport," he said. "For God's sake, what did you think I meant?"

Adam shrugged. "I don't know," he said. "But here's the deal. Tell me the truth and I'll go voluntarily."

"You've already had the truth."

"Then tell me all of it," said Adam. "Or at least enough to persuade me I'm wrong about Moreno."

Gardiner shook his head in apparent disbelief. "You don't get it, do you?" he said. "You're in no position to bargain with me."

"I'll go quietly if you tell me."

"You'll go quietly if I don't," said Gardiner, but Adam sensed a subtle shift in his tone, as though he were wondering whether to fall back on to a different position, one he had already prepared, one he had been holding in reserve in case Adam proved to be truly recalcitrant. Adam decided to push harder. "How are you going to manage that?" he said. "Is your friend Tim going to knock me unconscious? Are you going to drug me? Don't tell me you really do stuff like that? And how will you get me on the plane?"

As he was speaking, Adam saw himself, in a subliminal flash, being strapped, unconscious, into a stretcher and slid into the rear of a private aircraft. But he dismissed this as ludicrous fantasy and ploughed on regardless, hoping that his confident exterior would disguise his uncertainty.

"Don't tempt me," said Gardiner venomously. He was silent for a while, then said: "Put the television on."

Adam was momentarily nonplussed, but he reached back for the remote control on the desk behind him and pressed the power button. A late-night discussion programme came on, with a group of serious-looking men in sombre suits arguing and gesticulating, speaking Spanish far too fast for Adam even to grasp the topic they were debating.

Gardiner heaved his heavy weight off the bed and went into the bathroom, gesturing to Adam to follow him. He turned on the shower and the taps in the wash basin.

"Bloody hell," said Adam. "*Our Man in Havana.*"

"Can't be too careful," said Gardiner. "Now listen. This is what I'm authorised to tell you, although personally I think it's a mistake."

Adam said nothing, concerned not to interrupt Gardiner's flow.

"What I told you yesterday was balls," said Gardiner. "Luis has been one of ours for the best part of ten years, from before he was employed by the Defence Section. In the early years he gave us a lot of good stuff about contacts between ETA and the IRA, although all that became less critical following the Good Friday Agreement. Since I've been in Madrid we've been more concerned about the possibility of Al Qaeda trying something in Britain based on their organisation in Spain."

"You're not telling me Moreno's capable of penetrating an Al Qaeda cell," said Adam. "ETA I can believe, but Al Qaeda?"

"That's where you're wrong," said Gardiner. "He's a Moslem convert. His wife's from Melilla and he converted when they got married. He also contrives to give the impression of being more papist than the Pope, if you get my drift."

"And the pensions fraud?" said Adam. "What's that all about?"

"That was Luis's idea. He'd got very close to someone who was on the fringes of a group we thought might have connections to the Madrid bombings. He knew they were suspicious of him, because he worked at the Embassy. So we concocted the story that we had blackmailed him into working for us. He *told* them he was a British spy. But he said he hated us and would work for them against us. He'd give them information about us and give *us* false information about *them*. Neat, eh?"

"And how do you know that's not exactly what he's doing?"

Gardiner looked affronted again. "You don't understand," he said. "He's our boy. He's giving us priceless stuff."

"Such as?"

Gardiner shook his head. "Nothing doing. Even the Spaniards don't know what we know yet."

"But that's crazy."

"It's common prudence," said Gardiner. "If the Spaniards know, it will leak and then we lose everything."

"Lose everything?" said Adam. "What is this 'everything'? What is it that's so important that you don't even tell the government most intimately involved?"

Gardiner looked momentarily unhappy. Then he said: "This is all I can say. Someone's planning something big in the UK in the next few weeks. If we play this right we can get the whole network. But we've got to let them think they're home free. If the Spaniards get wind of it now they'll want to start arresting people at once, and then we'll lose half of them."

"But you're on their territory," said Adam. "You must work with them all the time."

Gardiner smiled, a not very nice smile. "Of course we do," he said. "We work with all sorts of people. But that doesn't mean we tell them every last one of our secrets, does it?"

Adam thought for a moment. "So, this man I saw with Moreno," he said. "You know who he is?"

Gardiner gave him a withering look. "What do you think?" he said.

"Shit," said Adam. "I'd better make a call."

***

Luke stood by the window in the darkened room looking through a pair of binoculars towards the pub at the end of the road. A very faint buzz and chatter reached him through the warm, still evening air, but the sound bore no direct relationship to anything he was watching. It was like a silent movie. He saw an intoxicated boy trying to grope the red-headed girl next to him. She pushed his hand away and pulled her t-shirt straight with a dismissive grin. *Not bad-*

looking, he thought. *I wouldn't mind a go at that myself, except she's probably underage.*

He moved the binoculars slightly to the right and scanned the faces of the rest of the group. Young, very young, all of them. Almost certainly too young to be drinking, but old enough for everything else. He moved the binoculars back to the left, lingering momentarily on the red-headed girl before moving on to the next table. *Three middle-aged farts*, he thought, *out with their wives after a game of golf probably*. He sized up the women – the brassy blonde looked as though she was up for it, but she was hardly worth making much of an effort for. Then there was a small table with just two people, a man and a woman, who seemed to be having a serious argument about something. He liked the look of the woman: thirtyish with dark hair, which she kept sweeping back from her forehead as she spoke, and a face which for some reason made him think of Snow White. Good figure, too. *I could kill the man and have her*, he thought. *Maybe not tonight. But if they ever came back . . .*

Well, maybe not. Better to find women on their own – it was less complicated. He turned the binoculars to the final table, which was a riot of saris and dishevelled suits. Indian women did nothing for him, so he wasted no time examining them. Then he saw the girl reading the newspaper.

Luke fine-tuned the focus of the binoculars. *Nice hair, mid-brown, shoulder-length, middle parting. Crooked nose, and eyes a bit too close together. Generous mouth. Interesting, definitely interesting. But also familiar.* He adjusted the focus again. *Yes, definitely familiar.* He stared at the girl for twenty seconds or more. *Suddenly, very familiar.* He trained the binoculars on the newspaper: it was *The Independent*. He looked again at the girl's face. There was no doubt in his mind now. He put the binoculars down and rubbed the back of his neck absentmindedly. Something else he would have to deal with. Well, perhaps he could combine business with pleasure. But he didn't have much time to spare.

***

"Adam, sorry. I can hardly hear you."

"Where are you? What's all that racket?"

"I'm outside a pub in Hounslow."

"It sounds like a riot. What are you doing there?"

Ali laughed mysteriously. "I'm on a stake-out," she said.

"Ali, that's not what I asked you to do," said Adam. "Go home at once."

"Hang on, there's a plane going over."

Adam waited patiently. He was lying on the hotel bed, now vacated by Freddie Gardiner, who had withdrawn on the understanding that Adam would be on the first flight out to London in the morning. "Tim will pick you up," Gardiner had said. "No need for taxis this time, eh?" In fact, Adam knew that Tim was almost certainly going to be sleeping on the sofa in the hotel reception that night to ensure that Adam did not try to give Gardiner the slip for a second time. But there was no real danger of this: Adam was sufficiently persuaded by Gardiner's final explanation to acknowledge that he had been on a false trail.

"That's better," said Alison. "Listen, Adam. I know where he lives. I just thought I'd hang around a bit to see if I could find out anything else."

"Look, Ali, I'm really sorry," he said. "I think I sent you on a wild goose chase."

"How do you mean?"

"I think this chap's entirely innocent," said Adam.

"But you said he was—"

"I know, I know. I'm really sorry. I was wrong."

"But we know where he lives now."

"Sweetheart, I'm really sorry. I've ballsed up pretty comprehensively. I'll be home tomorrow and I'll talk to the police."

Ali's voice did not conceal her annoyance. "Honestly, Adam," she said. "Sometimes I wonder…"

"I'm truly sorry, Ali," said Adam. "Meet me off the British Airways flight tomorrow morning and I'll tell you everything. Hang on," he said and gave her the flight number. "I've got a lot of explaining to do to the police and I'll need some moral support."

CHAPTER 9

Fox and Coker were waiting in the immigration hall, their jackets spattered with rain spots. A sudden shower had fallen at the moment Adam's aircraft touched down and had evidently caught them by surprise between their car and the terminal building. Fox was looking mildly unhappy, Coker clearly in his element. Gerry Baxter from Security was also there. His slightly-too-small jacket was dry, but he looked even more uncomfortable than Raymond Fox.

"Hello, Gerry," said Adam. "Are you here to see fair play?"

A grimace flickered across Baxter's plump features. "Sorry, Adam," he said. "After Friday's fiasco, the Permanent Under Secretary wanted to be assured you'd turned up."

"Well, here I am," said Adam. "So you can put her mind at rest." He turned to Fox. "Don't look so sad, Raymond," he said. "I know you're just doing your job. But I promise you, it's a mistake. Have you seen Alison, by the way?"

Fox looked puzzled. "Alison?" he said. "No, why?"

"She was supposed to be meeting me," said Adam. "Maybe she's been held up."

The group walked through the baggage hall and out into the waiting crowd. There was no sign of Alison.

"She said she'd be here," said Adam.

"We can't hang around waiting for your girlfriend," said Coker. "This isn't a family picnic."

"Let me at least call her," said Adam, reaching into his pocket. Coker shook his head, but Fox gestured to him to be still. "Just keep moving while you talk, Adam," he said.

There was no reply from Alison's mobile, and after several seconds the dialling tone changed and Adam heard her standard message. He left a request that she call him, and then telephoned Alison's father.

"I haven't seen her since yesterday afternoon, Adam," said Harry. "She said she was going back to the flat to make sure everything was alright there." It was typical of Ali, thought Adam, not to tell her father anything which might worry him. He called the flat. There was no reply, so he left a further message.

"Doesn't look like you're in much luck, does it?" said Coker, as they climbed into the waiting police car. Baxter, having made a call to Gillian King's Private Secretary, had excused himself and made for the Underground.

A few spots of rain were still falling as the car headed into the tunnel and towards the M4. The three men sat in silence. Adam sought to compose himself. Ali had been delayed for some reason. She was on the Underground and getting no signal. She'd call him in a matter of minutes. Nothing could have happened. Not to Ali. It wasn't possible.

***

"I hope you don't mind my presumption, Mrs Ballesteros, but I thought you might welcome some of these lovely tomatoes. Fresh from the farmers' market, they are – I caught them before they'd even set up their stalls."

Ginny smiled her thanks to the man at the entrance to her flat. Edward Harrison, her next-door neighbour, belonged to another age. He was dressed, in mid-August, in a three-piece beige tweed suit, a cream-coloured shirt and a red tartan tie, with a pair of sturdy brown brogue shoes on his feet. His only concession to the summer was a battered Panama hat, now clutched in one hand while with the other he extended to Ginny a well-filled brown paper bag.

"That's so very kind of you, Mr Harrison," said Ginny. "How much do I owe you?"

"Please," he said. "Have them as a gift from me."

Edward Harrison had taken Ginny under his wing from the moment she had moved into the flat some six months previously. The gift of tomatoes was just the last in a series of small kindnesses he had shown Ginny. From a younger man, such exaggerated solicitousness might have engendered suspicion, but Edward was in his eighties and his actions appeared to be inspired by nothing more than courteous decency. At the very worst, he exhibited the exaggerated desire for contact of someone who had lived alone for too long. Ginny had happily entrusted him with a spare key to the flat in case of emergency and had taken his in return.

"You're too generous," said Ginny. "Can I offer you a coffee or something?"

"No, no, thank you," he said. "I won't disturb you. I know you're busy with your writing."

After Edward had left, Ginny sat at the open window for ten minutes or more watching people organising their stalls at the farmers' market on the small paved triangle at the end of her street. Watching, in the sense of being vaguely aware of the stall owners moving busily around and their displays of plants and vegetables gradually taking shape. But not really seeing. She was seeing Diego, Diego when still apparently in full health, Diego in those extraordinary days when she had still not understood that she loved him. They were riding in the mountains above Santiago. The sky was a heart-rending blue, the city haze now far behind them. Diego was talking about his flight from Chile following Allende's death, of the shame he felt at abandoning the girl he was to have married. His face was lined and sad, he had an air of anguished nobility, the memory of which wrenched at Ginny's heart. He had not yet spoken to her of María Carmen: that fateful day lay some weeks away in the future. How could this Diego, her Diego, be the same Diego who had loved María Carmen with such ferocity, who had ended that relationship with a momentary act of blind violence? What would the youthful Diego have made of her, Ginny, when she was still a naïve, Home Counties undergraduate in thrall to her adulterous Spanish language teacher? Or she of him, the permanent exile, preaching Marxist revolution? Thank God they had found each other at the right moment, brief though that moment had been.

The sudden rain shower took Ginny by surprise and she rapidly closed the window. Even so, some rain had blown in and spotted the papers on her desk. She took some tissues from a box at the side of the desk and patted the documents dry. The writing was continuing to prove more difficult than she had expected. The research had been a pleasure – no, the right word was joy – because she and Diego had done so much of it together. And the planning of the book, the devising of its structure and the provisional allocation of the supporting material, had been a welcome discipline in those terrible, empty days after Diego's death. Why, then, could she not translate all this preparatory work into a coherent narrative? She knew the material, she had a working hypothesis to inform the story. Why would the words themselves not flow? Why did she spend more time staring out of the window than actually writing? Why had she allowed the meeting with María Carmen to upset her so much?

The latter thought had come unbidden, but perhaps this was part of the answer to her difficulty. It was as though the wound of Diego's loss had been clawed open, as if Ginny's memory of him risked infection by exposure to María Carmen's own very different memories. *I shall not see her again*, Ginny decided. It had been a mistake to meet her at all.

Ginny went into the kitchen to make coffee. She switched on the radio in the middle of *Desert Island Discs*. The guest was a woman, a writer. Waiting for the water to boil, Ginny tried to work out who the woman was from the questions about her early life. The accent was familiar, but she could not bring a name to mind to match it.

The telephone rang. Ginny had left it on her desk, and she retraced her steps to pick it up. Once, twice, it had rung, now three times, now four... Ginny shook her head impatiently and pressed the button.

The harsh accent was unmistakable. "Virginia," said María Carmen. "I must speak to you urgently. Please. Please, don't say no."

***

The cupboard door opened silently, but Alison could sense the sudden light around the edges of her blindfold. Instinctively, she cowered back, but a hand gripped her powerfully by the arm and hauled her out. She felt the faint prick of something sharp against her throat.

"I'm going to take off the tape," said the man. "If you make a noise, I'll kill you. Nod to say you understand."

Alison nodded. "Just do as you're told," her father had once said to her, long ago when she was a teenager. "If anyone threatens you or abducts you, always do what they tell you. Don't give them the slightest pretext for anger."

The tape was of the kind used for sealing cartons of

personal effects. Alison had inhaled the unmistakable smell of the glue, mixed with the cloying, sweet remains of the chloroform, throughout her night of terrified incarceration. She winced involuntarily as the tape was ripped from her mouth, but the relief was tremendous. "I've got to go," she said. "My bladder's bursting."

"Yeah, yeah," said the man. He led her across the room into what she supposed was the bathroom. She could feel the edge of the toilet bowl against the back of her legs. Now she felt the tape being torn from her wrists.

"Go ahead," he said.

Alison wanted to scream for privacy, but knew she must not. She did what she had to do, fear outweighing her embarrassment.

He led her back into the other room and sat her on a chair. He pulled her arms behind her and applied fresh tape.

"Water," she said. "Give me some water, please."

"In a minute," he said. "If you're good."

"Please," she said.

"If you're good, I said. Now, Alison. Why are you following me?"

It was a mildly lilting accent, a young voice, with a curious quality of immaturity about it. "Come on, I just need to know the truth," he continued. "I know where you live, I know what you do, I know how many speeding points you've got on your licence. What's your interest in me?"

Alison realised that he was going through her wallet as he spoke. She remained silent, thinking as fast as she could.

"Oh, what's this?" said the man. "A husband?" he paused. "No, a boyfriend, maybe. Oh, and this must be Mummy and Daddy."

Still, Alison said nothing. Suddenly, she felt the knife at her throat again. "Come on, Alison," said the man. "I haven't got much time."

Alison forced herself to speak. "I wasn't following you," she said. "I don't have any idea who you are. Please, just let me go."

"Hmm," said the man. "That's not the right answer, I'm afraid."

Alison gasped as the knife briefly penetrated her skin at the edge of her jawbone just below her right ear. She felt a slow trickle of blood down her neck.

"Try again," said the man.

Alison heard the sudden clatter of rain against the window pane, the sound heightened by her temporary blindness. What was the right thing to say to this man? There was no point in deluding herself. Sooner or later he was going to kill her. If she said she suspected him of involvement in Kate Thomas's murder, he would probably do it there and then. She was tempted to say she was working with the police, that they knew where she was, that the game was up, that he could not win. But that would still not stop him from killing her. She decided she had to stick as near as possible to the truth.

"My boyfriend saw you in Madrid," she said. "He asked me to follow you and find out where you live."

"Why did he do that?"

"The police think he murdered someone," said Alison. "He thinks you can help prove his innocence."

"Who is your boyfriend?"

"Adam White."

There was silence for several seconds. What did this denote – surprise? Did Adam's name mean something to the man? Then Alison felt the pressure of the knife against her throat once more.

"Does he know my name?" the man said.

Alison hesitated momentarily. "No," she said. She had to tread a fine line between panicking the man and making him overconfident. "But I told him your address."

"Is he coming here?"

Alison thought fast. "No," she said. "He was going straight from the airport this morning to the police. He thinks I'm at home."

Again there was silence. Then the man shoved her mobile phone to her ear. There was a ringing tone. "It's your boyfriend you're calling," said the man. "Get him to come here. Today. Alone."

The phone rang out unanswered for maybe thirty seconds. Alison desperately used the time to collect her thoughts. She had had to say Adam knew the address to stop the man killing her there and then. How could she convey this information to Adam now without enraging the man when he discovered her deceit? She would have to give Adam some clue which would not be too obvious. But what? *Come on, Alison, think. Think.* Suddenly, it came to her. The pub. If she could give him the name of the pub, that would be a start.

Alison sensed the man becoming restless. "I've just realised," she said. "Adam doesn't have his normal phone with him."

The man cursed and ripped the phone from her ear. She felt a sharp pain and gasped as the knife penetrated her skin again, this time just below the jawbone. Blood flowed freely down her neck into the collar of her blouse. "Where is he?" the man said.

Somehow, Alison was able to speak through her terror. "Look at my last text message," she said. "That's the number he's on now."

She heard the man punching the keys on her phone, swearing under his breath as he did so. Suddenly the phone was rammed against her ear again and she heard it ringing.

"Get it right this time, Alison," said the man, suddenly

calm again. "Because if you don't, being killed will be the last thing you'll have to worry about."

***

Whenever she got the chance, particularly in the summer months, Gillian King would spend the weekend at the house she had inherited from her parents some fifty miles north of Aberdeen. This weekend, however, there had been no possibility of getting away from London. Things looked as though they were coming to a crunch and she needed to be in continuous contact with the group.

There were seven of them sitting drinking coffee around the kitchen table in Gillian's flat, while Hilary Price sat alone behind a closed door in the sitting room, making a series of telephone calls. They had gathered originally on the tiny balcony looking down on to the inner courtyard, but the sudden rain had driven them inside. Jonathan Blood, the head of MI6, a lanky, scholarly man, dressed over-warmly in grey flannels and a sports jacket, mopped his bald pate with his handkerchief. "I don't know," he said. "First it's too warm, then it rains. I can never get it right."

The others in the group had judged the weather better. Sam Lampard, the Head of GCHQ, was elegant in chinos and a white t-shirt. Anthony Mills, Permanent Secretary at the Home Office wore a cool linen suit. Simon Shakespeare's bony frame was clothed in tennis shirt and shorts, but he had a rainproof jacket hanging on the back of his chair. Gillian herself had also ventured to wear shorts, although she was conscious enough of her broadening figure to choose the longest pair she had and put a loose, long-sleeved shirt over them. No such worry would have afflicted the other woman in the group, Dame Evelyn Powell, the Head of MI5. Her slender figure, clad in a faded floral dress, was much as Gillian remembered it from their time together at LSE.

The seventh person in the kitchen was dressed for a cricket match and appeared impatient to be about his business. His name was Mohamed Shaukat and he was the Assistant Commissioner at Scotland Yard responsible for Special Operations. "So, what do you think, Gillian?" he said. "Are we still on track?"

"I'm not sure that's really my call," said Gillian, looking at Jonathan Blood. "All I can say is that White's back in England and talking to the police."

Blood was now wiping the back of his neck. "As far as we can judge, he bought the story," he said. "You tell us he's an honest citizen, Gillian. So we just have to hope he keeps schtum."

"But what about Moreno?" said Shaukat, waving away with a quick, tight smile the coffee pot Gillian had raised towards him interrogatively. "Has he been upset by all this?"

"I think Freddie's convinced him White was just being overzealous about the pensions fraud," said Blood.

"If this goes wrong, there'll be trouble," said Shaukat.

"I'll second that," said Mills.

For a while, no one else said anything. What was there to say? Shaukat had done no more than voice everyone's thoughts. In ordinary circumstances, such a high-risk operation would have been vetted and triple-checked through a series of committees until, when every last wrinkle had been ironed out, officials finally submitted the proposal for ministerial approval. Then a well-oiled, bureaucratic machine would have moved into action to set up the necessary mechanisms and monitor every stage of the process. Instead, the scheme had been devised around Gillian's kitchen table by these same seven people, with no more than a handful of key operational staff involved in each of their organisations, not one of whom knew the whole picture. It was against all the rules. It was reckless. But the circumstances were not ordinary. They had felt they had no choice.

It was Evelyn Powell who finally broke the silence, in a voice whose authority belied her fragile looks. "Then we must all ensure it doesn't go wrong," she said.

***

Sitting in a kosher restaurant on the Vanderkindere Straat, Hussein made much of eating his lunch with relish. It had been a long three months, and the beard and clothing had been tiresome, but it had been worth it to get all the necessary arrangements in place without attracting attention to himself.

Assembling the team in Spain had required several weeks of patient negotiation with the individuals concerned. They were people on the periphery of Al Qaeda's operational cells in Spain, who were anxious for action after the prolonged clampdown following the Madrid bombings and – best of all – were prepared to die. Their participation had been ensured by dangling such a tempting target in front of them, together with generous promises of compensation for their families – promises made possible by the drug money flowing into a number of Swiss bank accounts from South East Asia. Arranging the necessary source of intelligence in London had, by contrast, required no negotiation, just old-fashioned seduction and blackmail.

Hussein had chosen to base himself in Brussels for a number of reasons. It was a highly efficient city in so many ways. Communications with London and Madrid were good, internet cafés were plentiful, and a wide selection of television stations from around the world was readily available. The passport-free Schengen Area had allowed him to travel unchecked from Sicily to Spain, and he could now move easily backwards and forwards between Brussels and Madrid (he had no intention of travelling to the United Kingdom). There were sufficient Modern Orthodox Jews in Brussels for him not to stand out, but not so many – as, for example, in Antwerp – that he would keep running into them: his French and Arabic were passable but he did not want to have to respond to an interrogation from a stranger speaking Yiddish. Most important of all, communication between the Belgian police and intelligence services – both of whom were woefully under-resourced – was notoriously poor: there were few places in Western Europe where he could more easily stay under the radar.

Living in a modest boarding house in a non-descript suburb, he would have told anyone who asked – nobody had – that he was conducting research into the historical interaction between Modern Orthodox Jews and the Haredi community. He had in advance analysed the essential elements of the Torah and the Halakha in order to avoid any obvious blunders in his appearance and demeanour. Now, between operational activity, he had devoted himself to a detailed study of the religious texts, originally out of a desire to maximise the authenticity of his disguise, but increasingly out of genuine fascination with their dense and complex teachings.

Hussein had sent members of the team to London separately on two reconnaissance trips. He wanted to familiarise them with the geography, but he also wanted to test the extent to which they were vulnerable to detection. On both occasions, one of the group had aroused the suspicions of the British intelligence services and had been pulled out urgently thanks to the inside knowledge available to Hussein. They would play no further part in the plan, but received handsome financial compensation to keep them quiet.

His meal finished, Hussein walked to the relative isolation of the Brugmannpark, where he made a call on a mobile phone.

"Can you speak?" he said, when the call was answered. "Good. Listen and don't interrupt. You've done well, but I'll need more frequent updating now – at least daily, and more often if anything unexpected crops up."

There was silence at the other end.

"I understand," Hussein continued. "You're worried. Don't be. We'll fix it."

***

Adam, Fox and Coker were back in the same interview room at Charing Cross Police Station. Coker seemed content, initially, to leave the questioning to Fox. He just sat, with a nasty smirk on his face, making doodles on his pad. He had placed his mobile phone on the desk in front of him, along with a pack of cigarettes and a lighter, as though to say: this may take some time, and we won't stop until we break you. Adam had to remind himself that he was still, theoretically, engaged in a voluntary process and not yet under arrest.

"Adam, I need to go back again to the second text message you got from Kate Thomas on Monday night," Fox said. "Can you just remind me what time that was?"

"It must have been some time after eleven. Probably closer to eleven thirty."

Fox consulted his notes. "According to our records it was sent at eleven seventeen," he said. "So you must have seen it almost immediately. Where were you at the time?"

"Somewhere on Archway. It was just before I got home."

Fox consulted his notes again and nodded. "And you tried to call her and got no response?"

"That's right."

"What did you do then?"

Adam said nothing immediately. "Do you need reminding what you told us before?" said Fox, leafing back through his notepad.

Adam sighed. "No, Raymond," he said. "I know what I said. I went to bed."

"Is that really the case?"

"Yes, it is."

Fox looked as though he had swallowed a lemon. "Can anyone vouch for the truth of that?" he said, as though he were painting by numbers.

"Ali was asleep already," said Adam. "So, I guess not."

Coker's smirk had turned into a broad grin. "Adam," said Fox. "We found your fingerprints and traces of your DNA in Kate Thomas's flat."

Adam drew a deep breath. "Is this what this is all about?" he said. "The fact that I was once in Kate's flat?"

"What do you mean, 'once'?" said Coker, finally breaking silence. "You were there on Monday night. You killed her. Why bother denying it?"

There was a look of slight relief on Fox's face. "What *do* you mean, Adam?" he said.

"I was there on Saturday," said Adam. "I went to pick up some papers Kate had been working on which I needed to see myself before Monday."

"Don't you people use e-mail?" said Coker, in ostentatious disbelief.

"These were original documents from the Uzbekistan government," said Adam. "They were too large and numerous to scan easily."

"So you went to see Miss Thomas in her flat," said Fox,

who appeared to want to give Adam the benefit of the doubt. "Had you ever done that before?"

"No. And anyway, I didn't go to see her, Raymond. I went to pick up the papers, that's all."

"But you did see her?"

"No, she wasn't there. It was all a bit of a mess. Originally she was supposed to bring the papers back to the office on Friday, but she forgot. Then she called on Saturday morning to say she had to go out, so could I collect the papers from her flat."

"You were her boss," said Fox. "Shouldn't she have brought them to you?"

"She was really apologetic," said Adam. "Something urgent had come up which she couldn't get out of."

"So, how did you get into the flat?"

"She left the key under the mat," said Adam.

"Do me a favour," said Coker.

"Raymond, this is the truth," said Adam. "And that was the one and only time I was in Kate's flat."

"Was anyone else with you?" asked Fox.

"No," said Adam. "Alison was at her father's."

"Did anyone see you at the flat?"

Adam thought for a moment. "Not sure," he said. "I didn't notice anyone. But someone looking out of their window might have seen me."

"We'll check that," said Fox to Coker. "Interview the neighbours again."

"Even if you were there on Saturday, that doesn't mean you weren't there on Monday night as well," said Coker.

"I'm telling you I wasn't," said Adam.

"Going back to Saturday," said Fox. "Can you tell me what exactly you did in the flat?"

"I went in, looked for the papers and left," said Adam. "I can't have been there more than a couple of minutes."

"Did you go into the bedroom?"

"You obviously know I did," said Adam. "Kate had left the papers on her bedside table."

"Why did she do that?"

"I don't know," said Adam. "She actually said they'd be on the kitchen table. Maybe she left in a hurry."

"So you went looking for them in the bedroom?"

"Well, I looked everywhere else first."

"But you said you were only there a couple of minutes," said Fox.

"It's a small flat," said Adam.

"Does your girlfriend know you went there?" asked Coker.

"No," said Adam. "The subject never came up."

Coker grinned, but said nothing.

"Okay, Adam," said Fox. "We'll see if we can find witnesses who saw you on Saturday."

"Have you found Kate's bag yet?" asked Adam.

"We ask the questions here," said Coker nastily.

"No," said Fox, ignoring Coker. "It's not in the flat or the surrounding grounds. Nor is it anywhere in St James's Park. We haven't even found anyone who saw her carrying it."

"Except for you, funnily enough," said Coker. "Maybe you know where it is – if it ever existed."

"What about Kate's pass?" said Adam to Fox.

"No," said Fox. "Nothing. Your security people are watching out in case anyone tries to use it." He paused, then went on. "Look, Adam, there's something else we need to ask you about. Archie Drysdale. You were with him on Wednesday night, weren't you?"

"Yes," said Adam, surprised. "He asked to see me."

"What about?"

Adam thought swiftly. He had promised Freddie Gardiner he would say nothing to the police which might draw their interest towards Luis Moreno's activities in Madrid. "He wanted to brief me about a case I was working on," he said.

"What time did you see him?"

"We had a drink at around eight," said Adam. "Why?"

"We have witnesses who saw you in the pub with him as late as nine thirty," said Coker. "They said you were arguing."

"We had a few words," said Adam. "Why? What's Archie been saying to you?"

"Oh, very good," said Coker. "When was the last time you saw him?"

"I can't remember exactly," said Adam. "I got home before ten sometime. It's about a fifteen-minute walk. Raymond, what's this all about? Is Archie claiming I assaulted him or something? It was only a scuffle for God's sake."

"Now we're getting somewhere," said Coker. "Tell us about this so-called scuffle."

"We were leaving the pub together," said Adam. "Archie was pretty drunk, so I offered to accompany him back to the hospital. But he wanted to go somewhere else, to go on drinking. He had a lot of loose cash in his raincoat pocket and he started waving it around and saying he could afford to drink and no one was going to stop him. I said I had to go and he swore and threw a punch at me. I grabbed him by the lapels and told him not to be such an idiot. He swore at me again and went back into the pub."

"Are you sure of that, Adam?" said Fox. "No one in the pub can recall seeing him come back after you left together."

"Yes, I'm sure," said Adam. Or was he? Drysdale had lurched back through the outer door of the pub, but Adam had not stopped to see whether he had gone right in. He had been too concerned to get home and talk to Alison. Maybe Archie had changed his mind and gone somewhere else. But what did it matter anyway? "I still don't get what the fuss is all about," he said.

"Archie Drysdale's dead," said Coker. "Someone pushed him off the Archway bridge sometime early on Thursday morning. You, would be my guess."

"Archie's *dead?*" said Adam, remembering with a shock Archie's apparently paranoid ramblings – maybe he had not been so paranoid after all. "Look, this is bollocks, Raymond. Christ, I had no idea Archie was dead. Are you sure he was pushed? He was very drunk. He could easily have fallen off the bridge."

"That's true," said Fox. "Or he could have jumped. We're keeping an open mind for now."

"What was he doing on the bridge at that time, anyway?" said Adam. "It doesn't make any sense."

Adam's mobile rang. "Can I take this, Raymond?" he said. "It may be Alison."

Coker began to snarl something, but Fox waved Adam to go ahead. Coker stood up, muttering about taking a leak, and left the room.

"Can you speak, Adam?" said Ali. Her voice sounded strange, strained and quiet.

"Ali, thank heavens," said Adam. He stood up and moved a few steps away from the interview table, his back turned towards Fox. "Where are you?"

"Are you alone?"

"No, I'm with the police."

There was silence at the other end, then a rustling noise and a man's voice came on to the phone. It was a young-sounding voice, with the barest of Welsh accents.

"It's Adam, isn't it? Now, listen carefully. If you get this wrong, Alison's dead. I want simple yes or no answers. Understood?"

In the sweaty interview room, Adam suddenly felt very cold. "Yes," he said.

"You know where we are?" said the man.

"Yes," said Adam, somehow sensing that, if he said otherwise, Ali would be lost.

"Get here as fast as you can," said the other. "If you tell the police anything, I'll not just kill her, understand?"

"Yes," said Adam. "Just as soon as I can get away."

"Giving you a hard time, are they?" said the other.

Adam looked over his shoulder towards where Fox sat, consulting his notes and making the occasional pencilled amendment.

"I'll need to speak to her on a regular basis," said Adam. "To make sure everything's okay."

"Just get here," said the other. "Or it won't be."

Adam glanced again at Fox, who remained busy with his notes. "Let me speak to her now or it's no deal," he said.

There was a pause, then a grunt, then Ali's voice again. "Adam, darling?" she said. "I'm really sorry. This is such a mess."

Before Adam could speak, Alison went on: "It was stupid of me to go to the County Arms like that. It was far too close. Only three houses away."

Then the man was back on the line. "You've got two hours," he said.

***

Ginny shifted uncomfortably on the park bench, holding her umbrella closer to her face. She wished she had told María Carmen she could not see her. Already she could feel her lovingly preserved image of Diego threatened by this second encounter. She did not want to hear any more about this woman's relationship with him. She would certainly tell her this was the last time they would meet.

Suddenly María Carmen was sitting beside her, breathing heavily, her face half hidden by the hood of her anorak.

"What on earth made you choose Regent's Park?" said Ginny.

"I feel safer here," said the other woman. "No one watching us."

"You're right there," said Ginny. "Everyone's very sensibly inside in the dry."

"I must be quick," said María Carmen. "You know – I think Diego must have told you – I was involved at one time with Sinn Féin."

"Yes, I do recall he mentioned that," said Ginny, wondering what the other woman could possibly be leading up to.

"It was at the time of the hunger strikes. You remember? Bobby Sands? She just let them die, the bitch."

Ginny said nothing.

"In any case," said María Carmen, "I have a friend who asked me to introduce him to some of my old contacts."

"A friend?"

The other woman looked awkward.

"Is this the man who picked you up at Sloane Square the other day?" asked Ginny.

"Yes, that's him." She looked momentarily embarrassed, then continued. "He's a journalist. He said he wanted to do some research into the history of the movement, you know. Get a first-hand account of what it was like on the streets of Belfast, why the IRA had to do what they did, that sort of thing."

Still Ginny remained silent.

"Anyway, I fixed the meeting like he asked. With a man called Gerry O'Leary. He was someone I used to see a lot of in the old days. It all seemed to work out very well."

Again, Ginny said nothing.

"Then yesterday I bumped into another old friend," said María Carmen. "Someone who's been closely involved in the

164

peace process. He told me he'd overheard Gerry in a pub in Londonderry laughing about how he'd found a novel way of decommissioning some of the IRA weapons the British were making so much fuss about and make a nice profit into the bargain."

Ginny frowned. "Are you suggesting—?"

"It appears there are still arms stored secretly in England," said María Carmen. Her face was agonised. "He'd sold some to my friend."

"This is very serious, María Carmen," said Ginny. "You must go to the police at once."

"No, please," said María Carmen. "I can't do that."

"But you must. Surely you can see that?"

"It's not that simple."

"María Carmen, it's very simple. IRA weapons being sold on the mainland? That's about as serious as it gets."

"I want *you* to go to the police."

What is it about me? thought Ginny. *First Gwyneth, now María Carmen.* "That's ridiculous," she said. "I don't know this Gerry O'Leary. I don't know your friend. You have all the information. You must go."

"You don't understand," said the other woman. "They'll throw me out if I go anywhere near the police."

"No, they won't," said Ginny. "They'll listen to you." She hesitated. "I'll come with you, if you want."

"I mean out of the country," said María Carmen. "I'm here illegally."

"But I thought you had political asylum."

María Carmen laughed. "That's what Diego told you?" she said. "Yes, he always had a romantic view of me."

"Are you telling me you've been here illegally all this time?"

"Yes. And somehow I've managed to avoid the notice of the police."

"But if you were mixed up with Sinn Féin in the 1980s, surely the Security Service will have a file on you?"

"You may be right. But by some miracle, they've never come after me. If I walk into a police station now and draw attention to myself, that will be it."

Ginny said nothing for a while. She looked at the sodden grass and the foliage of the nearby ash trees, heavy with rain. The rain itself had abated somewhat and a lone dog-walker had appeared in the distance with a golden retriever. She could not believe María Carmen. Diego might have idealised her in his memory, but surely he would not have lied to Ginny about something as fundamental as María Carmen's flight from Nicaragua. There must be some other reason why María Carmen would not go to the police. Was she afraid? Could it be that this woman who, when young, had fought heroically in the Sandinista cause, now genuinely feared for her life?

"Alright," Ginny said finally. "Tell me as much as you know. What's your friend's name?"

"John Jones."

"Are you serious?"

María Carmen shrugged. "It's the name he gave me."

"Where does he live?"

"I have no idea."

"Phone number?"

"A mobile."

"How did you meet him?"

"He had a Sunday job working in an estate agent's in Kentish Town. I was thinking about moving flats. He asked me out for a drink."

"And?"

"And, well, you know…" The sentence hung, unfinished.

"He said he was a journalist?"

"Yes. Freelance."

"And you weren't at all suspicious when he started asking you about your Sinn Féin connections? He might have been with Special Branch or something."

María Carmen shook her head. "He didn't ask me anything. He was just talking about his plans for a series of articles on Northern Ireland. I volunteered to introduce him to some people, that's all."

"Why did you do that?"

María Carmen turned to look at Ginny from under her dripping hood. The dark eyes flashed. With anger? With shame? "Because I wanted to keep him around," she said.

Ginny thought for a moment. "He stayed at your place?"

"Sometimes."

"Did he leave any belongings there?"

"No."

"So all we have is a name, a mobile number and where he works on Sundays."

"Used to," said María Carmen. "He told me he was going to quit to devote all his time to his project."

"I'll need more than that if I'm to go to the police," said Ginny. "Can I give them this man O'Leary's name?"

María Carmen looked unhappy. "I suppose you'll have to," she said.

"He may give the police your name if they arrest him."

"I don't think so," said María Carmen. "That's not the way they are."

"But you've given me *his* name."

"Look, Virginia, I'm trying to do the correct thing here and stop some violent stupidity. Anyway, I was never really one of them."

"Alright," said Ginny. "Now can you give me a detailed description of his appearance? I know he's blond and has blue eyes. I guess he's around thirty, or maybe younger even."

María Carmen gave a dry laugh. "Of course," she said. "That's no problem at all."

***

Coker was still out of the room. Adam momentarily wrestled with the idea of telling Raymond Fox everything. But Fox might not believe him. Even if he did, the slightest sign of the police would be the end of Ali. No, he reasoned. This was something he had to deal with himself.

"Are we going to be much longer, Raymond?" he asked, keeping his voice as level as he could manage.

Fox looked up from his notes, a slightly distracted expression on his sharp features. "As long as it takes, Adam," he said. "We've still got quite a lot of questions to ask."

"Can I at least take a pee before we start again?"

Fox nodded. "Jack will take you."

The constable at the door opened it to allow Adam to pass and followed him out. "Down the corridor to the end and then turn right," he said. "I'll be right behind you."

Adam reconstructed in his head the route he had taken with Fox and Coker when entering the building. It had taken around thirty seconds to walk from the front desk to the interview room, including the stretch of corridor he was now walking down. It would be risky, but he had no choice.

Just before the end of the corridor, Coker appeared around the corner, still fiddling absently with his trouser zip. It was now or never. Adam leaped forward, grabbed Coker's tie and hit him hard on the side of the jaw. Coker's head snapped sideways. Adam hit him again, at the same time swinging him round and hurling him into the face of the policeman. Jack went over backwards, swearing, as the dead weight of the now barely conscious Coker bore him down and pinned him to the floor.

Adam ran, like he had never run before. When he had tried out for Celtic, at the age of sixteen, the youth trainer had persuaded him to abandon his initial dream of playing centre back. "You're strong enough, laddie," he had said. "But you're too fast to spend your time just stopping the opposition. If you don't fancy midfield, play at right back and overlap. Surge, laddie, that's what you've got to do. Surge."

So Adam surged down the corridor. A policewoman appeared in front of him, pushing a trolley piled high with files. He yanked at the trolley as he swept past her, overturning it and spilling the files over the floor. There were more trolleys parked further ahead, and he set them all rolling backwards down the corridor as he heard shouts behind him. He emerged into the holding area, miraculously, at the precise moment when a violent drunk was being admitted, and charged through the still open electronic door, leaving more police – and the protesting drunk – stumbling in his wake.

Outside, the rain had stopped and large groups of people were converging on an anti-war rally in Trafalgar Square. Adam thrust himself, crouching, into the crowds entering William IV Street, and was already through them and halfway across the Strand before his pursuers emerged on to Agar Street. Adam hurled himself desperately down the slope into Villiers Street and raced into Embankment Tube station. He leaped down the steps on to the platform, thanking the God he did not believe in for his monthly travel card. Again he had luck, given that it was Sunday. A District Line train bound for Richmond arrived almost immediately.

But where in hell's name was he supposed to be going? Ali had given him the name of the pub. But where was it? He had heard a plane go over, very low, while they were talking the night before. That meant she must have been still very near the airport. He tried to use his mobile, but there was no signal. He waited, frustrated, until the train arrived at South Kensington, and jumped out on to the platform. He rang Directory Enquiries. "County Arms," he said. "It's a pub. Somewhere near London Airport, not sure exactly where. Could be Hounslow."

"I'll need an address," said the operator.

"That's all I've got," said Adam. "Please, it's important."

"Haven't you got a postcode?"

Adam watched despairingly as another train pulled away from the platform. He had already used up nearly half an hour of his precious two hours.

"No, I've told you—"

"I'm sorry, I can't help you. Have you tried *Yellow Pages*?"

Swearing to himself, Adam leaped up the steps two at a time to the exit. *An Internet café*, he thought. *I have to find an Internet café*. He ran out into Pelham Street and raced, without looking in either direction, towards the restaurants and cafés in Brompton Road. A taxi braked urgently in a desperate attempt to miss him, catching him with a glancing blow so that he fell backwards on to the road.

"Are you bloody mad?" shouted the taxi driver, as Adam dragged himself to his feet and saw, with disbelief, that the orange light above the windscreen was illuminated.

"Are you free?" said Adam, hauling himself round to the passenger door.

"Christ, mate," said the taxi driver. "All you had to do was wave."

"It's urgent. County Arms – it's a pub, somewhere near Heathrow," said Adam, stumbling into the cab. "Could be Hounslow?"

"Isleworth," said the taxi driver, performing a U-turn and heading for Cromwell Road.

"You know it?"

"Grew up there. Prefer the London Apprentice myself, but if it's the County Arms you want, the County Arms you shall have."

***

Luke hummed a repetitive snatch of a recent number-one hit as he assembled the timer on the kitchen table where he was seated. White was on his way and before too long he and his interfering woman would be safely eliminated. All the same, part of Luke regretted not having been able to kill the girl immediately. It would have been decisive and irreversible, just as it had been with Kate. And with Major Whitlock.

Funny how he'd been thinking about Whitlock again recently. He'd been a nice enough bloke. He'd always had a joke and a laugh with the lads and didn't try on any old-school-tie bullshit like some of them. But he hadn't understood the business with the Iraqi prisoner – Christ, what a fuss he'd made. It would have been too risky to let him live after that. It was Whitlock's bad luck that they were about to go on patrol – and that they were ambushed by insurgents in the southern suburbs of Basra...

Yes, it might have been more satisfying to kill the girl straight away, but he had had to keep her alive for the time being. He had needed to know if she was acting on her own – and why. It had been a shock to discover that he'd been seen in Madrid. Now he needed the girl alive to lure White to the flat. If White got any hint that she might already be dead he would bring in the police, and Luke was not ready for that yet. The flat had outlived its usefulness, but he needed time to sever all connection between it and him before he moved on.

Ideally, he should have interrogated her the previous evening, although a night in the cupboard had probably helped to soften her up. But he had, in any case, had no time to question her earlier. He would have been late for his meeting with Gerry if he had done, and he could not have been late for that. He'd had no qualms about keeping the gutless Spaniard waiting, but not Gerry. Because Gerry would simply have walked away and that would have been the end of it. And he needed Gerry. He needed what Gerry could give him if he was going to do the job properly.

He smiled to himself as he finished attaching the wires to the black metal box and began to unroll them slowly and surely, walking backwards out of the kitchen and down the stairs towards the front door. The girl had been so surprised when he stepped out from the gateway as she walked past. Luckily for him, the street had been deserted, all the other pub-goers having departed in cars. Shocking really, all that drinking and driving – he was minded to report them all to the police. He giggled at the thought, as he attached the wires to the detonator. She had tried to pull away as he seized her wrist, but he had his arm round her neck and his hand over her mouth and nose with the chloroform pad before she could begin to struggle. Not too much chloroform – he didn't want her being sick. Just enough to slow her down, to allow him to pick her up and get her into the flat before anyone saw her.

He looked at his watch. Time to call White again to give him some encouragement.

*****

The rain had faded to a light drizzle. Adam stood where the taxi had dropped him outside the pub. So far so good, but he was still not quite where he needed to be. *Only three houses away.* That should have made it simple. But the pub stood at the intersection of three roads and he had no idea which of them was the right one.

His mobile rang. "Getting close, I hope," said the man.

"Five minutes away," said Adam. "Let me speak to Ali."

"Don't you trust me, Adam? Shame on you."

"If I can't speak to her, I'll call the police."

There was a rustling and Ali came on the line.

"Which road?" said Adam, praying that the man would not have had the wit to put the phone on speaker. "Hall?" Nothing. "Worton?" Nothing. "Heath?"

"Yes, I'm fine, Adam," he heard Ali say. And then after a short pause: "He's left me alone."

He's left me alone. The house was on the left-hand side. It was thirty seconds away if he ran. The man was not expecting him for another three or four minutes. Maybe he could find a side window or some other way of getting into the house unnoticed.

The man came on the line again. "If I don't see you at the front gate in exactly one minute, she's dead."

***

The man had placed Alison in an upright chair by the open sash window, facing towards the front of the flat. He had removed her blindfold but sealed her mouth again, this time with translucent medical tape which would be invisible to any casual observer on the street. He had also cleaned the blood from her neck and taped the two wounds. He had previously given her some water and allowed her to use the bathroom again. She sat now, with her hands and feet bound, but not, for some reason, tied to the chair.

"Don't get any ideas, Alison," he said, in his curiously childish voice. "The path is made of stone. You'd look a pretty mess."

173

The man disappeared into what Alison supposed was the kitchen, where she could hear him humming to himself. She looked around her in desperation. The room was starkly furnished, with a square of dirty carpet in the middle of the floor. The walls were entirely bare, save for a calendar advertising motor tyres. There were some old newspapers and magazines and a dirty coffee mug on the table. There was no hint of the man's identity anywhere.

He came back into the room with a backpack over his shoulder and Alison's mobile pressed to his ear. "Stay where you are," he was saying. "You can see her from there."

Alison twisted round to look out of the window. Her heart leapt. Adam was standing at the front gate staring up at her, talking into his mobile.

"He wants you to nod your head if you're okay," said the man. "Do it or I'll slit your throat."

Alison nodded, while her eyes stared in terror as she tried to convey some sense of warning to Adam. What was this madman planning to do? He could surely have no intention of letting either of them live.

"You're to wait exactly thirty seconds when I say 'now'," said the man. "Then you can come in. It's the door on the right – it's on the latch. If you move any earlier, I'll kill her. Now."

The man turned and ran from the room. Alison twisted in the chair to follow his movement, but he was already through the door and gone towards the back of the house. Through the now open kitchen door she glimpsed something on the table and some trailing wires. For maybe two seconds she did not know what she was looking at. Then suddenly she understood.

She turned back to the window. Adam was standing, grim-faced, at the gate, poised like a wild animal waiting to pounce. She shook her head at him vigorously, but he already had the gate open and was striding through it.

She rocked urgently backwards and forwards and pushed herself upright off the chair. She tried to half-hop, half-jump to the window, and stumbled and began to fall. Somehow she got a purchase with her elbows on the sill and dragged herself up and thrust her head and shoulders through the open space. Summoning all her strength, she swung her legs up and round, so that she was teetering on the edge. She saw Adam look up in alarm and start to shout something. She gave a final heave and fell.

At the last moment Adam, still shouting, opened his arms and took Alison's full weight on his chest, twisting sideways as he did so and dragging her with him off the path and on to the muddy lawn. *This must be what a car crash feels like,* thought Alison, as her body was struck in several different places and she rolled over and over on the grass. There was wet earth in her nose and eyes and the taste of blood in her mouth. Then Adam was leaning over her, blood streaming from his face, making soothing sounds and loosening her bonds and, after what seemed like an age, the tape on her mouth.

"Bomb," she spluttered. "There's a bomb. He wired the door."

They dragged each other through the gate and out on to the pavement. Adam collapsed on all fours in the gutter, cursing and clutching his knee. Alison crouched by him, her arms around his shoulder, aware in a curiously calm way that she felt no pain. Then there was the roar of an explosion behind them and something flew over their heads and into the middle of the road. It was the front door of the house. They turned in shock to see the house engulfed in flames.

"Jesus," said Adam, spitting out a tooth. "He wasn't planning on taking any chances."

Suddenly Alison was aware of the pain whose absence she had only moments ago observed. It was everywhere: in her head, her neck, her legs, her left arm in particular. And she was trembling, shaking, filled with terror at the enormity of what she had just experienced.

"Adam," she said. "I think I'm..." And then the world went black.

CHAPTER 10

Detective Sergeant Coker's card lay on Ginny's desk in front of her as she waited for him to answer his telephone. She had opened the window a little to bring some fresh air into the tiny flat. Despite the masses of grey clouds still overhead, the rain had ceased altogether now and there was some light left in the evening. The damp streets outside were virtually deserted. The participants in the farmers' market had long packed up their rain-soaked stalls and departed. It would soon be dark, and she would be alone with her thoughts once more.

Coker was not going to answer his telephone. It was Sunday. Why would she expect him to be at work on a Sunday? For some reason she had assumed the police were always on duty, but of course that was ridiculous. And yet the number on the card was a mobile number. Surely he would not have it switched off?

"Detective Sergeant Coker's phone," said a man's voice.

"Is Detective Sergeant Coker there?"

"No," said the other. "He's... he's indisposed, I'm afraid. I'm Detective Inspector Fox. Can I help you?"

Fox. She might have known. He had been involved in the investigation into the deaths for which her first husband had been responsible. She had met Fox only once, after her husband's own death, when he had interviewed her to clarify information about James's movements and behaviour on certain dates so that the case files could be conclusively closed.

He had been courteous, sympathetic and to all appearances deeply embarrassed at subjecting her to such an ordeal. Courteous or not, she had no desire to meet him again. Better to speak to Coker. Uncouth, thoughtless Coker, who at least was ignorant of her past. Or was he? If he worked with Fox he probably knew just as much about her as Fox did. Knowing that, could she face talking to him? But somehow the prospect of a meeting with the thoughtful, patient Fox seemed even worse. She would take her chance with Coker.

"No, thank you," she said. "It's a personal matter. Will Detective Sergeant Coker be there tomorrow?"

"I hope so," said Fox. "Can I give him a message or get him to call you?"

"No. I'll call again, if I may."

"Can I say who called?"

She hesitated. "It's Virginia Ballesteros," she said.

The name appeared to mean nothing to Fox. "Fine," he said. "I'll let him know."

Ginny put the telephone down. She read again through the sheet of paper on which she had written the closest she could get to a verbatim record of her conversation with María Carmen. She felt a sudden twinge of conscience. Perhaps she should ring Fox back and talk to him tonight. She shrugged to herself and folded the paper and placed it between the pages of her Spanish dictionary. Tomorrow morning would surely be time enough.

***

Alison started from unconsciousness, aware simultaneously of voices, the dryness in her throat and a relentless throbbing in her left arm.

"Adam, are you alright?" she cried, trying ineffectually to raise herself from the bed.

"Take it easy, Alison," said a female voice.

Alison could see now the nurse who was gently restraining her. "Where's Adam?" she said. Then she heard her father's voice.

"He's not here, Ali," he said, reaching down and taking her hand. "He rang me to tell me you were in hospital and I got here as soon as I could."

"But, Daddy, is he alright?" said Ali. "There was this terrible explosion. Is he badly hurt?"

The nurse interrupted, laughing. "Oh, he'll live, I think," she said. "He had a couple of cracked ribs and some quite considerable cuts and bruises, including a nasty bang on his knee. We should probably have kept him in for observation, but he insisted on leaving."

Alison heard now a third voice and became aware of a uniformed policeman who had been standing silently on the other side of the bed, by the apparatus dispensing a saline drip into Alison's wrist. "In fact, Miss Webster, we'd be really grateful if you could let us know where you think Mr White may have gone."

"You'll have to wait before talking to her," said the nurse. "She's suffering from a fracture of the upper arm and severe dehydration. She needs to rest."

"It's alright," said Alison. "I've no idea where's he's gone. But it's not Adam you should be looking for – it's the man who tried to blow us both up."

***

Luke parked the BMW in a public car park in Chalk Farm and walked the mile to María Carmen's flat. Everything was now in the car, and he needed to keep some distance from it for the next couple of days.

Luke sucked absentmindedly on a small graze on his

thumb and thought about Kate. He'd thought about her a lot over the years. He'd been tempted to make contact earlier, but prudence had kept him away in the early years, and then she'd moved on and he'd had no means of knowing where she'd gone. The army had in any case given him other things to think about and, after all, there'd been no shortage of women. One-night stands were best. No names, no telephone numbers, no complications. Whenever anything lasted longer, there were problems. Women didn't understand when he moved on. Sometimes they wouldn't take no for an answer. Like the one in Paderborn, and that other in Sarajevo. In the end, he'd had to shut them both up. No problems there, because he'd been very careful. If you planned things carefully, they always worked out. With Whitlock, it had been different. He'd had to move too fast.

He'd told the court martial he'd tripped as the shooting began. At that range, the burst of fire from his SA80 had nearly taken Whitlock's head off. The expert witnesses had differed as to the credibility of Luke's explanation, but in the end they had to give him the benefit of the doubt. There was no obvious motive and Luke's previous record in the army was unblemished, save for one charge of drunken assault on a non-commissioned officer, to which he had pleaded guilty. He had not been drunk. On the contrary, he had been soberly enjoying systematically beating up a lance-corporal called Rooney who had been careless enough to suggest that Luke did not know who his parents were. But the defending officer had persuaded the court that both men had been drinking and as a result Luke received a relatively light sentence. Thinking about this again, Luke decided he might look Rooney up and finish the job he'd started.

It was a pity about the army, because it had suited him very well. But there were other ways of getting what he wanted, and this job was especially gratifying.

In the end, he'd met Kate again by pure accident, in St James's Park, of all places. She was special. She was different. If only she hadn't been so nosey…

The taste of blood from his thumb was slightly salty. How had that happened? He noticed also, as he walked, a nagging pain in his right ankle. It was nothing to worry about, but irritating all the same. He had stumbled on landing when jumping the back fence into the garden of the rear neighbouring house. Having to carry so much had affected his balance, but there had been nothing he could do about that. At least he had got well clear, and into the street behind, before the bomb had been detonated. He'd had the BMW out of the lock-up garage and almost as far as Twickenham rugby ground before he heard the first sirens.

All in all, things had worked out well. White had done exactly what he was told, and now he and the girl were gone and the trail was dead. John Jones, who had rented the Hounslow flat, was also no more. (The original owner of his identity was underneath the foundations of a new block of flats being erected close to the airport.) Abandoning Hounslow had come sooner than he'd planned. But, in the event, he was rather pleased with the neatness of the solution.

Now he would spend the night at María Carmen's flat. He needed to assure himself that she had no suspicion of his real interest in meeting Gerry O'Leary. If he detected any hint of that, he would kill her. He might have to kill her anyway, to be on the safe side.

**

One of Gillian King's strongest attributes was the ability to focus on one issue at a time without becoming distracted by the myriad other problems with which she was dealing. 'Old laser brain' was her affectionate nickname in the Service and she took this, rightly, as a compliment. So, despite the horrendous situation she had been discussing earlier in the day with her police and intelligence colleagues – and despite the abiding sadness about Andrew Singleton, of which she would never be finally free – she was totally absorbed in the final version of the briefing for the Iraqi President's visit when her doorbell rang.

Gillian looked through the peephole in the front door and saw the distorted image of Adam White's face, wild-eyed and grotesque in close-up.

"For heaven's sake, Adam," she said, as she let him in. "You look as though you've been in a car crash."

"I'm sorry to burst in on you," he said, as he limped towards the centre of the room. "But you've really got to level with me now."

"Sit down, Adam," said Gillian. "You look all in. I'll get you a coffee."

She started to move towards the kitchen, but, with an obvious effort, he stepped across to bar her way. "Please," he said. "No calls to the police. Not until we've talked."

There were several panic buttons installed in the flat, including one by the front door. *Why didn't I press that before letting him in?* she thought. Why had she let him in at all? Why hadn't she left him down on the street when he first rang the bell?

"Assaulting a police officer is not something to be taken lightly, Adam," she said.

"Listen to me," said Adam. "Please." He gestured to a chair. Gillian sat down. Adam remained standing.

"The police think I killed Kate Thomas and Archie Drysdale," he said. "You know that's not true."

"I don't know anything, Adam," said Gillian. "I certainly find it difficult to believe."

"I went to Madrid because I thought Kate's death might have something to do with the pensions fraud," said Adam. "Freddie Gardiner warned me off. He said Luis Moreno was one of his agents. He implied that someone was planning a serious terrorist attack in the UK and that Moreno was somehow going to help identify the terrorists."

Gillian said nothing. Gardiner had gone exactly as far as he had been authorised to go.

"So, like a dutiful citizen I laid off Moreno and came home and gave myself up," said Adam. "And what happened? Alison was kidnapped by the man I saw with Moreno in Madrid. He threatened to kill her if I didn't come to the house where he was holding her. And then he tried to blow us both up."

"Blow you up?"

"Yes. Hasn't it been on the news?"

Gillian remembered now something she had seen on the early evening news. "You were involved in the explosion in Hounslow?" she said. "I thought it was a gas leak."

"Yes, I was," said Adam. "And no, it wasn't. If Alison hadn't been incredibly quick-thinking, we wouldn't be alive now."

Gillian was silent. "Go on," she said finally.

"I just want the truth," said Adam. "By now I think I'm owed that."

Gillian thought for several seconds. She considered Adam carefully. For all the scrapes he had got himself into in the last few years, his central characteristic was integrity. He had been bull-headed. His judgement had sometimes been faulty. He had broken the rules more than once. But she could not fault his trustworthiness.

"Yes," she said, "I think you are." She gestured to him to sit down.

"I'm not authorised to tell you what I'm about to tell you," she said. "I'm doing so because I want you to understand how important it is that nobody touches Luis Moreno."

Adam was silent, his face a mask of scepticism.

"About two months ago we began to suspect that we had been penetrated," said Gillian.

"We?"

"The Met became suspicious initially. Twice they came near to picking up people linked to Al Qaeda who disappeared at the last moment. Someone was tipping them off."

"Someone in the Met?"

"Not necessarily. The intelligence leading to these people came from different sources – MI5 informants in this country, MI6 agents overseas, GCHQ intercepts and so on. And it was all processed through the Joint Terrorism Analysis Centre. Even on a need-to-know basis, the number of people was too large to pin down an obvious suspect – and we could be talking about more than one person."

Adam said nothing. He was clearly digesting what Gillian had said.

"Then, coincidentally or not, Moreno came up with a piece of sensational intelligence. A group with links to Al Qaeda in Spain was planning to assassinate the President of Iraq when he visited London. This was so much bigger than anything Moreno had previously produced that Freddie Gardiner flew to London and reported orally to the Head of MI6. This gave us the idea for the plan."

Gillian saw a look of incredulity spread across Adam's face. "You're using the President of Iraq as bait?" he said.

"Of course we're not," said Gillian. "Moreno's report was processed in the normal way, the Iraqis were warned of the threat, all the necessary precautions are being taken at this end. And we have a pretty good idea who the people involved are – apart, that is, from the person who is controlling them. All Moreno knew was that he had come from South East

Asia and was based somewhere in Belgium. We're working with the Belgians on this, but I'm afraid they're literally clueless."

"I don't get it."

"In parallel to all the standard activity, we're running a separate operation," said Gillian. "The only people involved are the heads of the relevant services and one or two key personnel. No JTAC, no JIC, no COBRA – in fact no ministers at all."

"No ministers?"

"It could conceivably be a minister we're looking for," said Gillian. "Or someone in a Private Office."

"So, how are you going to find them?"

"During the twenty-four hours before the visit we shall plant false information on a very limited basis in each agency about a planned raid on the terrorist suspects. Even I don't know the exact details, but each piece of intelligence in each agency will be different, and differently timed. We'll be monitoring the terrorists' activities. Depending on when, and how, they react, this will point to the agency concerned – and possibly to the individual."

Adam appeared to be struggling to understand what he was being told. "Wouldn't it be simpler – and safer – to suspend all the people concerned from duty?" he said.

"If we suspend them all, the system won't function," said Gillian. "It's a calculated risk, but we have to take it."

"And what happens if the terrorists don't react at all?"

"Well, at least we get them," said Gillian. "And we're no worse off than we would otherwise have been."

Adam looked no more convinced than when he had first entered the flat. "I still don't understand. If the Met have these people under surveillance, how did they allow Alison to be kidnapped and why did no one try to stop me from entering the house?"

Gillian felt a sense of acute unhappiness. "Because the people they're watching aren't in Hounslow, Adam," she said. "And I have no idea what you're talking about."

***

Ginny opened the door on the chain and peered through into the corridor. A large white envelope lay on the floor some six feet from the entrance. Why would someone go to the trouble, so late at night, of coming up and ringing her doorbell and then not wait for a reply? And how had they gained entrance to the building? Or was this, perhaps, some surprise gift from Edward Harrison?

Her question was answered as soon as she released the chain and stepped outside to collect the letter. The man came from behind the door, clamped his hand across her mouth and dragged her back into the flat.

He pushed her on to a sofa and sat beside her, his hand still held fast to her mouth. "You must be Virginia," he said, his blue eyes dancing. He sounded the 'g' in her name with a mischievously aspirated 'h'. Immediately, Ginny understood.

The man put a knife to her throat. "I'm going to take my hand away," he said. "One sound and you're dead." There was a curious cadence to his voice which reminded Ginny of something or someone.

After the initial shock of terror, Ginny felt a sense of great calm. "There's money in my desk drawer," she said. "This chain is gold. The watch isn't new, but it's a Cartier."

"I've no time for games," he said. "Have you spoken to anyone else?"

"I don't understand."

She started as the knife pierced the skin beneath her chin. "Yes, you do," he said.

I've nothing to gain either way, she thought. *But at least I can unsettle him.* "Yes," she said. "You're right. I've told the police everything."

For a moment, he looked uncertain. Then he laughed. "Nice try, Virginia," he said. "But I don't believe you."

Who did his voice remind her of? It scarcely mattered at this stage, she thought. But the question nagged at her.

He reached behind him for a cushion and brought it round to within an inch of her face. "You should have minded your own business," he said, pressing the cushion into her mouth and nose.

She fought the instinct to struggle, for there would be no point. The man was vastly stronger than her, and the final outcome would never be in doubt. She had not expected it to be this way, so soon, so violent. The book would never be finished now. But, no matter – now they would soon be together, she and Diego. She saw him, smiling and holding out his hand to her. *Soon,* she thought, *let it be soon.* And then, just before the blackness closed in, at the very moment when she heard Edward Harrison shouting at the opened door that the police were coming, she knew who the man's voice reminded her of. It was Gwyneth Thomas.

LUIS

CHAPTER 11

Raymond Fox had just dropped his two daughters at school when his mobile rang. He had planned to take the morning off to compensate for his lost Sunday and to try to placate Nicole. It was a sunny day, but with a slight breeze to take the edge off the temperature. They were going to drive to Beckenham and walk the baby in Kelsey Park, then eat the sandwiches Nicole had been making as he drove off half an hour previously.

It was Andy Baker, his DCI. "You'd better come in, Ray," he said. "We've had two murders overnight. It's all hands on deck."

There goes the picnic, was Raymond's first thought. "Are they linked, Andy?" he said.

"It looks like it. One of the victims was a woman who was suffocated and had knife wounds to her throat. The killer tried to do the same to another woman, but a neighbour interrupted him – and got his throat slashed for his pains, poor bastard."

Raymond felt the small hairs rise at the back of his neck. "Jesus," he said. "Was it the same location?"

"No," said Andy. "One was in Kentish Town, estimated time of death around six p.m. The other was in Pimlico around midnight. Another thing, though. Both the women had Spanish surnames."

Something awful stirred at the back of Raymond's mind. "What were the names?" he said.

"Dominguez and Ballesteros. You know, like the golfer."

"My God," said Raymond. "Not Virginia Ballesteros?"

"Yes. Why, what is it, Ray? Do you know her?"

"She rang yesterday to speak to Phil."

"Bloody hell," said Andy. "Well, she's in no condition to talk to anyone at the moment. She's only alive at all because of some smart first aid by the officer who found her. You'd better get in as fast as you can. I'll speak to Phil meantime."

"Is he working?" said Raymond. "He looked pretty rough when I saw him last night."

"You know Phil," said the other. "He's a tough bastard. He's all gung-ho to catch up with your friend White."

"Any sign of him yet?" asked Raymond.

"We had a report in just before midnight from the Head of the Foreign Office," said Andy. "Apparently the cheeky sod went to see her around ten o'clock for a chat."

"Why didn't she call us straight away?"

"She says he prevented her from calling until after he left."

"What did he want?" said Raymond.

"He claimed his girlfriend had been kidnapped and someone had tried to blow them up."

"Someone did try to blow them up from the look of it."

"We don't know that yet, Raymond," said Andy. "Special Ops are taking the lead. All they're saying is that there was an explosion and that White and his girlfriend were injured. But they're not yet saying what caused the explosion, and we don't know if anyone else was involved."

"What else did White say?" asked Raymond.

"He gave her a full physical description of the man," said Andy. "But no name or any idea where he might be now."

"And why did he think this man was trying to kill them?"

"Because he'd also killed Kate Thomas – according to White."

A sudden gust of wind blew the discarded pages of a newspaper into the air and sent them dipping and fluttering across Lewisham High Street, causing a number of cars to brake suddenly before the traffic resumed its uneven flow. "Sounds a bit far-fetched, doesn't it?" said Raymond.

"It does that, Raymond," said Andy. "I'm sorry. White's a friend of yours, isn't he?"

"Not a friend," said Raymond. "We knew each other. I thought I knew him."

A sudden, disturbing thought came to Raymond. "Where does this Foreign Office person live?" he asked.

"Westminster. Why?"

Raymond felt a sense of dizziness. Westminster. That put Adam White halfway between the locations of the two murders at exactly the right time to make it possible for him to have committed them both.

"Never mind," he said. "I'll be there in half an hour."

***

Gillian scrolled rapidly through her morning telegrams. The whole world seemed to be seething with menace: Iraq, Afghanistan, Gaza, Lebanon, Sudan, North Korea – was there anywhere offering good news this troubled Monday morning? The European Union was again in crisis, with the unprecedented threat of senior politicians being dragged from their beach or mountain retreats to attend an emergency meeting in Brussels. There was a trade war looming with the United States, China and Taiwan were growling at each other again, Russia was making threatening noises about Ukraine's ambitions to join NATO. Only Latin America seemed to be temporarily quiescent.

Gillian closed her eyes, momentarily exhausted. The world would have to manage on its own for the next forty-eight hours – or rather her excellent staff would. She had to concentrate on one thing only.

Even as she thought this, however, an image flashed unbidden into Gillian's mind of Andrew Singleton, lying on the floor of a hotel bedroom in Catania, dead from a gunshot wound to the temple, the weapon lying by his outstretched hand. It was an incredible scenario: the Andrew she knew would never have committed suicide. Had his ordeal really so transformed him? And how had he obtained the gun? Despite this unanswered question, the local police had seemed in no doubt that he had killed himself, and Andrew had no surviving near family in a position to pursue an independent enquiry. *Sweet Lord, Andrew,* she thought. *What a way for it to end.*

Gillian wrenched herself back into the present. Had she pitched her report to the police correctly? She could not simply ignore Adam White's story, and she had a citizen's duty to report what might be a genuine lead in the investigation into Kate Thomas's murder. At the same time, she dared not prejudice the operation – although she was beginning to have grave misgivings about the entire plan, because there was clearly something going on which had not been expected. All but one of the terrorists the Met were looking for had been identified with some precision. Two were Algerian, one was Saudi and a fourth was from the Spanish North African enclave of Ceuta. There was also the so far unidentified controller, who was in hiding somewhere in Belgium and thought to be of South East Asian origin. Who in God's name, then, was this blond-haired man Adam White claimed to have seen in Madrid?

A series of cryptic telephone conversations had enabled Gillian to fix an emergency meeting of her interlocutors in the Met and the agencies at ten that morning. Until they had been able to discuss the situation, she had to remain economical with the truth.

Gillian had tried unsuccessfully to persuade Adam White to surrender to the police. "I've already been suckered once," he had said. "If I go to the police, I'll tell them the whole bloody story. If your scheme's going to work, you're better off with me at large."

"But doing what, Adam?" she had said.

"I'm going to find him," he had said. "He tried to kill Ali. One way or another, I'm going to find him."

Hilary Price interrupted Gillian's thoughts. "I've got Assistant Commissioner Cambridge on the line," he said. "He says it's urgent."

At the back of her mind Gillian filed a personal note to herself to have a heart-to-heart talk with Hilary once the visit, and the operation, were safely out of the way. He looked exhausted, as though he were not sleeping properly. His exquisite manners were unimpaired, and he was doing his job efficiently enough, but there was something wrong. She would speak to him on Friday.

"Put him through, Hilary," she said.

"Gillian," said Cambridge. "I'm really sorry. I always seem to be bearing bad news these days. Someone has tried to kill Virginia Ballesteros. Another woman you probably don't know *has* been murdered. And it looks very much as though your man White was responsible in both cases."

***

Luke had slept until five in the morning in María Carmen's flat. It was risky, but at least it was well clear of Pimlico. Things had not gone quite to plan there, thanks to that interfering old wanker, although he had been easily dealt with. It had just been necessary to get out fast before the police arrived.

A number of María Carmen's friends had telephoned late at night and left messages on her mobile, but luckily none had suggested a meeting that evening. He had left the building at five thirty and walked to Paddington, where he had shaved and changed his clothes in a public lavatory. Now he sat in an Internet café in Shepherd's Bush, drinking coffee and watching Sky News on a television mounted high on the wall in the corner. He glanced at his watch, fingering his split lip and the bruise on his chin. It was nearly eight. The cleaner would have found María Carmen's body by now.

There was only a relatively brief reference to the Hounslow explosion, which came third in the news coverage after the latest suicide bombings in Iraq and a public spat between the British Prime Minister and the President of France. The newspapers Luke had bought were equally reticent. The police had said that, pending a full forensic investigation, it was too soon to determine whether the explosion had been deliberate or accidental. There had been no serious casualties, both flats in the house being unoccupied at the time. Two passers-by, a man and a woman, had been taken to hospital with minor injuries, but the man had subsequently discharged himself. Political analysts were expressing scepticism about a possible link between the explosion and the imminent visit of the President of Iraq.

Luke began to hum to himself again, his mind meanwhile making a series of rapid calculations. No serious casualties. How could that be? Just when he thought he'd covered his tracks, things were looking messy. Maybe he should have killed the girl as soon as he had White in view. But that would have been very risky – he had needed to get White into the house. *Move on, Luke. You can't change the past.* What did they know, anyway? They had seen his face. They knew he'd been in Madrid and met the Spaniard. But they didn't know his name, or where he was, or what he was planning to do. Even if they told the police everything, even if the Spaniard was arrested, by the time they sweated the truth out of him, it would be too late to stop him. If he felt there was a real danger of exposure, he could always abort the whole plan – and he'd still have half the money. But he didn't want to abort, because he was having too much fun. And the Spaniard didn't know his real name, so they wouldn't be able to find him. He would have to disappear afterwards, but he'd done that before.

Luke finished his coffee and paid the girl behind the bar. She was very young, pale-skinned and pretty. She reminded him a bit of Kate. He flashed his blue eyes at her as she gave him the change. "Where are you from, sweetheart?" he said.

She smiled shyly. "Estonia," she said.

"If you're free later on, maybe we could have a drink," said Luke.

The girl giggled and said nothing.

"I'll take that as a yes," he said.

***

The sudden sound of the horn of an approaching ferry sent a flock of seagulls wheeling and screeching into the air. Adam counted the tour buses lined up at the entrance to the ferry terminal. There were nine altogether, and his guess was that they were all booked on the next ferry to Calais. The British buses were mostly filled with school children, although there was one that looked like a pensioners' day trip. Two were evidently French and German tours returning home. It would be a toss-up between one of them and the pensioners. He wanted to avoid a British bus driver if possible, but would a French or German be any better? As he was deliberating, another bus arrived at the end of the queue. It contained a rather somnolent group of middle-aged couples. The wording on the side of the bus was Polish. That was the one.

Adam could detect no police presence in the immediate environs of the port, but he knew they must be inside, sitting with the customs and immigration officials or patrolling the terminal and studying foot passengers. His plan was madness. He would never get away with it.

Adam had slept rough the previous night. He had assumed that the police would be watching the flat. They were probably also watching Ali's father's house, but in any case Adam did not want to compromise Harry in any way. He had toyed with the idea of going into the Foreign Office to run through the files again in case anything had escaped him earlier. This was arguably the last thing the police would expect, but he guessed that, even so, the police would cover all possible bases: the moment he used his office pass the system would alert the police.

What he really needed, he had decided, was to get back to Madrid. He had no idea where to begin looking for the blond-haired man in England. All the information he had would have been passed on to the police by Gillian King. If they gave it any credence, they would be better placed than him to track the man down. Adam's only real lead was Moreno, whom Gillian King was clearly still anxious to protect from police scrutiny. So Adam would have to go after Moreno himself.

But how? The police would be watching all airports and sea ports. Eurostar would also be under surveillance. After leaving Gillian King's flat, and for want of a better idea, Adam had caught a slow commuter train from Victoria to Bromley South, where he had changed to another slow train to Dover Priory. He had left the train at Shepherds Well and walked across fields until he was within a couple of miles of the port. Then he had settled himself down in the corner of a disused barn and tried to figure out a plan.

The plan he had come up with was thin in the extreme, but he could think of none better. The buses were now moving slowly through the customs and immigration checks. Adam came out of the shadows and, hanging his Foreign Office pass on its chain round his neck, marched boldly towards the final bus with his right hand raised in the air.

"Security check," he said, as the driver let his window down.

The driver scratched his black moustache and looked puzzled. He reminded Adam vaguely of the young Lech Wałęsa.

"Just routine," said Adam, conscious of his overnight growth of beard and creased suit. "A spot check."

The driver released the door and Adam climbed into the bus as casually as he could. "Please have your passports ready," he called out. He moved slowly down the bus, pretending to study the passports proffered to him. The bus moved forward slowly. Crouching towards the back of the bus, with a batch of passports in his hand, Adam could see through the front window that an immigration officer had boarded the bus in front. Was this a random check? Would he be lucky?

He couldn't risk it. As the bus began to move again, he handed the passports back to their owners, grimaced and clutched his stomach and made his way swiftly back down the aisle to the middle doorway, where the lavatory was situated. He locked himself in and waited. The bus stopped again, but only momentarily, and then moved on. After a while, he felt it gradually ascending, then turning in a wide curve before descending again to the waiting area. It was the last bus. If he was lucky again, the others had already begun to board. The bus stopped, but the engine continued to run. After a few minutes the bus pulled away again and Adam felt it climbing the ramp and slowing as it approached the ferry. He flushed the toilet and emerged, still clutching his stomach and muttering words of apology to no one in particular. He stood behind the driver's seat, smiling confidently at the ferry workers as the bus entered the bowels of the vessel.

"Thank you, sir," he said to the driver, as he descended from the bus. "Have a pleasant crossing."

Adam made his way to the nearest cafeteria and found himself a corner table. By some miracle, his hair-brained plan had worked. In an hour and a half he would be in Calais. All he had to do now was work out how to get to Madrid. And what to do when he got there.

***

Raymond briefed his team, including a worse-for-wear Coker, as soon as he had come from the DCI's office.

"We're leading on both of these," he said. "The assumption has to be that the murderer also killed Kate Thomas. We'll be getting preliminary forensics by midday." He paused. "Our prime suspect remains Adam White, so the priority is to find him and bring him in. But there's still a lot of routine questioning of neighbours to be done, so let's get on with it. And let's look at these women's personal details and see what they've got in common, whether they knew each other, what friends they might both have had, anything which links them. There's also another lead we have to look into. Phil, let's go and look at the crime scenes. We can talk on the way."

"Can we interview Ballesteros yet?" asked one of the team.

"*Mrs* Ballesteros is still under sedation," said Raymond.

"The hospital can't forecast when she'll be able to speak to us."

In the car, Coker spoke with some difficulty. "We know it's White, Ray," he said. "Why do we have to bother with this bullshit he's feeding us about some mysterious blond-haired man? He knew Thomas. He knew Ballesteros. We'll find a link with the other woman."

"I'm still puzzled about motive," said Raymond. "Why would Adam White want to kill Virginia Ballesteros, let alone María Carmen Dominguez?"

"Perhaps he was having some kind of mid-life crisis," said Coker. "What do I know? But all the material evidence points to him. We'll find the motive when we catch up with the bastard."

"Maybe you're right," said Raymond, suppressing the urge to defend Adam in the face of such damning facts. "But we can't just ignore all other possibilities. Why do you think Virginia Ballesteros wanted to speak to you yesterday?"

"I've no idea."

"But why did she call you personally?"

"Because she knew me, presumably."

"She knew you?"

"She was looking after Kate Thomas's mother when we questioned her."

"Bloody hell, that can't be a coincidence," said Fox. Or could it? *She knew me too*, he thought, *but she hadn't wanted to speak to me*. Maybe if she'd said something the previous night she wouldn't have been lying comatose in hospital now. But he wasn't to know that at the time. Her name had meant nothing to him – he had known her as Virginia Carter. Reading the file that morning had brought a shock of belated recognition.

"Maybe she was scared," said Coker. "Maybe White had already threatened her."

"She didn't sound scared," said Fox. "She seemed almost reluctant to be making the call."

Apart from the piles of papers on and around the writing table under the window, the flat in Pimlico was almost unnaturally tidy. There seemed to have been no struggle, no forced entry.

The forensic team were just finishing their investigation. "We've picked up a few odds and ends, Ray," said the female officer in charge. "Not much though. Quite a lot of prints. Some hair and fabric fragments, mud from shoes, that kind of thing. We're going back to look at them all now."

"What colour hair?"

"Some blonde, some black."

"There were two of them?"

"Not necessarily. The hairs may have been left at different times. You might want to ask when the flat was last thoroughly cleaned to narrow it down a bit."

Raymond nodded. "Nothing else?"

"We've left you her desk diary and phone book, and bagged up the mobile and laptop. Can't see anything else on the desk, but you're free to look for yourselves. It seems to be all stuff about Chile."

"Can we look now?"

"Help yourselves."

As soon as the forensic team had gone, Raymond looked rapidly round the flat searching for anything out of the ordinary, but there was nothing. He flipped through the desk diary, noting immediately the two appointments – one the previous day – with someone described as 'MC'. He sat down at the desk, opening and closing drawers idly, riffling unsuccessfully through the contents for something which didn't fit. He made a start on the piles of research, but stopped after five minutes. "Get them to take all this in," he said to Coker. "And get someone to look at every page – just in case."

Raymond continued to sit at the desk, swinging gently from side to side on the swivel chair. Somehow Virginia Ballesteros had been tricked into letting her assailant in. Perhaps she knew him. (She certainly knew Adam, he reflected unhappily.) She had let the man in and she had not resisted when he tried to kill her. It was possible he'd drugged her: the hospital had yet to provide a definitive report. But, in his heart of hearts, Raymond sensed that she had simply given in. If it had not been for her suspicious neighbour, she would have died. She'd been lucky. He had not...

Raymond's eyes moved casually along the desk, past the piles of paper to the shelves of books next to the window. He stood up to read the titles of the nearest books. They were mainly historical and sociological studies of Latin America, and of Chile in particular, although there were novels, collections of short stories and anthologies of poetry as well, all in Spanish. Closest to the desk was a set of dictionaries, Spanish-English, English-Spanish, and several Spanish-Spanish. A battered copy of a large Collins Spanish-English dictionary was protruding very slightly from the otherwise neatly stacked row of books. Unthinkingly, Raymond pushed it gently with his extended forefinger to bring it level with the others. And then, for no good reason he could later explain, he grasped the book by its spine with both hands and pulled it out. There was nothing hidden behind it. Of course there wasn't. That would have been ridiculous. He opened the book and saw a neatly folded foolscap sheet between the front covers. He put the book carefully on the table and opened the sheet of paper.

Coker came back into the room as Raymond was halfway

through reading the notes written in Virginia Ballesteros's neat handwriting.

"Bloody hell, Phil," Raymond said. "This is not as simple as we thought."

***

Once the secure conference call had been set up, Gillian closed the door of her office. Hilary Price would listen in, but she did not want the secretaries in the outer office to pick up anything by accident.

Gillian spoke first. "Things are getting out of hand," she said. "It's not just fraud we're turning a blind eye to now. Four people are dead. One of my officers is under suspicion, but he's claiming the real murderer is someone linked to Luis Moreno. We can't just ignore that."

"We mustn't lose our nerve," said Jonathan Blood. "We need forty-eight hours to flush out our man. Let's focus on that."

"I agree," said Evelyn Powell. "There's too much at stake to halt the operation now."

"But can we trust Moreno?" said Gillian.

"He's never let us down before," said Blood. "Why would he now?"

"I'm for going ahead as well," said Mohamed Shaukat. "But I think you should know what the murder squad just told my people. Virginia Ballesteros had written a note about a man she heard had been obtaining arms from the IRA. She described him in some detail. The description closely matches that Gillian gave to the police following her meeting with Adam White last night. And it's pretty much in line with what we got out of White's fiancée following the Hounslow bomb."

"So it *was* a bomb?" said Gillian.

"Yes," said Shaukat. "We've just got the preliminary report through from the explosives people. Whoever it was used Semtex."

"That's very bad news," said Evelyn Powell.

"Yes," said Shaukat. "The worst imaginable."

***

The girl was called Karin, and she shared a cramped flat in Camberwell with a Latvian girl who, conveniently, was away visiting her family in Riga. All Luke needed was a bed for a couple of nights, but he had never been averse to mixing business with pleasure. He had told her he was a television film producer and had spent much of the evening, in a Chinese restaurant at the back of Waterloo station, telling her the story of his current project. She had listened with wide-eyed fascination as he described the story of a lone assassin single-handedly outwitting the collective might of the British security forces and hitting his target before melting away and leaving the greatest of all mysteries unsolved.

"You mean, he get away with it?" asked the girl, partly impressed, partly shocked.

"Yes," said Luke, imitating the girl's accent. "He get away with it." He'd had a couple of beers to let him relax and was enjoying himself.

In the flat she turned towards him as soon as the door closed behind them. "You want coffee or...?" She left the sentence hanging in mid-air, her lips slightly parted. She was wearing a skimpy green cotton top and low-slung blue jeans. Her bare, flat midriff gleamed in the subdued light. She no longer reminded him of Kate. Kate, the first time, had been surprised, not expecting anything, had almost resisted. This girl had no qualms.

205

"I can wait for the coffee," he said, slipping his index finger under the strap on one bare shoulder.

*****

Raymond sat at his desk with his eyes closed. He had just endured a gruelling argument with Phil Coker, at the end of which he was beginning to believe Coker was right.

"How much more do you need to convince you, Ray?" Coker had said, his face a picture of exasperation. "We've got White's DNA and fingerprints in both Thomas's and Ballesteros's flat. He was screwing Thomas and we know he knew Ballesteros. He was in the right place at the right time to attack both Dominguez and Ballesteros. It's practically cut and dried."

"He says he wasn't having an affair with Kate Thomas," said Raymond, wincing inwardly at his partner's crudeness. "And he's explained why he was in her flat. As to Virginia Ballesteros, the presence of his DNA and fingerprints in her flat isn't proof of anything – you said yourself, he knew her. And there's no trace of Adam White in María Carmen Dominguez's flat."

"I've sent the team back," said Coker. "They'll find something. You saw for yourself they hadn't done a thorough job." This was not entirely fair. Fox and Coker had gone to María Carmen Dominguez's flat immediately after the visit to that of Virginia Ballesteros. There had been evidence of a prolonged struggle, with lamps smashed and furniture overturned. The forensics team had done no more than a preliminary sifting in order to produce a provisional report, and were in any case intending to return for a more detailed examination.

"What about this other man?" said Raymond. "The man with the blond hair? We've got two independent descriptions of him which match. We've got his DNA in Virginia Ballesteros's flat and in María Carmen Dominguez's flat. We've got diary and phone records linking the two women."

"We don't know the hairs found in the women's flats necessarily belong to the man in the descriptions," said Coker. "They could be anyone's – a girl friend's even."

"But we can't just ignore the existence of this man," said Raymond.

Coker shrugged. "I'm not saying we have to ignore him," he said. "I'm simply saying we don't know anything about him. Whereas we know all about White and the evidence all continues to point to him."

"But you still can't explain to me what motive Adam White would have for wanting to kill these women."

Coker shrugged again. "I'm sure the CPS will come up with something," he had said. "All the other evidence is rock solid – or it will be when we can prove White was in Dominguez's flat."

Raymond opened his eyes and looked at his watch. It was nearly seven. He should be on his way home – Nicole would be furious with him again. But something was niggling away at the back of his mind, something which might make sense of the apparently asymmetrical relationship between the three women; something which might exonerate Adam – or conceivably implicate him beyond doubt.

The one common factor in all three assaults was the method employed. Otherwise the links were partial only. Virginia Ballesteros and María Carmen Dominguez knew each other, and it required no genius to deduce that María Carmen was the person who had told Virginia about John Jones's contacts with the IRA. If the man was the same as the one whose DNA had been found in both women's flats, then Coker was wrong and the blond man was the obvious candidate to be their assailant. But neither woman appeared to have known Kate Thomas, although Virginia had met Kate's mother after Kate's death – could that really be a coincidence? The only direct link between Kate and Virginia was Adam White, but he had no known connection with María Carmen. Coker appeared determined to establish such a link. But supposing it proved impossible to do so? Supposing the missing link was actually that between John Jones and Kate Thomas?

Raymond read again through the photocopy of the note written by Virginia Ballesteros. He had asked the Belfast police to interview Gerry O'Leary, but the latter was on a visit to the United States and his precise whereabouts was unknown. Apart from the physical description of Jones, the only information about him was his place of work. Enquiries at the estate agent concerned had revealed that there had indeed been a John Jones answering to that description who had been employed there on a casual basis at weekends, but he had not been seen for the best part of a week and had left no forwarding address. One of his work mates thought he might have been Welsh, but couldn't be sure – Jones kept himself pretty much to himself, they said.

The smallest of thoughts began to form at the back of Raymond's mind. He called the Central Registry and asked them to e-mail the transcripts of Kate Thomas's mobile telephone calls. He printed them out and placed them on his desk alongside the lists of calls made in the previous month by Virginia and María Carmen. He could find no calls in common between Virginia and Kate. But there were several in common between Kate and María Carmen. And they were all to the same two numbers, one a mobile, the other a landline.

Raymond dialled the landline number, but he knew what he would hear before the phone was answered. "This is Axworthy and Blunt," said the recorded message.

"Our opening hours are between eight thirty to five thirty, Monday to Friday, and—"

Raymond terminated the call. He was satisfied. John Jones was the common factor. Adam White was innocent.

CHAPTER 12

Even at seven in the morning the Madrid summer heat was beginning to penetrate the shade of the plane trees lining the street outside Luis Moreno's apartment building. Adam absentmindedly massaged his sore ribs as he watched the entrance to the block. Conscious, suddenly, of his actions, he reflected wryly on how much damage a slender girl like Alison could do when travelling at speed. He hoped she was alright. He hoped she understood why he'd had to leave her alone.

Entering France the day before had generated a few tense seconds, because the French police appeared to be on some kind of security alert and were much in evidence around the port of Calais. But they seemed uninterested in Adam, who passed through with a large group of day-trippers evidently bent on stripping the town's supermarkets of their entire stock of wine and beer.

If the French were not looking for him that suggested the British police did not yet know he had left England. Luckily he still had a hundred pounds or so of euros in his wallet, which meant he could postpone the inevitable use of his credit card for a few more hours. He bought a rail ticket to Paris and took a taxi to Charles de Gaulle. There he finally had to resort to his American Express card to buy a plane ticket to Madrid.

Arriving at Barajas again had brought on a strange

sense of déjà vu. Was it only four days ago that he had first set off to Madrid to begin his investigation? Out of a sense of perversity he had gone to the same hotel where Gardiner had harangued him. He ordered a meal by room service and collapsed into a sleep filled with dreams of such incoherence that he had been unable to recall any of the detail when he finally awoke in the early hours of Tuesday morning.

Adam knew he had to get Moreno alone. The Embassy began work at eight thirty. It was, at a guess, no more than a twenty-minute bus ride away from Moreno's flat. So Moreno would probably leave for work at around eight. With luck, the children's school would start earlier. But what of Moreno's wife? Would she take the children to school?

At ten past seven his question was answered. Moreno's wife and children emerged and walked down the street towards the Castellana. When they were out of sight, Adam moved swiftly across the road and rang Moreno's bell.

"It's Freddie," he said, summoning up all his powers of mimicry to suppress his Glaswegian accent and reproduce the gravelly elegance of the voice of Moreno's controller. "It's urgent."

The buzzer went and Adam entered the building. The lift was of polished mahogany with a glass window, through which occupants were clearly visible even when the external metal grill was closed. Adam could conceal his face, but there was no way he could simulate Gardiner's bulk. If Moreno was waiting for him on the landing, he would see at once that something was wrong.

Adam bypassed the lift and sprinted up the three flights of stairs to Moreno's floor. Moreno, wearing a dark green silk dressing gown, was standing in the doorway to his flat, looking expectantly at the lift shaft. Adam ran straight at him and bundled him into the apartment before he had a chance to cry out. Adam closed the door behind him with his foot and manhandled Moreno into a chair.

The apartment was well-furnished in an expensive, understated way. This had cost more than Moreno could afford on his Embassy salary. Did Moreno's wife have a high-powered job? Did either Moreno or his wife have independent means? Or was their lifestyle subsidised by money defrauded from the British taxpayer, or by Gardiner's secret funds?

Moreno's face betrayed no emotion beyond a flash of mild surprise.

"Oh, it's you," he said. "I thought you'd returned to London."

"I'm back," said Adam. "I've got some more questions for you."

"I thought we covered the ground pretty comprehensively last time," said Moreno. "I doubt I can be of any further help." His tone was even, with no suggestion of either reproach or sarcasm. But there was something irrationally irritating to Adam about the idiomatic fluency of his English.

"I'm not talking about the accounts."

"Really? I thought that was your field of expertise." Again, the tone was not aggressive, the words no more than a flat statement. Disconcertingly, Adam experienced a sudden temptation to hit Moreno in the face.

"Who was the man you met in the Vaso de Oro on Saturday?" said Adam.

Was it Adam's imagination, or was there a momentary flicker of uncertainty in Moreno's eyes? Then his face took on a look of weary patience. "I thought all that had been explained to you," he said.

"Look," said Adam. "I'm not interested in your work for Freddie Gardiner. It's quite simple. The man you met tried to kill me. More to the point, he tried to kill my fiancée. And I have a strong suspicion he killed one of my colleagues. So I need to find him. And you're the only person I know who knows him."

"I'm sorry," said Moreno. "I really can't talk to you." He looked at his watch. "In any case, I should be getting ready for work."

"I just need a name," said Adam. "A genuine name and if possible some form of contact information."

Moreno sighed. "You have no understanding of what this is all about," he said, as though speaking to a young child.

"You're right," said Adam. "I'm totally confused. But one thing I am sure of is that the man I'm after is a murderer. And if you don't tell me where he is, you'll be shielding him."

"I have no idea what you're talking about," said Moreno.

"Perhaps I should call Freddie and tell him what I know," said Adam.

Moreno shrugged. "I have no secrets from Freddie," he said.

Adam was frustrated by Moreno's insouciance. Was Gardiner really aware of the actions of the blond-haired man? Was his operation so vital to national security that he was prepared to tolerate murder? "Your wife will be back soon," Adam said. "Tell me what you know and I'll be gone by the time she gets here."

Moreno laughed, a dry, humourless laugh. "You're scaring me with my wife?" he said.

"I'm sure she's unaware you're mixed up with murderers," said Adam.

Moreno shook his head. "I've told you, I don't know what you're talking about," he said. He made to rise from the chair, but Adam shoved him back, to his own surprise slapping the other man hard round the face as he did so.

213

"Now you listen," said Adam, conscious of the adrenaline flooding through his body. "You're going to tell me, one way or another. And I'm not expert at this, so I'll probably use too much force. I'm really sorry." He hit Moreno again, this time with the back of his hand, wincing inwardly as he did so. The other stared at him, fingering his reddened cheek in disbelief.

"You're mad," said Moreno.

"You're right," said Adam. "I'm mad as hell." He hit Moreno again with the flat of his hand, harder even than before. *I never believed I could do this*, he thought. *This is not me.* But then he remembered the flash of unexpected pleasure when he had hit Coker and wondered whether this was really true.

Moreno yelled and tried again to rise from the chair. This time, Adam's fist met him square on the nose. Moreno fell back, clutching his face. Blood trickled through his fingers.

"Please," he muttered. "Don't hit me again."

"Then tell me what you know," said Adam, holding out his handkerchief.

Moreno held the handkerchief to his face and was silent for several seconds. Finally he spoke. "What time is it?" he said, his face still covered by the increasingly bloody handkerchief.

Adam glanced at his watch. "Seven fifty," he said.

Moreno appeared to come to a decision. He removed the handkerchief from his face. "Most of what Freddie Gardiner has probably told you is true," he said. "I went to the Plaza Mayor on Saturday to meet my contact to pass on new intelligence about MI6 operations in Spain."

"Fabricated intelligence?"

Moreno shrugged. "What do I know?" he said. "Maybe parts of it are true. It has to be convincing enough to maintain my cover."

"What's his name, Moreno?" said Adam. "What's the name of your contact?"

"Tarik Benhamadi."

Adam grasped the lapels of Moreno's dressing gown and hauled him to his feet. "Don't mess me about, Moreno," he said.

"Don't hit me, please," said Moreno. "I'm telling you, Benhamadi is my contact. He's a waiter in the restaurant where we had lunch."

Adam released the dressing gown and pushed Moreno back into the chair. "Then who the hell's the man you met in the Vaso de Oro?" he said.

"I don't know what you're talking about."

"I saw you, Moreno."

Moreno said nothing, as though gathering his thoughts.

"Come on, Moreno, you've come this far. Spit it out, for God's sake."

Still Moreno was silent. Adam pulled him to his feet once more. "Tell me!" he shouted into the other man's face.

"Okay," said Moreno wearily. "You saw me."

"And?"

"It was – a private matter."

Adam raised his fist. Moreno lifted his hands to cover his face and cowered back into the chair. "I'll tell you," he said. "I'll tell you."

Adam lowered his hand. "I wanted a job doing in England," said Moreno. "I hired him to do it."

"Him?"

"He called himself John. That's all I know."

"You must have an address, or a phone number."

Moreno shook his head, trying vainly to staunch the blood still flowing from his nose. "No. We communicated by e-mail."

Adam felt himself becoming desperate. "Moreno, I

swear to God I'm going to hit you really hard if you don't tell me something useful and soon. Where did you meet him?"

Moreno removed the handkerchief again. "In a bar in Tangier. I was there on holiday, but I was also doing a bit of business for Freddie."

"What business?"

"Nothing to do with this."

"So, what happened?"

"We got chatting and drank a few beers."

The man was playing for time. "Get to the point, Moreno," Adam said.

"He was ideal for my purposes," said Moreno, almost as though he were beginning to warm to his theme. "He was at a loose end and badly needed money. He didn't know me any more than I knew him. If anything went wrong, neither one of us could implicate the other. That suited him as well as it suited me."

"So, what was the job?" said Adam. "Has he done it yet? Why did he kill Kate Thomas?"

"Soon," said Moreno. "He's going to do it soon. And I don't know anything about anyone called Kate Thomas."

Adam hesitated. He was reasonably sure Moreno was telling the truth. But none of this was getting him any closer to his quarry. "What was the job, Moreno?" he said again.

Moreno paused before replying. His expression, through the blood on his face, was impassive. "Oh, why not?" he said at last. "Have you any idea what my life is like?"

Something told Adam to play along with this shift of mood. He looked around the apartment. "You don't do so badly, from what I can see," he said.

"That just shows how little imagination you have," said Moreno. "You don't understand what it's like to know you can never be free to be yourself. Always acting a part, deceiving your comrades, lying, misrepresenting."

"It was your choice, according to Gardiner," said Adam. "He told me even the pensions scam was your idea."

Moreno shrugged. "In the early days it was exciting enough. It gave me a feeling of power, being the only one who really knew what the truth was. But it soon wears off and the life gets you down in the end. If my friends ever discovered what I was really doing, I'd be dead."

"So why not retire? You look pretty well-heeled."

"You really are very stupid," said Moreno. "They won't let me retire. I'm far too valuable. In their gentlemanly British way, they point out that a discreet word from them in the wrong ear and that would be the end of me."

"Didn't you think of that when you started out on all this?"

Moreno gave a mirthless smile. "I was helping to defend Western liberal democracy against the forces of evil – why *would* I think of it? What hypocrites you British are. You make such a fuss about Guantánamo and extraordinary rendition. You won't deprive even the basest of criminals of his freedom without due process. You argue for years about detaining terrorists without trial for a matter of a few days. But you have no compunction about condemning me to a lifetime of hell for the sake of your precious national security."

"Fine," said Adam, who was beginning to wonder where this could all be leading. "So, you can't retire. What's this got to do with this man John?"

"He's going to exact revenge for me," said Moreno. Once again, Adam was struck by the precision of the Spaniard's English.

"Revenge?"

"Yes," said Moreno. "My life is in permanent pawn to

Her Majesty's Secret Service. Someone is going to have to pay for that."

"Someone? Who?"

Moreno lapsed into silence again, apparently lost in a private reverie. "It will be wonderful," he murmured. "Something monstrous that will shake their beloved country to the core. And I alone will know the truth of it all."

"What's the job, Moreno?" said Adam. "Who's going to pay?" As he spoke, he heard the sound of the elevator arriving outside the front door. "That's your wife, I assume," he said. "Tell me quickly and I'll leave in the service lift. You can say you ran into a door or something."

Moreno said nothing. Adam leaned down until his face was only inches from the other man's. "Tell me now!" he hissed, as a key scraped in the door behind him.

Moreno spat a mixture of blood and saliva into Adam's face. "Go fuck yourself," he said.

"*¿Qué demonios pasa acquí?*"

Adam, still shocked by Moreno's sudden, violent defiance, turned and saw the diminutive figure of the Spaniard's wife in the doorway. She was dressed in a long-sleeved white blouse and crimson jeans, the latter tucked into what looked like extremely expensive, decorated white leather boots. Her handbag matched the boots, and a small diamond-studded crescent hung on a simple silver chain around her neck. In each ear nestled a discreet diamond stud. Close to, she was even more beautiful than he had previously noticed.

The woman let the bag drop from her hand to the marble floor. "*¿Quién es este tipo, Luis?*" she said. "*¿Qué te ha hecho?*"

"*Él sabe,*" said Moreno. "*Sabe más o menos todo. Bueno, casi todo.*"

For maybe two or three seconds, no one moved or spoke. Then, without warning, Moreno's wife took two rapid strides towards Adam. He did not see the movement of her hands.

But he felt a jarring blow to the throat, followed immediately by another to the side of his neck. Choking, gasping for breath, he fell to his knees on the polished marble floor. For a moment, a long, uncomprehending moment, he found himself staring at the patterns on the polished toecaps of the woman's high fashion leather boots. Then one of them exploded agonisingly under his chin, and he rolled over into a tunnel of darkness.

***

Luke had awoken early, not much after five. For nearly an hour he had lain, unmoving, alongside the naked girl. He could see now, in the dawn light, that she was not nearly as beautiful as Kate. The features were marginally blunter, the teeth less even, the complexion marred by poor childhood diet.

It was really a shame about Kate. She had paid the price of curiosity. *Curiosity killed the Kate* – that was quite funny, he hadn't thought of that one before. How surprised she had been, and horrified, as she looked up from his e-mails to see him standing behind her. Yes, it was a shame. He had believed that meeting up with her again was fate. Maybe she would stay with him, he had thought, really understand him like none of the others had done. But no, she'd begun to cool, he could tell. Even when they made love on that last evening, she'd seemed distracted. Maybe she had already guessed that he was planning something. Maybe she had even said something to this man Adam White – but no, that was not possible, because White clearly had no idea who he was. How stupid she'd been to open up his laptop when she thought he was asleep.

Karin stirred beside him and opened her eyes. "Hello, John," she said. "I must go to work soon."

He looked at her blankly, his thoughts still on Kate. Oblivious to his mood, she grinned, rubbing sleep from her eyes. "But not yet, if you want," she said.

***

"He's in Madrid again," said Coker exultantly. "He bought an air ticket in Paris yesterday with his credit card."

Raymond looked up from the hastily assembled, and distressingly thin, file on John Jones. The man had been a casual part-time summer relief worker at Axworthy and Blunt, paid in cash. The company had no National Insurance number and no address or telephone number. The people he worked with knew him only as 'John' and he had not socialised with them after hours. One girl recognised the description of María Carmen Dominguez as fitting that of a woman Jones had attended to a few weeks back. A number of staff members remembered that Jones had frequently taken private calls. "Always from women," said the girl who had recognised María Carmen's description. But an analysis of calls to the office in the time Jones had worked there had revealed no fresh leads, only several calls from Kate Thomas and rather fewer from María Carmen.

The trail in Hounslow had also gone dead. The John Jones who had allegedly rented the flat had disappeared without trace in West London two months previously. His description did not in any case match that of the blond man.

The various detailed descriptions of the man posing as Jones had been used to produce an identikit photo, which was at that moment being refined with the help of the Axworthy and Blunt staff. The Americans had still been unable to track down Gerry O'Leary. The only other useful piece of information had come from Virginia Ballesteros's note, in which she recorded once having seen Jones driving a blue BMW convertible. This had rung a bell with one of the Hounslow neighbours, whose brother had rented a lock-up garage to Jones in a nearby street. A cursory examination of the garage had revealed it to be empty, but there had been prints and what appeared to be skin fragments on the handle to the sliding door, which were being analysed.

"Adam White will come back of his own accord," said Raymond. "John Jones is the man we're looking for. I'm putting out the call as soon as we get the identikit picture."

"I want to go to Madrid," said Coker.

"This shouldn't be personal, Phil," said Raymond.

"Well it is," said Coker. "He bloody nearly broke my jaw."

***

By means of a technological trick only approximately understood by Gillian the subtly varied false memoranda had now been inserted into the secret information circulating within the three intelligence services, the Foreign Office, the Home Office and the Metropolitan Police. The suspected terrorists were confidently believed to be distributed between three addresses in south London. Each of these locations featured in isolation in three of the memoranda, which described them as the only location where the suspects were now known to reside. One memorandum spoke in similar terms of two out of the three addresses, while the fifth identified all three. The memoranda all spoke of a police raid planned for midnight that night. They were given highly restricted circulation, their recipients enjoined not to share the information with anyone else in advance of the raid. No memorandum had been put into circulation in the JTAC.

Now began a period of tense waiting. All three addresses were under massive police surveillance. The police involved, from their commanders down, knew only that they were monitoring suspected terrorists. Their instructions were to detain, with maximum discretion, anyone who left the premises before midnight. Which group, or combination of groups, made an attempt to escape would point to the organisation housing the informant. If no escape was attempted, the problem in all probability lay within the JTAC. Whatever happened, all three houses would be raided shortly before midnight, some eight hours before the President of Iraq was due to arrive on British soil.

What can go wrong? thought Gillian. *We shall be arresting the terrorists under any circumstances, so the President will never be in danger.* The controller in Brussels was probably beyond reach, given the state of Belgian intelligence, but that wasn't really the point of the exercise. The worst that could happen would be that the informant in London suspected a trap and did nothing in order to avoid attracting attention. Or he suspected a trick and warned all three groups. At least in the latter case the police interrogators would be likely to get a lead of some description. And, even in the worst possible case, they would be no worse off than they were at present.

And yet, she reminded herself, there was an unknown man at loose in London whom the police suspected of murder, who was reported to have obtained weapons from the IRA and who Adam White claimed had a connection with Luis Moreno. How did he fit into the carefully planned scenario?

Her telephone rang. It was Bill Cambridge.

"Are you still averse to our bringing in the Spanish police, Gillian?" he said. "White's in Madrid again and the murder boys want to send someone to look for him."

"Oh, sweet Lord," said Gillian. "Is he really still a suspect?"

"We can't rule him out altogether yet, Gillian," said Cambridge "And in any case he's wanted for assaulting a police officer."

Gillian agonised for several seconds. Finally she said: "Could you bear to wait another twenty-four hours, Bill? Then you have an entirely free hand."

***

Alison lay on the sofa in the front room of her parents' house in Pinner, her left arm in a sling, resting awkwardly across her chest. It was a cool, grey day, much cooler than of late, and she had a tartan rug draped over her for warmth, a rug the family had used for picnic outings in days of distant memory. She had discharged herself from hospital early in the morning. Her father, grey-faced and drawn after two disturbed and uncomfortable nights at the hospital, had driven her home and fussed around with cups of tea and painkillers before she had sent him off to rest himself.

She desperately wanted to speak to Adam, but had hesitated to call him. She assumed the police would be monitoring her telephone calls and she did not want to betray Adam's whereabouts to them. And yet, she thought, would he not in fact be safer in police custody? Surely the blond man would be the man the police would now be looking for. The bomb had been real, their injuries genuine. Why would the police not be likely to accept their story? Adam on his own might be in serious danger if he came up against the man who had already tried to kill them.

Gradually she came round to the belief that she could do Adam no real harm by calling him. She fumbled for her mobile and called the number. She immediately got a woman's voice telling her that the mobile she was calling was not responding and might be switched off. Alison felt herself suddenly infected by a sense of undefined dread. She tried to persuade herself that she was being irrational. Adam would have switched the phone off for a perfectly good reason. The battery was flat. There was no reason to assume anything sinister. But the fear would not leave her, and when she finally drifted off into an uneasy sleep her dreams were peopled with armies of strangers with blond hair and piercing blue eyes.

***

In his plain, but neat and clean, room in the boarding house, Hussein made a call.

"We're very close now. I'm texting you a direct number for last-minute warnings. Text messages only – and dispose of the phone as we agreed."

***

"Twenty-four hours?" snarled Coker. "Again? That's fucking ridiculous!"

"It's what the boss says, Phil," said Raymond. "Now can we just concentrate our efforts on Jones, please?"

"You don't need me for Jones," said Coker. "You'll have every copper in London looking for him within the next hour. And I know you, Raymond. You're soft on White and you think he's off the hook. Well, he's not – not yet anyway. And no one takes a swing at me and gets away with it."

Raymond felt the situation slipping from his grasp. There was much about Coker he disliked, but the latter's instincts were frequently right and he was a determined and dedicated hunter of criminals. Raymond did not want him as an enemy, nor did he want to get him into trouble.

"I tell you what, Phil," he said. "Why don't you take a day off in lieu of all the work you put in over the weekend."

Coker grinned, suddenly mollified. "Good idea, Ray," he said. "I might just do that."

***

At twenty minutes to midnight Gillian was telephoned at home by Mohamed Shaukat and advised that no person had been seen to attempt to leave any of the three houses under surveillance.

"So it looks like someone in the JTAC," she said.

"Well, we can't be entirely sure of that," said Shaukat. "But it's certainly the current front runner."

Gillian felt an enormous sense of relief. The strong probability was that there was no traitor within the Foreign Office. She allowed herself a final cup of coffee and ten minutes with *The Economist*. She was cleaning her teeth when Shaukat telephoned again. He sounded uncharacteristically subdued.

"We raided all three houses," he said. "There was no one in any of them."

CHAPTER 13

The security arrangements at Buckingham Palace were tougher than any Gillian had ever before observed. A row of armed, uniformed police formed a solid barrier along the exterior walls, and many more were to be seen through the railings in the outer courtyard. Gillian knew there would also be camouflaged snipers stationed around the extensive grounds, and armed plainclothes police mingling with the crowds outside. A small group protesting about the British presence in Iraq had been courteously contained by a cordon of unarmed police some hundred yards or so from the Palace.

The President's stay in the United Kingdom had been designated a working visit, which stripped it of the more extreme ceremonial content that marked the comparatively rare state visit. The Queen would host an intimate lunch, at which she would confer on the President the title of Grand Master of the Order of St Michael and St George, but there would be no processing along The Mall in an open carriage, and no state banquet at Windsor Castle. The President would go by car straight from Buckingham Palace to Oxford, where he would deliver a speech and attend a dinner hosted by the Centre for Islamic Studies. The substantive element of the visit would be on the second day, when the President would have discussions with the Prime Minister in 10 Downing Street, followed by a seminar on security and economic development to be hosted by the Foreign Secretary in the Locarno Suite in the Foreign Office.

Gillian recalled that there had been something of a tug-of-war with the Palace about the date of the lunch. As originally conceived, it was to be the climax of the visit, to be held on its second day. But the Queen's Principal Private Secretary had been quietly insistent that the Thursday lunch period was already reserved for a staged walkabout at the foot of Constitution Hill to allow the Queen to meet participants in a large rally of disabled sportsmen and sportswomen for whom access to the Palace grounds was judged impractical. The date of the rally had been arranged many months previously and the Palace felt unable to renege on such a long-standing commitment, even for the President of Iraq. As a result, the meeting at Number Ten had been switched to the Thursday, thus rendering it vulnerable to last-minute cancellation if the Prime Minister decided instead to attend the extraordinary meeting in Brussels provisionally scheduled that day to seal the negotiations on the reformed EU budget. Irritating though this had been for those planning the Iraqi visit, Gillian had been quietly impressed by the Queen's decision to stick to her principles (for Gillian had no doubt it was taken by her personally). It was in any case no bad way to start the visit with a meeting between the two heads of state.

Despite the greyness of the day, Gillian had opted to walk through the park to the Palace. The fact that she arrived on foot seemed to be unexpected by the police at the main entrance, and she had to produce all manner of identification, as well as her invitation card, before she was allowed to enter.

The Queen was a charming and thoughtful host. If she was aware, as she surely must be, of the heightened security attending the visit, she made no reference to it. She asked

227

intelligent and sensitive questions about the situation in Iraq and about the President's own extraordinary life of imprisonment and torture, exile and ultimate rehabilitation. The President responded with great modesty, his self-deprecatory remarks frequently requiring amplification in more generous terms by the British Ambassador in Baghdad, who had returned to London to accompany the President. The latter too gave no hint of concern. He had been offered the option, while still in mid-flight, of cancelling the visit and returning to Baghdad. He had politely declined. "I am grateful for your honesty," he had said. "But we really must not let these people dictate our actions in this way."

Who would want to kill this man? thought Gillian. But she knew the answer to that. The real question was why they would want to do it here, when the opportunities to do so in Iraq must surely be so many more? What were they seeking to prove? That the Americans and the British could not protect a man deemed by his enemies to be their puppet?

We've been outwitted, she thought, *all of us*. A group of terrorists with known intentions was at large. An unidentified man was also at large, probably in possession of firearms and explosives, and no one had any idea what he planned to do. Well, there would be no more tricks, no subtle games, no more trying to be too clever. Security for the visit had been doubled and a manhunt for the terrorists and John Jones had been launched in the small hours of the morning. The Spaniards had been asked to arrest Luis Moreno pending his extradition to the United Kingdom on charges of aiding and abetting terrorists. It was an unholy mess.

"I'm very much looking forward to meeting the Foreign Secretary again," said the President to Gillian as he made his farewells. "I believe you will also be there tomorrow, Dame Gillian?"

"Indeed I shall, Your Excellency," said Gillian. *Don't*

doubt that for one moment, she thought. *For every second you are in the Foreign Office you will be my personal responsibility.*

***

Luke, suddenly fully awake, stared incredulously at the face on the television screen. How had the police created such a realistic picture, even down to the tiny mole just below his mouth and the barely visible scar above the right eyebrow? Neither White nor the girl could have seen enough of him to provide that degree of detail. María Carmen had had no photograph of him, he'd made sure of that. Could the police have somehow discovered he had worked at Axworthy and Blunt? But none of the staff there would have known about the birthmark on his left flank, a description of which he now saw was included in the explanatory notes below the picture. Only María Carmen could have known about that. But María Carmen was dead, of that he had no doubt. She must have given a description of him to Virginia Ballesteros. So, had the latter after all been telling the truth when she said she had already spoken to the police? Or had she survived? No matter, he had to act fast now. Even as he moved to get out of bed, Luke heard the announcer say that the wanted man had been seen driving a blue BMW convertible. "If you see him, or the car, do not approach them. The man calling himself John Jones is extremely dangerous. Call the police immediately…"

Luke looked at his watch: it was nearly two in the afternoon. Karin had left at eight thirty. "I see you tonight, John," she had said, showing her crooked teeth through her smile as she ran her fingers along his naked leg where it emerged from the rumpled sheets.

"Sure thing, sweetheart," he had said, turning his face to bury it in the pillow. Then he had slept, as he had promised

229

himself he would, to recover his strength. What had been intended as no more than a necessary refuge for a couple of days had turned into a sexual marathon. When Karin had returned to the flat the previous evening, she had suggested they eat in. Although he had been in the flat all day, this had suited Luke well enough, given his need to lie low. They had drunk two bottles of Bulgarian wine and then had sex repeatedly until the small hours of the morning.

Luke had no recollection of switching on the television. Karin must have been watching it over breakfast. Had she seen anything before she left? Surely not, or she would not have bid him such a careless farewell. But she would have seen the news by now at the café. And, however stupid she might be, she could hardly mistake the birthmark. Would she come back to confront him? No such luck – she would simply call the police.

He had to leave now, but he dared not walk on to the streets as he was. He slipped on his underpants and moved rapidly into the bathroom. He searched the medicine chest until he found scissors and a razor. Humming to himself, he cut off his hair, lathered the stubble with soap and shaved his head smooth. He hurriedly shovelled the golden locks of hair and a mess of lather and stubble into the lavatory and flushed it several times before swilling the sink around with water. He wiped the razor and scissors with a towel and put them back into the medicine cabinet. What else had he touched? He made a rapid tour of the bedroom, picking up bottles and glasses and the two discarded plates with the congealed remains of the previous night's spaghetti. He shoved them all in the sink and ran hot water over them before wiping them roughly with a towel. But what about his DNA? Well, they'd find that all over the place, so there was no point in fussing about it. And in any case they had nothing to match it with.

But he needed different clothes. Didn't Karin say her absent flatmate had a boyfriend who was around nearly all the time? Luke went into the other bedroom and pulled open the wardrobe door. There was nothing but female clothing on the hangers. He pulled a black unisex t-shirt off a hanger and looked around the room. Nothing. Then, as he went to leave, he saw some dry cleaning hanging in a translucent cover on the back of the bedroom door. He ripped off the cover and found a skirt and blouse and, yes, a pair of blue denim jeans. They were a bit baggy, but they would do until he could get to the car. His shoes were standard boaters, by which no one could identify him. He slipped on the jeans and pulled the t-shirt over his head. There was a pair of sunglasses on the bedside table, which would disguise his eyes. He put them on, stuffed his own clothes into his backpack and put that in turn into a large carrier bag he found hanging in the kitchen filled with supermarket plastic bags.

There was no one on the stairs as he left the flat. Lucky for them. And lucky for Karin. Oh yes, how lucky for Karin that she had not been with him when the police notice flashed on to the screen.

***

Scotland Yard has a tried and trusted system for filtering calls from the public when it puts out an appeal for help. It is inevitable that a large proportion of such calls are either mistaken or, worse, mischievous. All reports are meticulously logged, but only a relatively small number get transmitted to the officer in charge of the investigation. Judicious questioning rapidly reveals something which does not quite fit, or leads the malicious or the deluded into betraying themselves in some way. Even so, Raymond Fox had seen some twenty reports of sightings of John Jones in the previous forty-eight hours which were individually credible but collectively impossible. He had been seen in Birmingham, Edinburgh, Belfast and Penzance as well as in various parts of London. The sightings in London included three within a mile of María Carmen Dominguez's flat on Monday, but there had been none since then.

Until, that was, the Estonian girl called and described the man with the birthmark. Raymond rang Ed Pilbeam, his opposite number in Special Operations. "I'm on my way, Ed," he said. "Please don't shoot him if you get there first."

As it was, Raymond had to wait patiently for twenty minutes or more in the street, close to Loughborough Junction, before being allowed into the flat. The door was swinging off its hinges and the smell of smoke hung in the air as he brushed past the SWAT team on their way out.

"Not exactly an uncontaminated crime scene," muttered Raymond to the sergeant who had accompanied him in Coker's absence. *Although in this case*, he thought, thankfully, *it isn't a crime scene*. Raymond left his forensic officers to negotiate with the Special Operations team over the handling of the physical examination and returned to Scotland Yard as rapidly as possible to participate in the interrogation of the girl.

Karin was terrified and initially barely coherent. "You protect me, yes?" she kept saying. "Or he kill me, I know it."

Gradually she calmed down and under the patient questioning of the Special Operations interrogators described where and how she had met Jones, how he had talked over dinner of the film he was producing, how she had invited him back to her flat, how he had stayed the night, and then a second night. "I don't know," she said. "I don't know he such bad man."

Finally they let her go to the flat of a friend, accompanied by a policewoman.

"The lone assassin," said Pilbeam. "Sounds like a total fantasist. I think this is still yours more than mine, Ray."

"Fantasist or not, he's got the wherewithal," said Raymond. "You saw the report from the Americans. O'Leary's admitted selling him an M82, as well as a handgun and a job lot of Semtex."

"That's true enough," said Pilbeam. "But is he likely to be able to use something as specialised as that?"

"Do you want to take the risk?" said Raymond.

***

Alison's father had persuaded her not to go back to work immediately, so she lay on her bed in the room which was still decorated with the same blue-and-white Laura Ashley wallpaper her parents had thought appropriate when she returned home from university with her law degree. That seemed an eternity ago – it *was* an eternity ago.

Alison's father was in the garden, where he now pretty much lived whenever possible. The rainy weather had accelerated the growth of weeds and grass in the last few days and he was keen to try to get everything back under control. "Just give me a shout if you need me," he said.

If only life could be controlled like a garden, thought Alison. If only conscientious care and hard work were enough. But the unexpected always intervened. Adam, her beloved, trusted Adam, had been tempted by another woman. Only briefly, possibly only for a matter of seconds, but still it felt like a betrayal. And now he was being pursued by the police for murder. Where was he? And where – and who – was the blond-haired man who had tried to kill them both?

Alison had rung Adam ten times or more since she had first awoken around dawn. Each time the automated message

233

had been the same. *I can't sit here doing nothing*, she thought. *I'd be better off in the office.* She was tempted to ring Raymond Fox, but refrained from doing so in case Coker answered the phone. She rang Lata Shankar, who had no news. Finally, she rang the Foreign Office again, and asked to speak to Dame Gillian King.

A man answered the telephone. "I'm afraid the Permanent Under Secretary is not in the office," he said, with elaborate courtesy. "This is her Private Secretary. Can I help in any way?"

"I'm Adam White's fiancée," said Alison. "I was wondering if there was any news."

"Not that I'm aware of," said the man, who sounded distracted. "Have you spoken to the police recently? They would be the most likely to know if, well, if anything new had occurred."

"No," said Alison. "No, I haven't spoken to the police. I know, I should do."

There was a pause, and for a moment Alison thought she had been disconnected. Finally, the man said: "Look, give me your phone number. I'll try to call you if we do hear anything. My name's Hilary Price – here's my direct number."

Alison manoeuvred herself awkwardly off the bed. She had decided. She would go to work. But Hilary Price was right. She could not avoid the police any longer. She dialled Raymond Fox's number.

***

Raymond was barely back in his office before the telephone rang.

"He's in Madrid again, Alison," he said. "That's all we know."

"But is he alright?" The strain was clear in her voice.

"Alison, we just don't know," said Raymond. "I promise I'll let you know as soon as we learn anything."

"What about the man who tried to kill us?"

Raymond hesitated, then decided that Alison deserved some degree of reassurance. "We know he's in London," he said. "We're very close to finding him. Adam's in no danger from him in Madrid." He paused, then added, "And in case you hadn't noticed, there should be a rather obvious police car sitting across the road from your father's house."

"Oh, that," said Alison. He could sense relief, even a hint of amusement in her voice. "I thought they were there to keep an eye on *me*."

"Well, they are of course," said Raymond. "There's no point in me denying that."

The forensics officer appeared as Raymond put the phone down. "We have a fingerprint match," she said. "From the lock-up garage."

Raymond sat very still. *Don't get your hopes up*, he thought. Jones had left no prints at any of the crime scenes. The print at the garage might not even be his.

"He has a record?" he said quietly.

"Not with us," said the girl, placing an open file on Raymond's desk. "He was in the army. Involved in a friendly fire incident in Iraq, although the case was never proved."

Raymond was conscious of a mixture of elation and dread. The face which stared up at him from the top right-hand corner of the first paper in the file fitted the various descriptions of John Jones perfectly: the mole, the scar, the bright blue eyes, the blond hair – although in the photograph the latter was much shorter than how those who had met Jones had described it.

But there were two other items of information on the

235

summary sheet which made Raymond go cold. The man was a sniper, and also had explosives experience. And his name was Gareth Lucas Thomas.

***

Adam was on his hands and knees, crawling across a seemingly endless desert. It was dark, and yet the heat was immense, and there was a great weight upon his back. His throat and nose were clogged with sand, so that he could hardly breathe, and his thirst was terrible. A woman, veiled from head to foot, kneeled and held a cup of water towards him. Could it be Alison? Let it be Alison. But no, the veil slipped off her shoulder and he saw that it was Kate. *What happened, Kate?* he wanted to ask, but he could not speak. And then it was no longer Kate, but Moreno's wife, petite and beautiful but with her teeth bared like a vixen, and as he watched she grew two more heads, and one was Moreno and the other the man with blond hair. *If I can kill it now,* he thought, *we shall all finally be safe.* He reached around him blindly for a weapon and his hand grasped something, something heavy, something he could use to slay the beast, but he could not rise from his knees because of the weight pinning him down. He roared in frustration, and the roar became the sound of an engine and he was hurled sideways against something hard...

Adam came to consciousness, still scarcely able to breathe, still afflicted by a terrible, all-consuming thirst, still unable to lift himself off his knees, but rolling now from side to side in the pitch darkness. He was bound and gagged. His neck and head hurt and he felt sick. His hand was clutching something which did in fact feel like a large spanner or wrench of some kind. He smelled petrol and rubber and grease, and finally understood. He was in the boot of a car, a car which had only now begun to move, which was ascending, on its way up from – where? Could it be the underground car park below Moreno's building? Was he still in Madrid?

More questions flashed through his mind. What time was it? How long had he been unconscious? It felt like days, but this was not possible. Jagged, intermittent flashes of memory came to him, of people speaking urgently in Spanish, arguing, sounding angry and afraid. Before that, he remembered hitting Moreno. And he remembered Moreno's wife hitting *him*, with hands as delicate and deadly as fine steel. The voices had come later, he was sure of that, so he had not been unconscious without break. And there had been the needle. Yes, now he remembered the needle. They had drugged him. And, judging by how weak he felt, he had been out for twelve hours, probably more. Much more, maybe even as much as twenty-four. What were they planning to do with him? Why was he not already dead?

The car had levelled out and slowed down, the engine turning over quietly. The driver would be waiting for the up-and-over door to open. Adam thought rapidly. They were going to kill him. They had to. But why not before? He could only assume they had needed time to concoct a plan and, in the meantime, had not wanted to attract suspicion. Moreno must have gone to work as normal. Maybe later they had had a social engagement to keep – in any case they would have needed to do something about the children. But now they were on the move. And they were taking him with them.

Adam had read somewhere that it was relatively easy to open a car boot from the inside, provided it was not locked. But whoever had written this comforting piece of information had not had his hands tied behind him. Adam released the spanner, rolled until his back was pressing

237

against the rear part of the boot and felt for the latch. The car began to move slowly forward and he scrabbled ever more desperately for the latch. He knew that once the car was out into the streets and moving at speed his chance would be past. His hands grasped something, something which felt like the tongue of the latch. He pushed up hard, but the piece of metal did not budge. He tried pulling down instead, but still there was no movement. He tried both directions, pushing and pulling and swearing to himself. It was no good. The boot was locked.

Suddenly he was aware of shouting, and a rapid surge of acceleration hurled him backwards and forwards within his confined space. Then came a single shot and more shouting. Still the car was moving, faster still now. Then came a rapid volley of shots and the car swerved sickeningly, amidst a blaring of horns, and came to an abrupt halt, throwing Adam forward at crushing speed against the back panel. There was more shouting, and then silence, and then the sound of sirens.

Adam scrabbled again for the spanner. He wriggled his body around until his back was pressing against the lid of the boot and flicked his wrist so that the spanner beat against the metal. The noise was almost imperceptible. He tried again, moaning meanwhile through the gag. And again, and again, though all he could hear were the sirens, coming ever closer.

And then, suddenly, his world was flooded with light. He rolled over on to his back, momentarily blinded, and found the snub barrel of a sub-machine gun pointing into his face.

"*¡Tranquilo! ¡No moverse!*"

Adam stared, bemused, at the faces of the policemen looking down at him. Then he heard another, more familiar voice.

"Well, well, well, look what we have here," said Coker.

The policemen, now apparently satisfied that Adam

constituted no threat, removed his gag and bonds and pulled him from the car.

"Did they get Moreno?" said Adam to Coker.

"I don't know who they got," said Coker. "And I don't give a stuff. The important thing is, I've got you."

Adam pulled away from the policemen and thrust his head into the window space of the front passenger seat of the car. There was shattered glass everywhere. Moreno's wife was dead, in the driving seat, shot several times through the chest and neck. Adam looked in disbelief at the blank beauty of her elfin face. The seat belt had restrained her body at the moment of the crash and held her now in an upright position, her arms trailing, limp, by her thighs. Her head lolled to one side, a stray lock of hair descending along one cheek, almost as though she had fallen asleep at the wheel.

"Where's Moreno?" Adam demanded, turning back to the policemen. But he could see at once that they did not know the answer to his question.

***

"No," said Gwyneth Thomas, her voice betraying her consternation. "I didn't mention it before because I didn't think it was relevant. We haven't seen or heard from him for so long, you see."

Raymond Fox, suppressing a sigh of frustration, looked up from the telephone and nodded at the members of his team surrounding his desk. He switched the telephone to loudspeaker.

"I understand he was older than Kate," he said.

"Yes," said Gwyneth. "We thought we couldn't have children, see. So we adopted Gareth. And then along came Kate almost straight after. I've heard these things happen, you know."

"When did you last see him?"

"Oh, it must be nearly ten years ago now. He left kind of suddenly."

"You mean you've had no contact at all with him since he left?"

There was a pause. Then, obviously choosing her words carefully, Gwyneth said: "No, we thought it best to leave him be."

"Why was that, Mrs Thomas?"

Another pause. Then: "Luke wasn't... he wasn't a normal boy. We'd had problems, you know. It was better that he just left."

"Luke?" said Raymond. "You didn't call him Gareth?"

"Luke was the only name he'd answer to," said Gwyneth. "He said Gareth was a silly name."

"Why did he leave?"

"We felt we couldn't trust him anymore," said Gwyneth.

"Mrs Thomas, I'm afraid you'll have to be more specific than that," said Raymond.

"I'm sorry," said Gwyneth. "I'm so very sorry."

Raymond waited. Then, in a small, frightened voice, Gwyneth spoke. "He was a beautiful child. Kate adored him, followed him everywhere, always competing, trying to run races with him, you know. But later, when he was in his teens, he seemed to change. It was small things at first. Complaints from school about what they called his lack of regard for others. And we found him lying about things, money he'd taken, that sort of thing."

"Why did he leave, Mrs Thomas?"

"We caught him with Kate one evening. We came back early from the cinema." Another pause. "She was only fifteen."

"So you kicked him out?"

"I was ready to talk about what had happened," said

Gwyneth. "But Kate's father wanted him out of the house that night. We gave him all the cash we had and put him on a train to London. My husband said he'd call the police if he ever came back."

"How did Kate take all this?"

"She was very upset at the time, but I think she got over it quite quickly. She was a strong girl."

Raymond scribbled some notes on his pad, before continuing. "Mrs Thomas," he said. "Did you have no idea that he had made contact with Kate in the last few months?"

There was a long pause before Gwyneth spoke again. "No, of course not," she said. She appeared to be about to lose control, but then she managed to force out the words. "He did it, didn't he?" she said. "He killed Kate."

"I'm very much afraid it looks that way, Mrs Thomas," said Raymond. He hesitated, then said, "I'll have to ask you to come to London for further questioning, you understand that, don't you?"

"Yes, dear," said Gwyneth. Raymond decided to leave it at that for the moment. But he made a mental note to himself that once the immediate crisis was past, someone would need to look again into the exact circumstances of the death of Gwyneth Thomas's husband.

***

"Kate Thomas's pass has just been used," said Hilary Price.

Gillian looked up, startled, from the latest report from New York about deadlock in the United Nations Security Council over sanctions against Iran. "My God," she said. "You mean he's in the building?"

"Security have alerted the police. They'll be here any minute."

"Which entrance?"

"Main entrance."

A loudspeakered voice suddenly echoed around the corridors of the building.

"This is a security announcement. There is an unidentified package in the King Charles Street building. Pending identification of the owner, would all staff please remain in their offices and stay there to await further instructions. Please do not try to leave the building. I repeat, do not leave the building – stay in your offices."

Gillian grimaced. "You don't think he'll know what that means?"

Price nodded. "Of course he will. But what can he do? If he stays in the corridors, Security will spot him immediately. If he tries to hide in an office, they'll pick him up in the search."

How haggard the poor boy looks, thought Gillian. *Maybe he's ill. I really must talk to him on Friday.* "For God's sake, Hilary," she said. "He'll take hostages." And yet, something deep inside her was saying: *This is all wrong. Why should Jones break cover now? If he's after the President, he's a day too early. So this must be a decoy. Or* – and the thought came on her with a sense of great fearfulness – *he's after someone else altogether.*

***

Alison had tried to slip out of the house without her father seeing her, because she knew he would try to stop her from returning to work so soon. But he had come into the kitchen to make tea at the critical moment and had persuaded her to wait, at least until the following day. In truth, she had felt distinctly odd after coming down the stairs and had not needed too much convincing. She called the office and spoke briefly to Richard's Personal Assistant, who promised to pass on the message that Alison would try to make it into the office the following morning.

Alison and her father had just finished their tea when the telephone rang. It was Raymond Fox.

"Adam's safe, in Madrid," said Fox. "He's no longer a suspect. We know now exactly who we're looking for, and it isn't him."

Alison began to cry, uncontrollably. Then, aware that Fox was waiting patiently on the line, she got a grip on herself. "When's he coming home?" she said finally.

"Tonight, I hope," said Fox. "The Spanish authorities are questioning him, but I think we're the only ones who have a criminal charge to bring against him."

"Oh, please," said Alison. "You must know he had to get away to try to rescue me."

"I know that," said Fox. "But he nearly broke my detective sergeant's jaw."

Suddenly Alison felt a great need, a physical longing to be with Adam which had been suppressed by injury and shock, and now hit her like a wave of pain.

"You can bail him, can't you?" she said.

"I don't know what time he's coming in yet," said Fox.

"Let me make some phone calls," said Alison. "Let me get this sorted out now. I'll meet him off any plane you tell me and take responsibility for him."

"It's not that easy."

"Please," said Alison. "Let me try."

***

Adam and Coker made the last British Airways flight out of Barajas. Adam had spent four hours with the Spanish counter-intelligence authorities, answering questions in the presence of a grim-faced Gardiner and a bewildered-looking

Christopher Robin. Through an interpreter, with Gardiner's acquiescence, he had told the absolute truth as he knew it. Several times during the interview his Spanish interlocutors had raised a quizzical eyebrow in Gardiner's direction, who had nodded, expressionless, in acknowledgement of the fact that he had withheld significant information from them about Luis Moreno and his comrades.

Of Moreno himself, there was no sign. He had apparently come early to the office and left almost immediately with a large, heavy shoulder bag, telling the Assistant Defence Attaché, whom he passed coming in, that he was on his way to deposit some documents at the bank. Staff at the bank had not seen him. No one had seen him since he left the Embassy.

Coker, to his undisguised fury, had not been admitted to the interview. "All this bloody secrecy, it's a joke," he said bitterly to Gardiner, when he and Adam eventually emerged. "Now, do I have to ask really nicely or can I have him now?"

"You can have him, as you so charmingly put it, when we get back to the Embassy," said Gardiner. "You don't mind travelling in the other car, do you?"

Coker clearly did mind, but there was not a lot he could do about it.

"I was totally wrong about Luis," Gardiner said to Adam in the car. "I'm sorry. It was a royal fuck-up. If it's any consolation, I'm almost certainly going to get the chop."

"You weren't alone," said Adam.

"True," said Gardiner, lighting up a cigarette and examining the ash carefully. "But he was my man, and I was the one who misread him. I don't think anyone further up is going to volunteer to take the heat."

"I'm still puzzled about Moreno's wife," said Adam.

Gardiner's features darkened. "Consuelo," he said. "God, what a tragedy. The Spaniards are such a bloody trigger-happy bunch."

"But she must have been in it – whatever it is – up to her neck," said Adam.

"I think she just loved Luis," said Gardiner. "Some women are like that – stand by their man and all that."

Adam detected a hint of envy in Gardiner's tone, as though he could not imagine such loyalty in his own wife. "I wonder where she learned to fight the way she did," he said.

Now Gardiner looked embarrassed. "I'm afraid we taught her," he said.

Adam stared at Gardiner in incredulity, but the latter went on before Adam could say anything. "They both did our standard self-defence course," he said. "It was part of Luis's continuing education. He insisted on Consuelo doing it with him."

Adam shook his head in disbelief. "What about Moreno's cover?" he said.

"Oh, it was all very discreet," said Gardiner. "They left the children with their grandparents and went off on what they called a second honeymoon. They went to The Mermaid at Rye. You know it? All ancient oak beams and four-poster beds. Our place is just down the coast, so it was very easily arranged."

"So she knew what Moreno was up to?"

"She knew he was a double agent. None of the details, of course, nothing she didn't need to know. But the general setup, yes. It's never been our policy to make a man keep that sort of thing secret from his wife – otherwise he can go completely mad."

"It sounded to me as if he'd gone mad anyway," said Adam. "And her with him."

"I'm telling you, it was just misplaced loyalty as far as she was concerned," said Gardiner.

Something in Gardiner's tone gave Adam momentary pause. Then he said, "I'm still puzzled. If Moreno had had all this self-defence training, why didn't he put up more of a fight?"

"Because he was useless, physically," said Gardiner, with unexpected vehemence. "She was absolutely magnificent and he was bloody, terminally useless."

Adam could see now that Gardiner was not just professionally shaken.

"I'm sorry," said Adam. "I had no idea."

Gardiner stubbed out his cigarette and brushed ash from his tie. "No," he said. "I hadn't really thought about it myself until today. Stupid of me. Well, it makes no difference now, does it?"

Coker ignored Adam on the aircraft, making the most of the food and wine on offer and trying to flirt, unsuccessfully, with a rather stolid air hostess. Adam was grateful to be left alone. He was desperately trying to work out where Moreno could have gone – and where the blond-haired man could now be.

Revenge, Moreno had said. What did that mean? What had he paid the other man to do? Kate had found out, and been murdered. Had Archie Drysdale also discovered something? But how could he have done, effectively incarcerated, as he had been, in Whittington Hospital?

The tone of the aircraft's engines shifted, as it began the slow descent to Heathrow. Adam, his body finally responding to the stress inflicted on it in the previous two days, slipped into an uneasy doze, to dream a meaningless dream of shadows and whispers which brought him no closer to understanding the truth.

***

"Security have tracked down Kate Thomas's pass."

Gillian looked at Hilary expectantly. Could it be all over?

Could the nightmare really be finished so easily?

Price looked awkward. She could see it was bad news.

"He's dumped the pass, hasn't he?" she said. "He's still in the building somewhere."

"It's a bit more complicated than that," said Price. "There's someone called Steve Alford who works in Financial Control."

"What about him?" *Oh God,* she thought, *not another victim.*

"He was wearing Kate Thomas's pass."

ALISON

CHAPTER 14

Adam was released on police bail at eight thirty on Thursday morning. The sky was an improbably bright blue as they emerged on to the street, the temperature already hinting at the prospect of an unusually warm day. Alison drove back to the flat, neither of them speaking. At the police station she had succeeded in maintaining an air of crisp efficiency, coupled with mild exasperation at Adam's fecklessness. Now, once they were inside the flat, she turned awkwardly into Adam's arms and began to weep into his chest.

"I was so frightened," she said. "You're such an idiot. Why can't you just let the police do their job?"

Adam stroked her hair and kissed her softly on the ear. "You're right," he said. "I am an idiot. But at least everything's out in the open now and no one any longer thinks I'm a murderer."

"You've got to promise me this is it," said Alison. "Please, Adam. No more heroics."

Adam sighed. "I'd still like to know what this man is planning to do," he said. "The police don't seem to have any more idea than I do."

Alison could feel a touch of irritation emerging through her relief. "Adam," she said. "I'm serious. I want us to get married and have babies and live until we're a hundred. I don't want any more of this nonsense."

He looked at her steadily, the slightest of smiles playing round his lips. "Okay," he said. "You win."

"Come to bed," said Alison.

In the old days, she thought, Adam would have made a ribald remark about the hazards involved in making love to girls who had their arms in a plaster cast. Now, he said nothing, just put his arm gingerly around her shoulder and led her gently into the bedroom.

They made love, not skilfully, but with an unusual urgency, as though Adam had just returned from an absence of many months. Afterwards, they lay for a while, not speaking. Alison thought Adam had fallen asleep, and was beginning to doze herself when he broke the silence.

"I'm not the man I thought I was," he said.

"I'd say you were," said Alison, smiling.

"No, you don't understand," he said. "I enjoyed it. I enjoyed beating Moreno up."

Alison moved, with difficulty, to look into his eyes. "Now, you listen to me, Adam," she said. "Whatever you felt, it wasn't enjoyment. Anger, maybe. Release of tension, I don't know. But not enjoyment."

Adam ran a finger lightly over her forehead. "You only see the best in me," he said. "I know what I felt."

"I do *not* only see the best in you," said Alison. "I'm a bloody fishwife, and you know it. I'm always telling you what's wrong with you. You're untidy, undisciplined, impetuous – and you're crap at buying birthday presents. There was a time when you were preternaturally good-natured, and I'm beginning to miss that lately. One thing you're not is a sadist or a bully."

"I don't know, Ali," said Adam. "I used to be reasonably sure of myself. The thing with Kate really shook me. And there's violence in me I'd never suspected."

"You're a man," said Alison, rolling awkwardly on to her

back. Why did she not want to look at him now? "You said that yourself. She was lovely. You were tempted, but you didn't do anything. And we all have violence in us. Yours came out under enormous stress."

Adam did not respond, and she saw that now he was asleep. Had he heard her? Had he believed her? Did she believe herself? *I'm so tired,* she thought. *I want things to be normal again, how they used to be.* Was that possible? Could things ever be as they were before?

Now she too could no longer keep awake, but no sooner had she drifted into sleep than she was awoken abruptly by a telephone call. It was the office. Richard was sick; if Alison was now sufficiently recovered, she was urgently needed at work.

***

Luke fingered the small black moustache with a sense of inner amusement as he sat on the bus making its way through the early morning traffic on the Cromwell Road. He had bought the moustache, as a precaution, some weeks earlier from a theatrical supplier just off Charing Cross Road, but he had not originally intended to resort to disguise. Events had pushed him in that direction, and he had to admit that it rather added to the fun. He ran his hand over his hairless head and wondered whether women would go for the new look if he decided to keep it. He'd have to shave it regularly, as he'd already discovered. It wouldn't do to have golden fuzz on his pate, or on his chin – or on his body, come to that – if he kept the black moustache. No, that was silly – he certainly wasn't going to shave his chest, or anywhere else, every day. The moustache would have to go, once the job was done.

When Luke had arrived at the car park in Chalk Farm

the previous afternoon, everything had been as he had left it. From behind a pillar he scanned the other cars on the floor where he was parked to be sure the BMW was not already under surveillance. Apart from a couple of kids in anoraks playing the fool on skateboards, the place appeared to be deserted. He waited until they disappeared in a clatter of noise down the slope to the next level and then moved swiftly to the car and got in. He changed, in the car, into a fresh pair of jeans, a long-sleeved green check shirt and his black jacket. Then he removed his backpack from the carrier bag he had taken from Karin's kitchen. He filled the carrier bag with the contents of the backpack plus the clothes he had stolen and worn that day. Then he sat, munching a cheese sandwich and sipping mineral water from a bottle, until it was dark. When he was satisfied that his movements were not being observed, he opened the boot of the car and transferred the packet of money to the backpack. His original plan had been to come back to the car afterwards, but the police seemed to have found out more about John Jones than he had expected. It was only a matter of time before they located the car. He would risk one night in the car park, but no more – and he certainly could not take the car on to the open road.

He had made two expeditions on foot that night, first to drop the weighted carrier bag into the Regent's Canal and then to hide the backpack. He had slept in the car, with the passenger seat fully reclined, until around six. Then he had removed all his things from the car, except for a small welcoming package for the first curious policeman who might come along. A quick stop at the public lavatory to freshen up and shave and he was set for the day. He had momentarily toyed with the idea, mischievously, of eating breakfast at Karin's café, but decided that on balance the risk was too great. He had settled instead for Starbucks in Camden High Street.

Luke's hand returned to the fishing bag nestling casually between his legs. An elderly lady opposite him emerged momentarily from her reverie and her eyes engaged his. He winked at her through his sunglasses. *If you only knew, sweetheart,* he thought.

***

Raymond took a call from one of his detective constables shortly before ten thirty.

"We know where he was last working full-time."

Raymond sat up straight in his chair. "Go on," he said.

"He was a security guard at the Treasury."

"He was what?"

"Apparently there's some kind of outplacement service for soldiers leaving the army. They fixed him up."

"Why didn't we know this before?"

"We were looking at the court martial file. We had to dig around a bit for this."

"When did he stop working there?" said Raymond.

"He hasn't stopped, at least not officially. But he's been on holiday for the last week."

"Have we got his Treasury records?"

"I'm e-mailing them to you now. I'm sending them to Special Operations as well."

Raymond called for Coker and the rest of the team. They read the attachment to the e-mail over Raymond's shoulder. The address Thomas had given on his application form was a hostel in Bayswater.

"Check his references," said Fox to his WPC. "They look like former commanding officers – I wonder if they were ever taken up. Come on, Phil. Let's take a look at this hostel."

For the first time in many years, Adam paid attention to the exterior architecture of the Foreign Office as he entered the main courtyard on the way to see the Deputy Head of Personnel. He had a feeling that he might not for much longer be able to enter these historic premises as of right. Assaulting a police officer, no matter under what duress, had almost certainly put an end to his Foreign Office career.

Adam paused momentarily to take in the grand, neo-classical lines of the great building. Born in the nineteenth century out of the creative tension between the very different styles of two architects, Matthew Digby Wyatt and George Gilbert Scott, the structure had been sooty black after a century of absorbing London pollution when those such as Gillian King had joined the service. Now it was resplendent in pale grey following years of painstaking cleaning. Adam promised himself that later he would take one final swing through the Locarno Suite, also lovingly restored after decades of neglect. It was there, in the form of the highly decorated vaulted ceiling, that Scott had finally smuggled in an example of his beloved gothic. Adam would then take himself down the grand staircase, leaving behind on the first floor the most politically incorrect murals ever to decorate a Victorian public building, past the bust of Ernie Bevin, the Foreign Office's favourite ever Foreign Secretary, past the pillars bearing memorials to members of the service killed by terrorists, and on and out of the building into a new life consisting of he knew not what.

Adam had planned to stay at home with Alison, but he could not ignore Jack Grey's summons. In view of Alison's own urgent and unexpected work commitment, they had made a virtue out of necessity and gone their separate ways.

The courtyard was empty of all parked cars, and there

was a large concentration of police at the King Charles Street entrance. Adam saw more police as he looked through the massive wrought-iron gates into Downing Street just before entering the main building,

The Deputy Head of Personnel was in a hurry, and made no bones about it. He handed Adam a letter. "This is a formal reprimand for bringing the Service into disrepute – again," said Grey. He smiled thinly. "That's just to be going on with, of course. Once the criminal charges have been dealt with, I've no doubt there'll be further action. In the meantime, naturally, you're suspended."

Adam nodded as he took the letter. "I'm slightly hurt that Julian's no longer taking a personal interest in me," he said.

"Julian's preparing for Madrid," said Grey. "I'm in charge for now, so think yourself lucky."

"Oh well," said Adam. "I enjoyed it while it lasted."

"We'll need your pass," said Grey. "Jason will escort you out."

Jason was a nervous-looking new entrant with a bad case of acne, who had appeared at the door as if by some prearranged signal.

"I'd like to get some stuff from my room," said Adam. *This is Singapore all over again,* he thought.

Grey hesitated. Then he said: "Okay. Jason will go with you."

Adam took Jason with him on his pre-planned route through the fine rooms of the Foreign Office, trying to put the young man at ease with jokey stories about the building's history. Sadly for Adam, the Locarno Suite was not accessible, because it was being readied for the Iraqi development seminar later that morning. He could not resist, instead, a detour via the India Office Council Chamber, where he showed Jason the portrait of a long-forgotten governor of

Jamaica, whose nephew was allegedly one of Colin Powell's ancestors. It was in this august room, Adam recalled, that he, along with James Carter and others, had been interviewed by Raymond Fox about the Argentina murders.

Lata greeted Adam with damp eyes and a hug. "We were so worried about you," she said.

"I'm sorry, Lata," said Adam. "I really am. I've been pretty irresponsible all round. Now I've got myself suspended." While he was talking, Adam was removing photos of Ali from his desk, and rummaging in his drawers for personal odds and ends, and an envelope large enough in which to put everything.

Lata's dark, tired face creased in concern. "Oh, Adam," was all she seemed able to say.

"Have I had any e-mails I should worry about, Lata?" said Adam.

"Well, you've had a good number," said Lata. "But I'll be getting Steve to look at them. I don't think there's anything you need bother yourself with."

As Lata spoke, a sheepish and exhausted-looking Steve Alford emerged from the neighbouring office. Adam saw he was wearing a temporary pass.

"What are you doing here?" said Adam. "I thought you were away until next week."

"I came in yesterday afternoon," said Alford. "Lata rang me and said I'd better get back."

"I had to, Adam," said Lata. "No one knew where you were. We've no replacement for Kate yet, and Ubaid's off with flu."

"You did the right thing, Lata," said Adam. "I'm sorry for giving you so much grief." He turned to Jones. "You'll be in charge of the office for a bit, Steve," he said. "I'm suspended."

Alford looked rueful. "I'm lucky not to be suspended

myself," he said. "If we weren't so short-handed, I probably would have been."

"How's that?" said Adam.

"The police had me in until two this morning," said Steve. "Kate and I swapped passes for a joke just before I went on holiday. We forgot to swap them back." His face showed he realised how lame his explanation sounded.

"A *joke*?" said Adam.

"Yes," said Steve. "You know how hopeless the photos on our passes are. And no one ever looks at them. So we thought it would be a bit of a laugh."

Adam could not contain his incredulity. "A bit of a laugh?" he said. "Jesus, Steve – sorry, Lata – that was just plain stupid."

Alford grimaced in agreement and said nothing.

"So whoever killed Kate must have *your* pass?" said Adam.

Steve looked unhappy. "I guess," he said.

"Christ all bloody mighty!" said Adam, forgetting Lata's presence altogether. "So he could have been in and out of the office any number of times already."

"Security have checked back through the records," said Steve. "He hasn't. At least, not yet."

Adam looked out of the window at the congregation of police. "If it's the Iraqi President he's after, he may be about to," he said.

Jason, who had been hovering in the corridor, coughed awkwardly.

"Okay, okay," said Adam. "I'll be right with you."

***

Luke Thomas's room at the hostel was bare of any trace of its occupant, other than a pile of old newspapers on the bed.

Raymond had telephoned ahead to the hostel manager

and ascertained that Thomas had not been seen for several days. He had therefore called Pilbeam and secured his agreement to hold off the armed team until Fox and Coker had made their preliminary examination of the room.

"He didn't say anything about leaving," said the hostel manager. "Sometimes we don't see him for days on end. He must have friends he stays with."

Raymond was beginning to form a picture of Thomas in his mind, a picture which was making him progressively more uneasy. Here was a man leading a double, possibly a triple life. At nights, as Luke Thomas, he worked as a security guard in a government office, with the Bayswater hostel as his proclaimed address. Using the name of John Jones, he had worked as a Sunday relief clerk at Axworthy and Blunt. As Jones, paying cash, he had rented the flat in Hounslow. He had paid cash for the illegal IRA weaponry. Also as Jones, and using the latter's credit card for the one and only time – as Fox's team's enquiries had finally that day established – he had hired the BMW, whose registration number was now, with luck, in the hands of every police officer in the United Kingdom. He had told María Carmen Dominguez he was a journalist, and the Estonian girl he was a film producer. In both cases, he had slept with these women in their own flats. By contrast, there was no evidence he had ever been in Kate Thomas's flat. What had he told her about his life? And where, and exactly why, had he killed her? He had murdered at least three times to cover his traces – and might have been successful, but for the meticulous note prepared by Virginia Ballesteros. Why – or even if – he had killed Archie Drysdale remained unclear. Even though as yet no body had been found, he must have killed John Jones, probably for no reason other than that the name would be convenient. And there could surely now be no doubt, however inconclusive the findings of the court martial, that he had murdered Whitlock.

They were dealing with a psychopath. Judging by the independent accounts of Adam White and Alison Webster, he had appeared to be enjoying the game he had played with them when luring Adam to the Hounslow flat. And Raymond had a creeping sensation that Thomas was now relishing playing cat and mouse with the police. However much Luis Moreno might have paid him, and whatever the purpose of the payment, Thomas was in this for enjoyment as much as the money. And he was at large in London, armed with a high-powered sniper rifle.

Coker's voice interrupted Raymond's thoughts. "He must have done a runner," he said. "We were so close."

Raymond shook his head. "He hasn't done what he planned to do yet," he said. "He won't run until he has. Come on." He made swiftly for the car.

Coker looked sceptical as they drove off. "If it's the Iraqi he's after, he must know the game's up," he said. "He's got more security than George bloody Bush."

"But Thomas probably doesn't know we know about the Foreign Office pass," said Raymond. "He may think we're still looking out for Kate Thomas's pass and try to get in using Jones's pass."

Coker shrugged. "It's a long shot," he said. "If I was him, I'd have pissed off out of it while I still had the chance."

As Coker was speaking, a thought occurred to Raymond, a thought which he cursed himself for not having had before. "Where's the Treasury?" he said.

Coker looked at him oddly. "You know bloody well where it is," he said. "It's in Great George Street. You can practically see it from your office window."

"And where's the back entrance?"

"I don't know. King Charles Street, I suppose." Coker's

weasel-like eyes widened. "Oh, fuck," he said. "I see what you mean."

***

Gillian had been in the office since seven, clearing her in tray – and trying to clear her mind – in anticipation of the visit by the Iraqi President. God alone knew, they had taken every possible precaution. If Thomas tried to use Steve Alford's pass, just about every armed policeman in London would fall on him. And yet she could not still a sense of impending disaster. They had all been wrong about Moreno. How could she be confident that things would not go wrong now?

Hilary Price appeared in the doorway. Surely the boy had not slept at all the previous night, thought Gillian. "Number Ten have cancelled," he said. "The Prime Minister's going to Brussels after all."

Gillian suppressed the flicker of irritation she felt at the gratuitous discourtesy represented by the lateness of the Prime Minister's decision – or rather of its communication. "It was always on the cards," she said. "He can't bear the Chancellor to get all the kudos when there's a major breakthrough in sight. I just wish he'd levelled with us earlier."

"He's sent a personal message to the President," said Price. "And Private Office seem pretty relaxed. It gives the Foreign Secretary a chance to shine in the boss's absence."

"I suppose that's true," said Gillian. "What's the President going to do with the spare time?"

"He was apparently talking about going shopping," said Price. "Harrods, I think."

"What?" said Gillian. "The diplomatic protection people will go into a flat spin!"

"I suppose, if it's an impromptu outing, no harm will

262

befall him," said Price. *What a quaint expression*, thought Gillian. No one said things like that anymore. She smiled her reluctant agreement and turned back to her computer screen, but Price did not withdraw.

"What is it, Hilary?" said Gillian. "Was there something else?"

"I was wondering," said Price. "Given Iran and North Korea and all that, perhaps you ought to give the seminar a miss yourself."

Gillian glanced at the endless list of e-mails on her screen, and then at the pile of papers in her in tray. "Don't tempt me, Hilary," she said. "You know I'm committed."

"But if you sat in on the bilateral with the Foreign Secretary, that would surely satisfy honour," said Price. It was unusual for him to be this insistent, thought Gillian.

"What are you trying to say, Hilary?" she said.

Price hesitated, then came and sat down in front of Gillian's desk. "You know as well as anyone that there could be an assassination attempt on the President. I just wonder whether it makes sense for you to spend so much time in his presence."

Gillian frowned. "Hilary, are you seriously suggesting that I should not expose myself to the same potential risks as all the other participants in the seminar? Including, in case you'd forgotten, the Foreign Secretary himself?"

Price looked very unhappy. "It's you I work for," he said. "I can't advise the others."

"Now, look, Hilary," Gillian said. "We all know what the threat assessment is. The decision's been taken to go ahead with the seminar. My attendance flows from that decision. So let's have no more of this nonsense."

"I just thought—"

"Besides," interrupted Gillian. "I'm surely just as much at risk in the Foreign Secretary's office during the bilateral as I would be in the Locarno Suite. So, what's the point of doing one and skipping the other?"

"I just thought," Price continued doggedly. "It just seemed to me that, in the light of the many other pressing issues with which we have to deal—"

Gillian interrupted Price again. "Enough, Hilary," she said. "I thank you for your concern. But the decision's been taken, and that's that."

***

Alison found it difficult to suppress a smile when she walked into Richard's office. He waved her feebly into a chair in front of his expansive, highly polished and paper-free desk. His delicate, dark features were pinched and sweaty, and his nose was red. He reached for a tissue and blew his nose.

"Thanks for coming," he said, his voice a painful whisper. "I seem to have picked up a particularly nasty virus."

"I must say that evening seems a long time ago now," said Alison, intimating none too subtly that she knew the precise origin of his affliction.

Richard grinned, disarmingly. Even stricken as he was, he could be infuriatingly charming. "I dare say it does," he said, not even bothering to protest his innocence. "Particularly in the light of everything you've gone through in the meantime."

"I'm basically fine now," said Alison. "I just have to put up with this wretched sling for a few weeks. What do you need me for, Richard?"

"I want you to represent me at the Iraqi seminar at the Foreign Office today," said Richard. "I can't possibly go like this, and you're the only person who knows the case well enough to make the presentation."

Alison was simultaneously flattered and disconcerted. "But, Richard, it won't be remotely the same coming from me."

"Nonsense," he said. "You'll be—" He interrupted himself with a bout of coughing, which brought tears to his eyes. "You'll be great. Come on, let's go through the slides together as fast as we can. You'll need to be there within an hour."

***

Fox and Coker had to negotiate three cordons of the diplomatic protection force before they were allowed into the main entrance to the Treasury. Pilbeam, small and intense, was already there, accompanied by a tall, gangly detective sergeant called Lancaster and an armed, uniformed policeman. The Treasury security guard, a silver-haired ex-police officer whom Raymond vaguely recognised, had been briefed by the Treasury Head of Security (who stood nearby, grim-faced) and was ready for their questions.

"You go first, Ray," said Pilbeam.

"Do you know where Luke Thomas is?" said Fox to the security guard.

"Haven't seen young Luke for a week now," said the guard. "He said he was going on holiday last time I saw him."

"Could he be in the building now?" said Fox.

"I haven't seen him," said the other. "And I've been here since six this morning."

"What about the other entrances?"

"No way. They're all locked shut today on account of what's going on next door."

"Could he have come in earlier?" said Raymond.

"Possible, I suppose. I'd have to ask Stan. He was on overnight."

"Wouldn't you know from your computer records if he'd used his pass?" said Pilbeam to the Head of Security.

The other laughed sourly. "This isn't MI6, you know," he said.

Fox could sense Pilbeam's growing impatience. He too had a nasty feeling of time running away from him. "This is urgent," he said to the guard. "Please call all your colleagues who've been on duty in the past week and ask them if they've seen Thomas in the building at any time." He turned to Pilbeam. "What do you think, Ed?" he said. "Should we get some of your people in here right now to search the building?" Pilbeam nodded to Lancaster, who turned away to issue some rapid-fire and largely incomprehensible instructions into his walkie-talkie.

"Can you put something on the tannoy about a fire drill or something similar?" said Pilbeam to the Head of Security. "Get people to return to their rooms and stay there until given further instructions."

Raymond spoke again to the guard. "Before you make your calls," he said. "Did Thomas have a locker, or some kind of a room he kept things in here?"

"There's a room back there which is supposed to be a rest room," said the other. "None of us bothers with it these days, seeing as how we're normally on our own here following the staff cuts."

"Is it locked?"

"Yes. I'll open it for you."

They walked a few yards down the corridor and stopped outside a wooden door marked SECURITY STAFF ONLY. The man searched through a ring of labelled keys and unlocked the door. At the end of a short passage there was a further door. This time, the key would not turn in the lock. The man withdrew the key, inspected it, checked the label and tried again.

"Strange," he said. "It doesn't seem to be working."

"He's changed the lock," said Coker. "We'll have to force it. Do you have a screwdriver or anything?"

"Hang on a moment, Phil," said Raymond. "He may be in there. He could have double-locked it from the inside."

"Sod it," said Coker. "It's worth the risk."

But Pilbeam's men had now arrived. "Better let us deal with this," said Lancaster to Coker. He turned to the guard. "Can you get some help and cordon off this corridor?" he said. As he spoke, the voice of the Head of Security came over the loudspeaker issuing a droning instruction to staff to return to their offices.

"Don't forget Thomas is an explosives expert," said Fox. "He may have booby-trapped the door, for all we know."

"Good point," said Lancaster. "Let's find out, shall we?"

***

Adam turned for one final look at the Foreign Office quadrangle before surrendering his pass to Jason and walking through the arched passage towards King Charles Street. He was suddenly at a loose end. Alison had left a message with Lata to tell Adam that she was en route to the Foreign Office, but he knew she would be preoccupied with mastering her presentation, so he had not called back to suggest they try to meet. He felt a momentary pang of concern that Alison was about to be sitting in the same room as a man threatened with assassination, but he was reassured by the massive security measures he knew were in place.

"Adam – you're back!"

Adam was shaken out of his reverie and looked up to see Ubaid coming towards him under the archway.

"Ubaid? I thought you were sick," said Adam.

"Oh yeah," said Ubaid. "I am. Some flu thing going

around. But Lata seemed in a bit of a panic. You know what she's like. So I thought I'd better make the effort."

"She'll be grateful, I know," said Adam. Ubaid did not in fact look unwell. Adam suspected he had some personal commitment he had not owned up to when calling in sick. Even in their relatively short time together, Adam had noticed that family and mosque business tended to take priority for Ubaid over work. But this was no time to be worrying about what Ubaid had been up to – the important thing was that he was now reporting back for duty.

"Steve's back as well," said Adam. "So things should be okay for a few days. And I suspect you'll be getting a new boss anyway."

"What's that?" said Ubaid. "Oh yeah. You hit that copper. But where've you been, man?"

"It's a long story, Ubaid," said Adam. "I'd better not hold you up now. Let's have a coffee or something later."

There was a barrier across the top of Clive Steps barring the way down into St James's Park, so Adam walked up King Charles Street, along the lines of armed policemen, and out into Whitehall.

At a loss to know what to do with himself, Adam walked towards Parliament Square. As he did so, he found himself puzzling again over his final conversation with Luis Moreno, which he had reported, as near verbatim as possible, to all his interrogators in the preceding twenty-four hours. The shared assumption on the British side seemed to be that Moreno had been operating a classic double bluff. The tip-off about the plot to assassinate the Iraqi President had been designed to focus attention on a group of Islamic militants who were already under suspicion. Had they been arrested, Thomas would then have enjoyed an unsuspected free run at whatever his target was.

But Adam had a niggling feeling that somehow this

assumption did not square with what Moreno had actually said. Admittedly, Moreno could have been lying – he had proved himself adept enough at that over many years. But Adam didn't think so. There had been something about his demeanour which betrayed not so much resignation as relief, almost, that he had been forced to let slip the bland, unworried mask, to speak the truth at last. But what was the sense of what he had said? He had had enough. The stress was wearing him down. He saw no legitimate way out. He wanted revenge. But revenge on whom, precisely? Would killing the Iraqi President in London represent revenge on Britain in the largest sense?

But then again, supposing the plot against the President was nothing but a gigantic feint? The suspected militants had not, in the event, been arrested. Had Moreno tipped them off – and if so, why? Whatever the reason, security had not been relaxed. But conceivably its focus was not on the right target. Supposing Moreno's desire for revenge was much narrower, more personal? Could the mark be Freddie Gardiner? That made no sense either – Moreno could have had Gardiner killed in Spain at any time without bringing in a complete outsider. It had to be someone in England. Someone Moreno held responsible for his predicament.

Adam, who was by this time across Parliament Square and into Millbank, stopped dead. All at once it seemed so obvious that it was astonishing no one had thought of it already. The object of revenge had to be whoever had recruited Moreno originally, the person who had been doing Gardiner's job in Madrid at the time. Adam did a rapid mental calculation to work out which would have been the relevant years. Whoever it was would now be very senior, if not already retired. But even as these thoughts were going through his mind, Adam remembered an article he had read in *The Times* a few months back, a feature on personalities in the British intelligence world – the sort of article which would have been unthinkable only a decade earlier but which had now become increasingly commonplace. It had included a slightly sniffy piece about a man who had gone from Eton and Cambridge to a series of inner circle postings in Washington, Berlin, New York and, yes, Madrid before taking up his current position. There had been a photograph – times really had changed – of a lean, academic-looking man with a bald head. *Holy shit,* thought Adam, *of course.*

Adam searched his pockets for the mobile, then realised, cursing, that he had – again (he could not believe it) – left it on the bedside table. Where was the nearest phone box? He had walked too far to make it worth trying to get back to the Foreign Office. He looked around him despairingly. There were police outside the House of Commons, but it would be all too difficult to try to explain everything to them. He had to speak to Raymond Fox. He had a sudden thought. Westminster Tube station – there would be telephones there. Adam began to sprint back towards Parliament Square, still clutching his envelope of personal possessions.

***

The door was not booby-trapped, and surrendered to a locksmith's drill in less than twenty seconds. The door swung open into a dark and windowless room. Lancaster switched on the lights and stood aside for Fox, Coker and Pilbeam to look in, before he went off to check the progress of the search of the rest of the building.

"Bloody hell," said Coker. "Bloody hell."

Raymond did not know what he had expected, but it was certainly not this. The bedroom at the hostel had been squalid and devoid of personality. Alison Webster had described the Hounslow flat in similar terms. This room, by contrast, was immaculate. A portable bed stood in the corner, neatly made, with a deep red Chinese silk coverlet. There were two simple chairs, with Chinese cushions, and the floor was strewn with rugs and matching cushions. A small television, a radio and a CD player sat on a low carved oriental chest, with CDs neatly stacked alongside. Soft lighting fell from three carefully directed standing lamps, leaving the walls, with one exception, in semi-darkness. The fourth wall was illuminated by a final, upturned standing lamp. On the wall hung a blown-up photograph of a teenage girl, dressed in jeans and a t-shirt, sitting on a stone wall eating an ice cream. The girl in the picture was young, but there was no doubting it was Kate Thomas.

"Get the forensic team, Phil," said Fox. He stepped carefully into the room and pulled back a curtain in the corner opposite the bed. The curtain concealed a rail with empty hangers. On the floor was a sports grip. Covering his hand with a handkerchief, Fox unzipped the bag. It contained a woman's underwear, a pair of jeans, a blue check shirt and a pink sundress, all neatly folded, together with a pair of fashion sandals. It also contained, in a zipped side compartment, a Foreign Office pass bearing the name of Steven Alford. *What a wild goose chase that turned out to be,* thought Fox. Thomas was probably never planning to use it – he might not even know it was in the bag.

Raymond could only imagine that lack of time, or arrogance, explained why Thomas had left such incriminating evidence lying around. He had been about to go on leave. No one used the room apart from him, so he must have felt reasonably safe leaving Kate's belongings there. The urgent problem would have been to move the body. He had dressed Kate in clothes which were presumably already hanging in the room from a previous visit. *Why did he do that?* thought Raymond. *Because he wanted us to think she had gone home and out again.* People knew what she had been wearing during the day and, if there was the faintest risk that anyone had seen her entering the Treasury building that night, it was important that her body was clothed in something different. Only Adam White had spotted the anomaly, that the clothing was inappropriate for such hot weather. *No wonder we had no witnesses who saw her going home that night*, thought Fox. She had simply crossed King Charles Street and disappeared from sight.

And then Thomas had moved the body. In the small hours of the morning, miraculously unobserved, he had carried it into the park and dumped it in the lake. Had he enjoyed the thrill of that as well? The danger of being caught, the satisfaction of eluding detection against the odds? Somehow this did not ring true to Raymond. There would have been too much light. And, even in the middle of the night, would Horse Guards Road have been entirely deserted? However Thomas had managed it, he had then hurried back to his post, from which he could not afford to be absent for more than a few minutes, and waited to be relieved in the morning. He had not dared leave the building again to dispose separately of the sports bag. Nor could he take it with him in the morning, because his relief would have remarked on it. *Later,* he would have thought, *later I can come back and get rid of it.*

Raymond looked at the bed, then at the rugs and cushions on the floor. Was that where it happened? Why had he killed her? He was obviously obsessed with her. Could he have been jealous of Adam? Or had she really discovered something which made it impossible for Thomas to let her live?

"Forensics are en route," said Coker, just as Lancaster reappeared, shaking his head.

"No sign?" said Pilbeam.

"Nothing," said Lancaster. "We're doing a second sweep though the boiler area to be on the safe side, but I don't think he's here. We did find something interesting, though. There's a door in the basement opening into a passage that leads to the Cabinet War Rooms."

"Don't tell me he's hiding under Winston Churchill's desk," said Coker.

"No," said Lancaster, apparently impervious to Coker's attempt at humour. "That's all sealed off now. But there's also a tunnel off the passage that comes out in the park."

"In the *park*?" said Raymond.

"Yes," said Lancaster. "It must have been some kind of emergency exit. It comes out on the island in the lake. It's obviously been disused for years – at least until now. There are signs of the door having been opened recently."

So that was it, thought Raymond. *A tunnel.* Aloud he said: "But no sign of Thomas?"

"No," said Lancaster. "Nothing."

"Looks like a dead end unless forensics come up with something useful," said Coker.

"He's not far away," said Fox. "I feel it in my bones."

"I don't get all this," said Coker, gesturing at the room. "He seemed happy enough to screw his other women in their own beds."

"She was special," said Raymond. "He wanted to keep her separate from his other life. He could be – he had to be – Luke Thomas with her."

Coker frowned. "But she must have known about John Jones," he said. "She telephoned him at the estate agent's."

Good point, thought Raymond. "Maybe he gave her that number for urgent calls only," he said. "She didn't make that many."

Fox's mobile rang. It was his WPC. Forensics had found traces in the bathroom at the Estonian girl's flat suggesting that Thomas might have shaved off his hair. "We'd better get out an altered description – and fast," said Raymond.

Raymond's phone rang again. He did not recognise the number.

"Raymond, it's Adam," he heard. "I think I know who Thomas is after."

***

Gillian had felt the tension in her chest gradually ebbing away as the seminar progressed. There was something almost therapeutic about sitting in the historic Locarno Suite, listening to a series of experts in law, economics, trade and development spelling out, calmly and logically, the steps they envisaged in the reconstruction of southern Iraq. It seemed so far away from the daily killings and the dire predictions of civil war in the press. She knew how finely balanced the situation was, and how pointless all this discussion would be if security continued to deteriorate. But without such positive planning there would be no long-term security.

The Foreign Secretary and the President himself had both spoken eloquently at the beginning of the seminar of the need for international cooperation and of the determination of the Iraqi people to make their newfound democracy work. Now they sat together, flanked by officials making detailed notes as the experts spoke. Gillian watched, with admiration, as a nervous but capable Alison Webster, moving awkwardly with her arm in a sling, worked her way persuasively through a PowerPoint presentation that only a few hours earlier she could not have expected to be making. Why didn't Adam White just marry that girl and focus on doing his job and raising a family? she thought. He would have saved himself a load of grief. *But no*, she thought, *that's absurd*. Without Adam White, they might have been blissfully unaware of the existence of Luke Thomas and whatever unspecified danger he represented, and Luis Moreno would have gone undetected and still be playing a double game in Madrid. With these thoughts, the tension returned again. She made herself focus on her notes, from which she would shortly be required to produce a summation of the seminar's conclusions. Then it would be a working lunch in the neighbouring room and afterwards straight to the airport for the President and his retinue. Two more hours and Gillian would finally breathe easy.

A young girl entered the room, trying to appear unobtrusive. She came round behind Gillian and slipped a piece of paper on to her blotter. Gillian glanced at it, nodded and slipped silently from her chair. She picked up the telephone in the anteroom.

"Hello, Bill," she said. "What now?"

"We think Thomas may be after Jonathan Blood," said Cambridge. "We've alerted Vauxhall Cross and are getting some armed police down there now."

"Oh, how obvious," said Gillian, a sense of relief flooding through her. "We might have thought of that earlier."

"It was apparently your man White who gave us the idea," said Cambridge.

Well, well, thought Gillian. *You never give up, Adam, do you?* She resolved there and then to do everything in her power to save Adam from losing his job.

***

Adam arrived on the south side of Vauxhall Bridge at almost the same moment as the car bearing Fox and Coker.

"I think you can leave this to the police now, Adam," said Raymond, gesturing to the rapidly assembled cordon which had been thrown around the headquarters of MI6. Coker was avoiding looking at Adam. He clearly could not bear the thought that Adam, of all people, had been cleverer than the professionals.

"If it's all the same to you, Raymond, I'll hang around," said Adam. "I'd just as soon make sure—"

He was interrupted by the dull sound of a distant explosion. The three men turned and stared, uncomprehending, down the river towards the direction of the sound. Beyond the Houses of Parliament a cloud of black smoke was rising. Suddenly there was a chattering of automatic weapons, then the thump of another explosion, then silence.

"That's the Foreign Office," said Adam, unbelieving. "Oh my God, Ali."

"Holy fuck," said Coker, the horror in his tone attenuated by the slightest hint of satisfaction. "We're in the wrong place again."

CHAPTER 15

Gillian found it impossible to register her sensations in the right order. Logic told her that the windows must have blown in before she heard the sound of the explosion. Indeed, it was almost certain that the shards of glass and chunks of masonry which escaped the bombproof curtains had already struck their victims before they knew what was happening. But, in her mind's eye, in retrospect, she first heard the sound of the explosion in the courtyard, then saw, or heard, the windows shatter into a thousand pieces, then saw her Private Secretary – who had stood up just before the explosion, a mobile telephone in his hand and a puzzled expression on his face – fall sideways noiselessly with a great gash in his throat. Then there was gunfire and a further explosion and the room was filled with smoke and dust, and people running and stumbling, holding each other and calling for help or barking rapid instructions.

As far as Gillian could tell, the President and the Foreign Secretary were both unscathed. She could also see Alison Webster, sitting quietly in her seat, her hair and pale face covered in dust and fragments of glass, trying to make her mobile phone work. Something salty trickled into Gillian's mouth and she became aware for the first time of a throbbing pain in her head.

"Are you alright, Gillian?" asked someone. It sounded like Gerry Baxter from Security.

"I'm fine," she said automatically, aware of a sense of debility sweeping over her. "What happened?"

"We think it was a mortar," said Baxter. "Thank God it fell short. Things could have been a hell of a lot worse."

Gillian made a determined effort to focus on her words. "No injuries on the ground floor?" she said.

"No," said Baxter. "Just a lot of broken glass. The courtyard itself was sealed off for the duration of the conference, so there were no casualties outside. We've been very lucky."

Yes, we have been lucky, thought Gillian, as she slipped into unconsciousness. *Except for Hilary.*

***

Raymond had not been able to restrain Adam, who had set off running back up the Embankment towards Whitehall. After conferring rapidly with the head of the armed police detachment, Raymond agreed that the latter should stay where they were pending further information. Already he could hear the sounds of ambulances and a fire engine heading towards the scene of the explosion. After several unsuccessful attempts, he got through to the duty room at Scotland Yard.

"One Foreign Office official killed, several more people injured, but no one else fatally, they think," he told Coker. "It was a mortar. Landed in the courtyard. If they'd had a second shot, they might have done a lot more damage."

"A mortar?" said Coker. "Where from?"

"Out of the back of a van in Whitehall Place," Raymond said. "They were spotted as soon as they parked, but got off one round before the armed squad took them out. The van was wired to blow as soon as they went down, because there's apparently not much left to look at."

"How many bodies?"

"Four. Special Ops reckon it's the people they had under surveillance, but they'll need to look at dental records to be sure."

"No sign of Thomas?"

"No," said Fox. "So we sit tight here until someone tells us different."

Raymond's mobile rang. It was Pilbeam. "Thought you'd better know there's been another explosion," he said. "Somewhere in Chalk Farm. We've got a team on the way."

***

Luke had cleaned, checked and loaded the rifle in a lavatory cubicle at Victoria Station before returning it to the fishing rod carrier and making his way back out on to Buckingham Palace Road. The automatic was thrust down the back of his jeans, its slight bulge concealed by the lime-green high-visibility vest with which he had replaced his linen jacket. It was hot to be wearing the vest, but he needed the near-invisibility that it, ironically, conferred – and it would not be for long. This was the most dangerous moment, when he had both guns about his person in the open. Once the mission was accomplished, he would jettison the weapons and the vest, and melt into the crowds. Now, for the first time, he felt something like a thrill of adrenaline.

There were athletes in wheelchairs along much of one side of Constitution Hill, and Luke could see more arriving from the Mall under the stewardship of a man with a loudhailer. He looked at his watch as he made his way around the head of the parade and crossed over towards Green Park. He was in good time.

He had chosen the tree, just within the south-western boundary of the park, during a reconnaissance the previous week. It was easy to climb, had plenty of foliage for camouflage and was in the right place to give him a clear shot. It was also surrounded on three sides by other trees, which would allow him to climb it unobserved. He would also be able to get out of it, fast and unseen, in the vital seconds afterwards, when chaos would prevail. As always, surprise would give him the advantage.

The explosion on the other side of St James's Park took him unawares. He threw himself to the ground and rolled over under the shelter of his chosen tree, pulling the handgun from his waistband as he moved. He was alert to every sound and movement around him, searching for the threat, seeking to identify it, planning to neutralise it. The bastards had never got him in Iraq. No one was going to take him out in fucking Green Park. Now he heard gunfire and another explosion, slightly further away by his reckoning. What the fuck was happening? His immediate thought was to abort, but then he thought, *why should I?* Whatever was happening was too far away to have anything to do with him. It could even provide a helpful distraction. He heard the man with the loudhailer close by, calling for calm, then the sound of sirens from the direction of Whitehall. He could not have asked for a better situation. He climbed rapidly into the tree and began to make his preparations.

***

"My fiancée's in there," said Adam desperately, gasping for breath. "You've got to let me through."

"I'm sorry, sir," said the policeman standing at the entrance to King Charles Street. "Emergency services only."

Then, miraculously, Adam saw her. She was walking, unaided, accompanied by a boyish-looking paramedic. "Ali!" he cried. "Oh, sweet Jesus, you're okay."

Alison looked at him, almost without recognition.

"Hello, Adam," she said tonelessly. "I seem to be making a bit of a habit of this."

"Are you family?" asked the paramedic.

"We're engaged," said Adam.

"She's a bit shocked," said the boy. "But she'll be fine. Take her home and give her a hot drink. We need the ambulance space."

Adam nodded and put his arm round Alison's shoulder.

"Come on, Ali," he said. "Let's get you out of here."

"I tried to call you," said Alison. "Where were you?"

"Chasing bloody phantoms," said Adam. "I'd left my phone at home again, today of all days. I'm so sorry, Ali."

The traffic was jammed to a standstill in all streets around Whitehall, which had been cordoned off in its entire length. There was no prospect of getting a taxi, and something told Adam this was no time to be using the Underground. "Come on, let's get out of this madness," he said, guiding Alison along Great George Street towards Birdcage Walk. "We'll get some tea in the park. Then when everything's calmed down a bit, I'll get you home, sweetheart."

***

Gillian regained consciousness in the ambulance and knew that something was wrong.

Why had Hilary stood up? No message had been passed to him, no one had summoned him from the room. Or had they? He had looked at his phone, frowned, glanced briefly over at Gillian – a curiously blank look, as though his thoughts were elsewhere – and then risen from his chair and begun to turn. His weight must already have shifted critically when the glass sliced through his carotid artery, because he had gone over sideways, taking the chair with him. There was no question of him simply standing to stretch his legs. He had planned to leave the room.

There was something else niggling away at the back of Gillian's mind. The attackers had used a mortar. In itself, that was unsurprising – with the benefit of hindsight, it was the most obvious of weapons. Not even the most determined suicide bomber would have been able to penetrate the security surrounding the Foreign Office, and a shoulder-launched rocket could not have reached a target so deep within the building. No, the use of a mortar made sense. The Provisional IRA had shown the way with their attack on Downing Street in 1991. And that, Gillian suddenly understood, was what was bothering her. This was a copycat attack. The original plan must surely have been to kill the Prime Minister and the President together at Number Ten. Somehow, the attackers had learned that the meeting with the Prime Minister had been cancelled. They had been obliged to adjust their target and the timing of the attack. How could they possibly have learned of the change of plan so rapidly?

Before Gillian could develop this disturbing train of thought any further, she realised that something else was worrying her, something of greater urgency. Luke Thomas was a sniper, trained to hit a precise target. A mortar lobbed from a distance was not obviously his handiwork. This meant that in all probability he had yet to strike. The police had Jonathan Blood well protected by now. But supposing he was not in fact the mark? The more Gillian thought about it, the more she was afflicted by doubt. Moreno had good reason to hate Blood, but the latter was a relatively soft target. With the level of public exposure MI6 received these days, a determined assassin could have caught up with him easily enough at any time. So why the extravagant double-bluff? Why had Moreno not simply paid Thomas to kill Blood in his own time? Why involve an unknown psychopath in his already labyrinthine schemes, when he could quite easily have kept them entirely separate?

And why, after pointing the finger at the members of the Al Qaeda cell, had Moreno then tipped them off? Surely he must have known that this would bring suspicion on him – as had in the event happened, with tragic consequences for his wife. Was he hoping that the mortar attack would flush the President out into the open, giving Thomas a clear shot? If so, he was wrong, because the contingency plan, in the event of any attack, had always been to take the President down to the underground shelter and hold him there until a secure departure could be assured.

Unless, and the conviction was now growing in Gillian that this was the case, it had not been Moreno who warned the terrorists off. Suppressing for the moment, because it was so painful, the temptation to consider the implications of this thought, Gillian forced herself to focus on Moreno and his motives. By alerting MI6 to the Al Qaeda plot he would have earned himself considerable brownie points. And by timing Thomas's mission to coincide with the Iraqi President's visit he would have ensured that there would be a diversion of security resources away from Thomas's target. There need be no direct connection between the two operations. The participants of each might well be ignorant of the existence of the other. The only link was Moreno – *and we would have been unaware of this,* Gillian reminded herself, *if Adam White had not stumbled upon Thomas and Moreno in a Madrid bar.*

None of this speculation was bringing Gillian any closer to understanding who Thomas's target might be. She closed her eyes and visualised the report she had read of the debriefing of Adam White in Madrid. *Come on, laser brain,* she said to herself, *the answer must be in there somewhere.* She tightened her focus on to the passage where Adam was quoting Moreno's words in the final part of their conversation, before they were interrupted by the arrival of Moreno's wife.

Gillian opened her eyes. "Get me a phone," she said to the young paramedic fussing with her drip. "Now, please."

***

Alison began to tremble as soon as she took the first sip of tea. For the first time since the explosion, it came home to her how extraordinarily lucky she had been. There had been injured people all around her, at least one of whom was almost certainly dead. But she was unscathed, apart from a few minor cuts.

"Sorry, Adam," she said. "It's beginning to get to me."

Adam sat next to her with his arm around her shoulder. "Let it all out, Ali," he said. "Christ, I'm so sorry."

"Sorry for what?" she said, already feeling better just to have him nearby. "It's not your fault."

His naturally sunny face was tight with strain. "I shouldn't have let you go to the seminar," he said. "And where was I? Going in completely the wrong bloody direction, as usual."

"Adam, I'm over twenty-one," said Alison. "I think it was my decision I should go to the Foreign Office, not yours."

"I thought he was after someone in MI6," said Adam. "Now I just don't know."

In the distance, to the east, there were still traces of black smoke to be seen in the sky above the Foreign Office. From time to time a siren blared into action. All around Adam and Alison in the park café, tourists and office workers stared and discussed the mysterious explosions or spoke by mobile to friends to see if they knew any more than they themselves did. Alison deliberately looked away, in the opposite direction, towards the junction of the Mall and Constitution Hill, where the Queen Victoria Memorial was just visible through the trees. She could hear someone in the distance, near the Palace, shouting instructions through a loudhailer, but she could not make out what they were saying.

"Now I feel really tired," she said. "I just want to go home."

"Let's give it another twenty minutes or so," said Adam. "Once the fuss has died down we can walk up to Piccadilly and get a taxi from there."

Alison nodded, too exhausted suddenly to argue, relieved to have Adam to make decisions for her. She leaned her head on his chest and watched a pair of squirrels which had been bold enough to approach a neighbouring table to steal fallen crumbs of bread. A little further on, workmen were putting banners of some kind into the trees, apparently undeflected from their work by the nearby hullabaloo. Beyond the trees, she could see a crocodile of young teenage children, French she would guess, emerging from Green Park and turning towards Buckingham Palace for their next sightseeing treat of the day. They too seemed undeterred by all the fuss on the other side of the park.

Alison felt suddenly restless again. She supposed this was all part of the shock she was suffering: one minute she was lethargic, the next, desperate to be on the move.

"Can we go now, Adam?" she said. "Please, darling. I can't stay here any longer."

***

Pilbeam rang again. "It was in a car park in Chalk Farm," he said.

"A car park?" said Raymond. "I don't get it."

"Your friend's car finally turned up," said Pilbeam. "Two kids tried to break into it. One of them was killed, the other's lost an arm."

"I don't like this," said Raymond. "He's playing games with us."

"Or he may have done a bunk already," said Pilbeam. "Could be he was just a middleman. We don't know how the terrorists got their hands on a mortar."

"O'Leary said nothing about a mortar," said Raymond. "Thomas has an M82. You can't tell me he's not planning to use it."

"You're right there, Ray," said Pilbeam. "And we've got no trace of any contact between Thomas and these guys. Maybe there's no connection between them at all."

"Except for Luis Moreno," said Raymond. "He's the one who seems to have been pulling all the strings. I reckon—"

"Hang on a minute, Ray," said Pilbeam, interrupting him. "There's some kind of red alert coming through."

There was silence for thirty seconds or so. Then Pilbeam came back on the line. "You are not going to believe this," he said.

***

Gillian had persuaded the young paramedic to allow her to sit up and continue making telephone calls. Her first, after the call to Bill Cambridge, was to her Assistant Private Secretary.

"Sophie, what's the news on Hilary?"

The girl was crying. "I'm sorry, Gillian," she said. "I just can't believe it."

Dear God, thought Gillian. Would the intellectual in Hilary have appreciated such a graphic illustration of the law of unintended consequences?

"Does his mother know yet?"

"No, that's the awful thing," said Sophie. "I took a call from her just after Hilary went into the conference. She wanted me to tell him that the lease extension on the flat had been agreed. She was…" The girl broke off, clearly distressed. "She was just off out to see a travel agent about an autumn break on the Italian lakes. And we don't seem to have her mobile number."

Gillian closed her eyes. "You'll keep trying to reach her, won't you, Sophie?" she said automatically.

"Welfare are on to it," said Sophie. "I said you'd want to talk to her as soon as you were able."

"Well done," said Gillian, although this would be a conversation she was already dreading. "Are the President and the Foreign Secretary okay?"

"A bit shaken," said Sophie. "Otherwise fine. But what about you, Gillian?"

"Still standing," said Gillian. "Well, you know what I mean."

Gillian called Jonathan Blood. "I hope you're still continuing to take precautions, Jonathan," she said. "It may have been a false alarm, but we can't be a hundred percent sure."

"Don't worry, Gillian," said Blood. "I'm confined to my office with what looks like half the Metropolitan Police surrounding the building. But listen. It can't surely be true what I've just heard?"

"I know it sounds crazy," said Gillian. "But we can't take any risks."

Finally she called Mohamed Shaukat. "We're pretty confident we got all those directly involved, Gillian," said Shaukat. "The man in Belgium is proving a bit more elusive, I'm afraid."

"I think you know who tipped them off, Mohamed," said Gillian.

"He was one of a number of people we'd been watching for some time, Gillian," said Shaukat.

"Why on earth didn't you say something to me?"

"I'm sorry about that," said Shaukat. "It was all very circumstantial. We wanted to keep everything as natural as possible until we were absolutely sure."

And were you also watching me? thought Gillian. *Until you were absolutely sure?*

"The funny thing is that we thought his motives were primarily financial," continued Shaukat. "Your people had drawn his difficulties to our attention, and he seemed pretty desperate."

"What do you mean?" said Gillian.

"It turns out his mother had just won the maximum prize on the Premium Bond."

"I don't understand," said Gillian, experiencing a surge of unrealistic hope. "If he didn't need the money, what possible motive could he have had?"

"Well, we know he was very unhappy about the Iraq war," said Shaukat.

"So were half the Foreign Office," said Gillian. "Can you really be absolutely sure it was him?"

"As sure as we can be," said Shaukat. "We're assuming he normally used a disposable pay-as-you-go mobile, but he must have panicked today when the Prime Minister cancelled. There was a text in a mobile phone that survived the explosion in the van. It came from his mobile."

Gillian again saw Hilary looking at his phone before standing to leave, only to be cut down by the flying shard of glass. He had seemed puzzled, distracted, as though trying to understand something.

"You've examined his phone," said Gillian. "Did he receive a message just before the attack?"

"No," said Shaukat. "The most recent message was the outgoing one to the terrorists."

"I still can't believe it," Gillian said. *Listen to yourself,* she thought. *You couldn't believe Andrew had killed himself. You can't believe Hilary was a traitor. What the hell has happened to your judgement?* Then, conscious of the need to focus on the still current danger: "Any news about Thomas?"

"Nothing yet," said Shaukat. "Bill Cambridge's boys and mine are sharing all they know. And we've concocted a scheme which might just get him to reveal himself – if your hunch is right."

"I'm assuming now that Thomas didn't in fact time this to coincide with the mortar attack – or that he even knew it was going to happen," said Gillian. "Otherwise he'd surely have realised there'd be a total security clampdown in the immediate area."

"I'm not sure he's actually that bright, said Shaukat. "But we'll find out soon enough."

"Maybe he's actually on the run already."

"Maybe," said Shaukat. "But the general feeling here is that he's lunatic enough to try it even now."

***

Hidden by the thick summer foliage, Luke squinted through the sights until he had the target area comfortably engaged. He caressed the trigger through the latex gloves, regretting the slight loss of sensation. In the army there had been no need for such precautions. But those days were gone – he would have to take his pleasures as they came. In this case, timing was everything. If all went as planned, he would get off two shots, one to the head and a second to the chest. Then he would have to move very fast to get clear of the danger zone.

He looked at his watch. It was time. For a moment a slight doubt assailed him, a doubt he realised he should have had much earlier. Would the walkabout be cancelled because of the unexplained explosions? Well, that would be the Spaniard's bad luck. Luke would just settle for half the money and move on.

But no. He saw now that the vast wrought-iron gates of the palace were opening. A Rolls Royce emerged, travelling at a crawling pace. He hadn't expected that. Why wasn't the lazy cow on foot? If the windows were bulletproof, it would all be a waste of his time. The car paused, preparing to turn left into Constitution Hill. He saw with relief that the rear window was down. Was she planning to greet the poor sods from inside the car? No matter, at least he could just about see inside. Ignoring the male passenger in the rear seat, Luke shifted the rifle slightly until it was trained on the woman beside him. She was wearing a pale lemon suit and matching hat with veil, and was peering into her handbag. *Through the top of the skull it is then*, thought Luke. *I'd have thought you'd at least be waving to the crowd.* As the car slowly turned, the target arrived in the optimum position. He released the first shot, switched his aim to the top of the body and fired again. The handbag went flying as the body jerked from the force of the shots. Although tempted, Luke could not wait to witness the ensuing chaos. He wedged the rifle into the cleft of a branch, ripped off the vest and climbed rapidly down the tree, turning as he dropped the final five feet to land with bent knees. The automatic was still thrust into his waistband: it would go into the nearest waste bin once he was clear of the scene.

***

The wheelchairs were backed up almost to St James's Palace. Adam led Alison around the back of the parade.

"I was serious about what I said this morning," said Alison. "About marriage and babies."

"Ali, you weren't happy when you gave up your career

the last time," said Adam. "Are you really sure you want to do it again so soon?"

Alison turned to look at him as they stepped on to the pavement on the north side of the Mall. "If we're in London, I don't have to stop working," she said. "Except when I'm really pregnant. Besides, if you get the sack I won't be able to afford to stop working."

Adam laughed and, turning her away from him, propelled her before him into Green Park.

"That's very true," he said. "I may have to be a house-husband."

Alison became suddenly aware of a disturbance close to the Palace. "What's going on?" she said.

"Just keep moving, Ali," said Adam, pushing her ahead of him again. "You've had enough excitement for one day."

Thus it was that Alison saw him first. Had their eyes not met, she would probably have walked past him, unknowing. The shaven head, the black moustache, meant nothing to her. But those piercing blue eyes, there was no mistaking them. She cried out involuntarily.

The man looked temporarily confused, but then he grinned as he reached behind him.

"Well fucking well," he said in his soft lilting voice.

***

Fox and Coker, who arrived at the Palace at the same time as a slew of bleating patrol vehicles, leapt from their car at the moment the Rolls Royce slammed to a halt. Bent double, they ran up alongside and looked in. The driver and the protection officer were unharmed and calm, but the Private Secretary was shivering as he patted his sweaty forehead with a handkerchief. "What a nightmare," he said, feebly pushing the dummy away from his lap, where it had fallen. Fox made a rapid assessment, based on the position of the bullet holes.

"From Green Park," he said urgently into his phone. "From a tree on the southern edge at a guess. We're on our way."

***

Adam saw the gun in Thomas's hand as it came up, as though in slow motion. Alison was a pace ahead and momentarily masking him.

Adam did not think. He did not calculate. He had no time to absorb the sudden sense of impending loss which overwhelmed him.

"No!" he roared, leaping forward and wrestling Alison to one side. Something punched him in the chest, and then he was on his back in the grass, unable to move, staring up at the amazingly blue summer sky.

***

Raymond could only shout and hurl his phone at Thomas, but it was enough to deflect the latter's second shot, which had been aimed at the transfixed figure of Alison Webster. Then there were police everywhere, and there came a chattering of automatic weapons, and Thomas went down, cursing and firing wildly into the air, until a bullet struck him in the head, and he was finally silent.

Raymond saw Alison kneel down beside Adam, discarding her sling so as to be able to cradle his head in both hands. A red stain spread across Adam's shirt front and he made no movement. Fox looked at Coker, whose coarse features were for a moment transformed by disbelief and shock.

"Now it really is over, Phil," said Raymond.

***

Adam had heard shouting and the crackle of automatic fire. Then Alison was kneeling by him, holding his head and pushing the hair back from his forehead. She was weeping and calling his name over and over again.

"Did they get him?" Was that his own voice?

A shadow fell over him and he heard Coker's voice. "We got him," said Coker. "Christ, you're an awkward bastard, you know that? Always in the wrong place at the wrong fucking time."

Now Fox was kneeling by him as well. "You'll be fine, Adam," he said. "We'll soon have you away from here."

"Ali," said Adam. The voice was only in his head now, for no sound would come from his parted lips. "Ali, I'm sorry. What a mess."

He heard sirens and running feet and more shouting. He felt cold. The sky was blue, but he felt so cold.

LOOSE ENDS

CHAPTER 16

"Are you absolutely sure?"

Rebecca Shearer tightened the focus on her binoculars until she had a more sharply defined image of the bird perched on a branch at the edge of the thicket. It was smaller and slimmer than a native British cuckoo, dull brown above and white below, with large white spots at the tips of the dark tail feathers. It had a yellow lower mandible, and – the clincher – Rebecca had observed a flash of rufous in the wings before it alighted. It was undoubtedly *Coccyzus americanus,* the yellow-billed cuckoo, a vagrant species from North America, a rare sight even in the remote part of Inverness-shire that she and Barbara had elected for their August expedition.

"I'm as certain as I can be," said Rebecca.

"That's just brilliant," said Barbara, who was adjusting the telescopic lens on her incredibly high specification camera in preparation for a definitive record of the sighting. Barbara Pendleton was a retired judge, who had never married. Her enthusiasm for ornithology had long preceded Rebecca's own interest in bird-watching, and she travelled with all the paraphernalia of a seasoned wildlife observer. Rebecca herself travelled light: binoculars, a field guide and a small pad and pencil were all she needed. She was touched, given her relative lack of experience, that the older woman trusted her judgement in identifying some of the rarer birds they had come across in their trips together around the British Isles.

Rebecca's ability to summon almost total recall of detail, a genetic inheritance from her father, had proved invaluable in the fleeting sightings of elusive species the two women pursued in their expeditions.

"Got it," said Barbara, as her heavy camera emitted a satisfying clunk.

Later, the two women sat companionably under the shelter of a rowan tree to eat their sandwiches.

"Is it my imagination, or are you a bit quieter than usual?" said Barbara. "We haven't really seen each other that much since your cruise, but now I've had you to myself for a few days…"

Am I so transparent? thought Rebecca. Aloud, she said: "You're very perceptive, Barbara. Yes, something happened on the cruise."

"Is it something you want to talk about?"

Rebecca realised suddenly that, after keeping silent for so many months, she very much did want to talk about it now.

"I met a man on the ship."

"That's a good beginning."

"No, Barbara, please," said Rebecca. "It's serious." She recounted as briefly as possible the story of the cautious relationship that had grown up between her and Andrew Singleton, of the surprising dinner invitation in Catania, of her acceptance, of the odd way Andrew had ignored her when she arrived in his hotel in the evening, of the stranger with Andrew, and of her indecision about how far to go in trying to find him. For some reason – she could not explain to herself why – she did not immediately identify Andrew by name.

"I nearly didn't knock on the door at all," she said. "I came close to going straight back to the ship."

"This man interested you so much?"

"I don't know. I didn't know myself what my motivation was."

"So, what happened?"

"At first there was no answer, so I knocked again. This time, Andrew answered."

A frown formed on Barbara's face. "Where did you say you were again?"

"Catania."

"Sicily?"

"Yes."

"Oh, my God!" said Barbara. "You're not talking about Andrew Singleton, are you? The British High Commissioner in Singapore?"

"Yes. I know, it was all over the media at the time," said Rebecca. "I couldn't – I still can't – help thinking I should have done more."

"Why, what happened?"

"When I knocked, he asked who it was and I told him it was me. He said something about having a headache and would I mind awfully if instead of dinner he looked me up when we both got back to England."

"That's all?"

"Not quite. He said something I simply didn't understand. He asked me to give his regards to the First Engineer on the ship."

"How odd. Were they close friends?"

"I didn't even know they'd met. In fact, the First Engineer was equally puzzled when I passed on the message."

"And that was it?"

"Yes. I said I hoped he'd be better soon and that he could write to me via the cruise company."

"When did you find out that he'd killed himself?"

"Not until the ship had sailed. I went ashore at Naples and gave the police all the information I had, including a detailed description of the man who had been with Andrew. They were very courteous and made a careful note of everything, but I had the distinct impression that they had accepted the verdict of the Sicilian police that it was suicide."

Barbara looked at her sharply. "Did *you* not think it was suicide?"

"I don't know. I found it difficult to relate such an act to the man I had been talking to only a few hours earlier."

"Did you try talking to the police in England?"

"Yes. I went to the police in Peterchurch when I got back. They were also very polite. They said they would get Scotland Yard to conduct some enquiries, but I'm not sure how interested they really were in pursuing it any further. I certainly heard nothing more from them."

"And what do you think now?"

"I think I probably let my imagination run away with me at the time. My friends in Singapore finally told me all about the ordeal Andrew had gone through there: being kidnapped, losing his daughter – and rather more, if all the gossip was to be believed. Maybe it all finally caught up with him."

"And yet you picked up no hint of this when you were talking to him earlier in the day?"

"No, but I think he was a very self-contained man. He may just have been suppressing it all."

"So you now think it *could* have been suicide?"

"I still don't know. What I do know is that I might have done more to save him."

"Don't be silly," said Barbara. "How could you possibly have known what was going to happen?"

They packed away the remains of the picnic into Rebecca's rucksack. "Let's try the other side of the valley now," said Barbara.

As they walked together down into the valley, and Rebecca was trying to put Andrew Singleton out of her mind, Barbara suddenly said: "Look, I have an old LSE friend at the Foreign Office. She was an undergraduate when I was finishing my doctorate. I think she was a contemporary of Andrew Singleton. If you're really still fretting about this, why don't I give her a ring and try to arrange a meeting?"

***

In the privacy of his room, and by piggy-backing on the unprotected Wi-Fi of the boarding house manager, Hussein had finished reviewing all the television coverage on his laptop. Now he was analysing some shaky amateur video segments on YouTube, a facility for which he saw a brilliant future, not least in the realm of terror.

A second mortar might have achieved the primary goal, but no matter. A powerful message had been delivered. The publicity value would also be significant, if somewhat impaired by the maverick attempt by some lone lunatic to assassinate the Queen – although, on reflection, there might be a way of claiming responsibility for that as well. And, as planned, the glorious deaths of all the participants had handily diminished any danger of a link back to him. There had also been an added benefit.

As if on cue, his mobile rang.

"Congratulations," he said. "You should be in the clear now."

"But he's dead," said the caller, evidently distressed.

"You said he suspected you," said Hussein. "So that's good."

She was crying now. "I didn't want this," she said.

"He was finished as soon as you used his phone," said Hussein. "Dead or in prison. Dead is better. Now he can't point the finger at you."

"Please," she said. "I can't do this anymore."

"Yes, you can," he said. "Remember, I still have the photographs."

***

On Friday evening, in the soft light of the bedroom, the habitual tiredness in Nicole's face was less evident, and she reminded Raymond, achingly, of how she had looked when they first met. Her simple white cotton nightdress, chastely tied with a ribbon at the neck, created a dramatic contrast with the olive of her skin and the jet black of her hair. She slid into the bed beside him and nestled into his shoulder.

"He's asleep," she said. "It's a miracle."

"You're the miracle," he said.

Nicole raised herself on one elbow and looked down on him. "That's a very serious thing to say," she said.

"I've been thinking how lucky I am," said Raymond.

Nicole pulled loose the ribbon at her neck. "Show me how lucky," she said.

Afterwards they lay on their backs, side by side in silence. Finally, she said: "You're still thinking about it, aren't you?"

It was always like this at the end of a case. While a murder was still unresolved, he had the usual policeman's problem of working all hours and pleading for Nicole's understanding. She had understood this when she married him – her own father had been a policeman. But when the case ended, when the paperwork was done, the formalities completed, he ought by rights to be able to relax, to draw breath, to be a husband and father before moving on to whatever came next. The fact that he could not do so, that he needed time to come down from the high of the investigation, had in the early days made Nicole angry. Now, thankfully, she had grown more tolerant.

"If we'd got on to Thomas earlier," he said. "No one else need have died."

302

"How could you have known?" said Nicole. "It was the stupid mother's fault for not saying anything."

"Kate Thomas disappeared from sight after leaving the Foreign Office that night," said Raymond. "And we didn't even think of the obvious reason – that she'd simply walked across the road to the next building."

Nicole turned towards him impatiently. "It seems obvious now," she said. "It can't have done then."

"He wasn't even all that clever," said Raymond, ignoring her. "He took enormous risks, travelling to Madrid under his own name, using childish aliases in his e-mails, leaving all that incriminating evidence in his room at the Treasury – he'd even left his laptop there. Then there was that stupidly elaborate business with the bomb in the house in Hounslow. On top of all that, he hid money in a hole in the wall of a pub car park and dumped incriminating evidence in the canal. He was an amateur. He just *thought* he was clever."

"And yet he came close," said Nicole.

"I thought you were supposed to be reassuring me," said Raymond.

Nicole rolled on to her back. "There's no satisfying you," she said, her tone betraying her exasperation. "And in any case he didn't. So stop agonising about it."

"It was only because of Adam White that we had any idea he even existed," said Raymond.

Nicole turned to him again and pulled his face round towards hers. "Stop it," she said. "I know what this is all about. It wasn't your fault, Ray. You know that."

***

"Barbara?" said Gillian, who had been about to fall into a doze. It had been a year or more since she had seen Barbara

Pendleton and she was mildly surprised to be hearing from her now, of all times. "How very nice. How's life in rural Herefordshire?"

"Oh, fine," said Barbara. "But how are *you*? My God, you must have had a terrible time." Then, apparently as an afterthought: "Oh, I'm so sorry, how thoughtless of me. I hope it isn't too late to call?"

"No, no," said Gillian. "I'm just resting at home, as instructed. I'm on painkillers, so you may not get too much sense out of me."

"What a ghastly business," said Barbara. "Look, this is probably the worst time to raise this with you, but I've just been in Scotland with a very dear friend who told me that she was with Andrew Singleton shortly before he died. She didn't seem one hundred per cent convinced that he had committed suicide."

Gillian was immediately wide awake. "Really?" she said. "What did she have to say?"

Gillian listened as Barbara told Rebecca Shearer's story. She was silent for a while before speaking. "I don't recall seeing anything about a stranger at the hotel in the police reports," she said. "I might have a word with Bill Cambridge at Scotland Yard about this."

"So, would you like to see Rebecca?" asked Barbara.

"Certainly," said Gillian. "When all this current kerfuffle has died down a bit. What do you think the business about the First Engineer was all about?"

"No idea."

"What was his name, do you know?"

"She did tell me," said Barbara. "Hang on. Yes. It was Muzafar Hussein."

Gillian was momentarily rigid with shock. "Did you say Hussein?" she said.

"Yes."

"And Rebecca Shearer can give an exact description of the man she saw with Andrew?"

"Oh, yes. The girl has a photographic memory."

"How soon can she get to London?"

"What? I'll have to ask her."

"Get her here tomorrow morning at the latest, Barbara. This is important."

CHAPTER 17

Hussein surveyed the room he had occupied for the last two months. Every last trace of his presence had been removed, either destroyed or, if still needed, packed in his battered Samsonite suitcase or the bag slung around his shoulder. He had paid a further month's rent in advance, explaining to the manager that he was spending a few days with his sister in Bruges and would be back some time the following week.

He was not going anywhere near Bruges. He would instead be taking a train to Frankfurt. During the journey he would go to the lavatory, where he would change his identity, becoming now a businessman with an Indian passport bearing a German visa and entry stamp dated mid-August that had been lovingly forged in a Bangkok back street four months previously. In the evening, having discreetly disposed of his previous clothing in a garbage bin at the station, he would take a taxi to the airport and board a plane to Kuala Lumpur. It was time to take a more hands-on interest in his drug-smuggling business while he planned his next project.

***

"Gillian, are you sure you should be out of bed?"

Mohamed Shaukat was visibly concerned as he welcomed Gillian, accompanied by Rebecca Shearer, into his office. Bill Cambridge was also there, standing by the window. He turned and grimaced when he saw Gillian's bandaged head. "Good grief, Gillian," he said. "Talk about walking wounded."

"It's nothing to worry about, Bill," said Gillian. "It could have been a lot worse."

After the initial niceties, and the serving of coffee, Shaukat invited Rebecca to tell her story, which she did in a straightforward, no-nonsense fashion.

"I'm going to ask you to spend some time with our identikit people, Mrs Shearer," said Cambridge. "Then someone will take a formal statement from you."

Rebecca Shearer seemed uncomfortable. "Why didn't I do all this earlier?" she said.

"But you did," said Gillian.

"Yes, you did," said Cambridge. "Between us, we and the Italians dropped the ball. It wasn't your fault, please remember that."

After Rebecca had left with a young WPC, Gillian turned to the others.

"You're the experts," she said. "But I see a number of things very clearly. The security authorities of every country in South East Asia have been looking for Mohamed Hussein for the last six months. What we knew about his appearance previously was useless because we assumed he would undergo plastic surgery after Andrew Singleton had seen his face during the kidnapping. We now have a sighting of him in Sicily in April, and shall shortly have a precise description, thanks to Rebecca Shearer."

Bill Cambridge smiled. He and Gillian went back a long way. "I'm sure there must be something else, Gillian," he said. "Otherwise, I don't know how this helps us now, four months later. We don't know how or when Hussein arrived in Sicily, or with what identity, nor do we know where he went subsequently. The other thing that puzzles me is how exactly he knew where to find Andrew Singleton. I think we'll have to ask the Singaporeans to do a little digging on that."

"I agree," said Gillian. Then she looked at Shaukat. "Mohamed," she said. "I think it highly unlikely that Hussein would have risked coming to Europe with the sole intention of killing Andrew Singleton, however much he may have resented him. I'm going to suggest that we have another look urgently at everything we have, little though it may be, on the man we think was behind the assassination attempt on the President of Iraq. I seem to recall that one thing we knew was that he came from South East Asia."

"Are you serious?" said Shaukat.

"I grant you it's a long shot," said Gillian. "But do you have any better ideas?"

"In that case, he could be in Belgium as we speak," said Shaukat.

"But not for much longer," said Cambridge. "We'd better get on to Europol right now."

***

Ginny had awoken in the early hours of Saturday, aware immediately of the drip in her arm and the inimitable smell of hospital. Her first emotion was disbelief. *I'm not dead,* she thought. *How can that be?* Then she recalled Edward Harrison's shouted warning, and understood that she had somehow been rescued.

Now, at midday, she was sitting up and eating soup. Detective Inspector Fox was by her bedside, patiently waiting for her to finish so that he might clarify some minor outstanding issues. When she was ready, he told her that both María Carmen Dominguez and Edward Harrison were dead, murdered by the man who had killed Kate Thomas, the man who had also tried to kill her, and had turned out to be Gwyneth Thomas's adopted son. Gently, courteously, Fox asked the necessary questions about her own experience, noting her responses carefully in his notebook. Thank God, she thought, that she had been spared further exposure to Detective Sergeant Coker.

When Fox had left, wishing her a speedy recovery, Ginny lay silently, trying to digest everything he had told her. *Why am I not grateful?* she thought. *Why do I not feel incredibly lucky to have been spared?* Then, immediately, she was ashamed at the selfishness of the thought. María Carmen had lived a life of passion and conviction. Kate Thomas had had her whole life before her. Both those lives had been arbitrarily extinguished. And what of Edward Harrison? Sweet, thoughtful, heroic Edward?

With this surge of compassion and guilt came a new resolve. She had been given a chance she did not deserve: it must not be squandered. She would finish the book, and she would return to Chile. Somehow she would arrange to stay permanently and would establish a cancer charity in Diego's memory, and she would throw herself wholeheartedly into running it. No more moping, no more withdrawal. She would act, act in a manner that would have made Diego proud.

***

Hussein handed his passport to the immigration officer before the departure lounge at Frankfurt Airport, who studied it at length and then looked at him carefully. "Please wait one moment," he said.

"What's the problem?" Hussein said. He felt confident. He was clean. The passport was genuine – even if the photo had been changed – and the owner had sold it on the clear understanding that he would not report it missing for six months, when he would receive the balance of his considerable payment. The forged visa and entry stamp were the best money could buy.

"Please wait one moment," the immigration officer said again, impassively. Hussein felt the hairs rise on the back of his neck. He made a rapid mental checklist of all the precautions he had taken. Both the unlinked identities he had employed in Sicily, Spain and Belgium had been totally suppressed. The Italian immigration authorities might be puzzled at having no record of the Tunisian businessman having left Sicily, but his passport and clothing had been destroyed, leaving no trace of him. The Orthodox Jew had never travelled outside the Schengen Area and would therefore feature in no immigration records. He'd held a Belgian passport and identity card, but these too had been destroyed. The only person to whom Hussein had revealed his true identity – it had been impossible to resist – was Andrew Singleton, last seen lying dead on the floor of his hotel room as Hussein carefully placed the gun in his outstretched hand. And the only person who could connect him, as he now looked, to Andrew Singleton was the woman who had knocked on the hotel door.

What had Singleton said to her? Something about a headache, about seeing her in England. What else? A message of good wishes to the First Engineer. He had never understood what that was about...

One small misstep, thought Hussein, *that's all it takes*. He should have told Singleton to invite her into the room. He could have concocted some kind of story involving a suicide pact, and then the trail would have gone stone cold. Well, he had only himself to blame.

Hussein was suddenly aware of large numbers of armed police closing in on him from all sides. *This would have been a good moment for the machine pistol*, he thought, but the gun was long gone, lying now, rusting, at the bottom of the harbour at Catania. Then he was face down on the floor, his hands yanked behind him and the barrel of a Heckler & Koch MP5 rammed into the back of his neck.

CHAPTER 18

Gillian's head wound had proved to be superficial and she was back in her office by the Monday following the attack. Her renowned ability to focus, without distraction, on the issue of the moment was sorely tested as she waded through a mass of outstanding paperwork. The President of Iraq was safely back in Iraq, those who had tried to kill him were dead, as was the man who, incredibly, had thought he could assassinate the Queen. Perhaps most satisfying of all, Mohamed Hussein was in custody in Germany while negotiations took place between several governments over who had priority in charging him.

And yet there were so many loose ends, so many unsatisfying uncertainties that could never now be fully resolved.

They would, for example, never know the full extent of Luis Moreno's duplicity. Was the plot to kill the Queen a one-off, insane act of revenge? Had Moreno originally intended to continue his double life afterwards? Or had he been involved in a deeper game of deception? Had he in any case planned to escape to a new life, to a new identity on another continent somewhere? The children had apparently been told the day before Moreno's disappearance that they were going on an unplanned holiday to a surprise destination, but he had never come back for them. Maybe some clue would be found in due course on Moreno's computer, but its hard disk had been wiped clean, so it would be a long and difficult task. Until then, there was no means of knowing what Moreno had intended.

For Moreno himself was dead. The Spanish had found his body, with a bullet in the back of the neck, in Algeciras harbour. Who had killed him? It could have been someone from the Al Qaeda cell who had discovered conclusively that he was playing a double game. It could have been the people who were helping him escape (in all probability to Morocco, at least in the first place), but who had decided to take all his money instead. It could even, conceivably, have been a casual street crime. No matter. With both Moreno and his wife dead, there could be no final answers.

Nor was there any clue as to who, if anyone, might have killed Archie Drysdale. It could well have been suicide – Drysdale was certainly disturbed enough to have been capable of killing himself – but it might equally well have been an accident, for Drysdale had been very drunk. The coroner's open verdict would probably therefore stand. Folklore would no doubt grow up around the death, invented by people who claimed to have inside information, but no one would really know.

Gillian looked at her watch. It was nearly eleven. She had earlier had a difficult half hour with Hilary Price's mother. Of all her responsibilities, Gillian found dealing with the next of kin of members of the service who died in the course of duty (a task she had had to exercise too often for comfort in recent weeks) the most difficult to get right. Different people needed different things from these meetings. Kate Thomas's mother had simply wanted to hear that her daughter had been a conscientious and well-regarded colleague. Archie Drysdale's sister had made clear that she held the Foreign Office responsible for the deterioration in her brother's health which had led to his death, and was threatening to sell his story to the *Daily Mail*. Hilary's mother was rather more personal in her accusations. Why, she asked, had Gillian herself not ensured adequate protection for her son? She had neglected her duty of care. The family's lawyer had already been instructed.

Gillian had been studying the woman as she spoke. So like Hilary, thought Gillian. So old-fashioned, and now incredibly elegant in her brand-new Jaeger suit. In so many ways, her life had been transformed by the sudden influx of money. The miraculous extension on the lease, the relief from the creditors, the prospect of a holiday on Lake Como, all these would have been unthinkable only a few weeks earlier. But she had lost her only son, and the rest was as nothing.

Aloud Gillian said, choosing her words with some care: "That is of course your right. But you might wish to await the results of the commission of enquiry before taking any action – so that you have all the necessary evidence at your disposal."

Afterwards, Gillian had asked herself again how she could have been so wrong about Hilary. She had been relieved, although still deeply saddened, to discover that she had been right about Andrew Singleton. But she had worked so closely with Hilary over the last two years that her misjudgement of him had been a blow to her self-confidence.

Even now, something was niggling away at the back of her mind, something she could not quite dismiss. The expression on Hilary's face when he stood in the moment before the explosion was not one of fear, but puzzlement. He had looked at his phone and frowned. But Mohamed Shaukat had said there was no incoming message after the damning outgoing one. So what was Hilary puzzled about? By the outgoing message? Had he meant to send it on another phone and used his own by mistake, thereby putting

314

a noose around his own neck? Was it the realisation of this that had brought him urgently to his feet? But surely then his face would have shown shock, not puzzlement. Supposing instead... But no, that was surely too far-fetched.

And then Gillian recalled once more the words Bill Cambridge had spoken on Saturday: "The other thing that puzzles me is how exactly he knew where to find Andrew Singleton. I think we'll have to ask the Singaporeans to do a little digging on that."

No, it wasn't far-fetched at all.

It was now eleven exactly. Sophie Smith rang through.

"Alison Webster is here, Gillian," she said. She still sounded distraught.

"Show her straight in," said Gillian. She paused. "And I wonder if we might have a quick word afterwards, Sophie."